He was a man, plain and simple—a man at the height of his powers

His tongue teased her lips and she parted them for him. The invasion was swift and painfully sweet.

Years ago there had been a tentative side to Michael, but there was nothing tentative about him now, just as there was nothing uncertain about her response to him.

"Tell me now, Sandy," he said, his breath warm and moist against her cheek. "If you're going to stop it, stop it now."

But it was going to happen; she couldn't stop it from happening.

"Don't trust me, Michael," she whispered as his hands slid under her sweater and lit fires along the ridges of her spine. "Don't trust me."

The need for revenge was small and ugly and unmistakable.

"I don't trust you."

"I've given you fair warning," she said. "That's more than you did for me."

ABOUT THE AUTHOR

Barbara Bretton's published works range
from stories in *Katy Keene* comic books—
written when she was ten years old—to
articles written in the *New York Times*,
to Harlequin romances. Barbara, her
husband, Roy, and their pepperoni-pizza-
eating parrot named Walter live in
New Jersey.

Books by Barbara Bretton

HARLEQUIN AMERICAN ROMANCE

HARLEQUIN INTRIGUE

Don't miss any of our special offers. Write to us at the
following address for information on our newest releases.

Harlequin Reader Service
901 Fuhrmann Blvd., P.O. Box 1397, Buffalo, NY 14240
Canadian address: P.O. Box 603,
Fort Erie, Ont. L2A 5X3

Second Harmony
Barbara Bretton

Harlequin Books

TORONTO • NEW YORK • LONDON
AMSTERDAM • PARIS • SYDNEY • HAMBURG
STOCKHOLM • ATHENS • TOKYO • MILAN

For Susan C.F., with love to the woman
with the best wind chimes in town
and
For Tom, Kevin, Linda, Bob, the three Kathys
and the rest of the crowd who were all there
for the summer of '66. Miss you.

"But the dreamers of the day are dangerous men, for
they may act their dreams with open eyes, to make it
possible."

—T. E. Lawrence
Seven Pillars of Wisdom

Published August 1987

First printing June 1987

ISBN 0-373-16211-1

Chapter One

With the back of her hand, Mother Nature had managed to obliterate most of the signs of the twentieth century and send Long Island—land of microwaves and MTV—plummeting back into the darkness of another time.

On Harvest Drive, a twisting, hilly road off the Sound near Port Jefferson, residents peeked out their windows into the gathering darkness and wondered how they would be able to hack their way through the tangle of fallen trees and collapsed roofs the next morning.

While a lot of Long Islanders professed a love of the great outdoors, most liked it best when the great outdoors gently splashed around their twenty-five-foot sailboats or rustled the wind chimes hanging over their redwood decks.

Hurricane Henry was Mother Nature's way of thumbing her nose at progress and reminding everyone exactly who was in charge here.

Five neighbors, all men, labored at the far end of Harvest Drive, trying to make the roadway passable. The night air was alive with the sound of wood splitting beneath an ax, the brittle crunch of leaves underfoot and the mumbled curses and shouted directions of the men who worked by the light of a kerosene lamp and the high beams of a Datsun B210.

Four of the men were out there because it was expected of them, and because they were men of accomplishment who believed in always meeting the expectations of others.

The fifth man didn't give a damn about what others expected. He was there because storms were his natural element, the raw beauty of untamed nature, his food and drink. He was bigger than the other men—taller and more powerfully made—but it wasn't his size that marked him as a leader. Rather, it was something indefinable, a sense of power, of certainty, that made others give way.

"Hey, McKay!" The voice belonged to an attorney whose list of triumphs could have filled the Manhattan Yellow Pages. "Enough already. Haven't you noticed it's dark out?"

Michael McKay raised the ax overhead one more time and brought it slicing down on the trunk of a once-beautiful oak tree.

"It's been dark for almost an hour," he called out, as he wiped the sweat from his eyes with the back of his hand. "If I get this one out, we'll at least have one lane open."

Jim Flannery, the attorney, took the opportunity to grab the ax away from Michael. "Forget it, pal. You're swinging blind, and I don't think Bernstein over there is in the mood to do any microsurgery tonight."

Michael adjusted the beam of the kerosene lamp on the ground near them. "I'm not a desk jockey like you, Flannery. Hard work doesn't scare me."

Flannery turned to Sid Bernstein, the surgeon. "I think he just insulted us, Bernie. What do you think?"

Bernstein feinted a quick right jab toward Michael's jaw. The other men—a psychologist and an engineer—joined in the good-natured ribbing.

"Hard work doesn't scare any of us, McKay," Bill Hughes, the psychologist, said, "but how in hell can I dial 911 when you keel over if the phone lines are down?"

In answer, Michael raised the ax overhead once again, and the other men quickly stepped backward.

"Can't convince you to stop?" Frank DeMarco, the engineer, called out.

The ax whistled as it cut first through the air, then the oak tree, freeing the last piece to be cleared from the street.

"You finally convinced me," said Michael.

With one motion he picked up the tree limb and tossed it onto the pile near the driveway to Sid's house.

"So now the problem is food." He turned to the rest of the men. "Any suggestions?"

"Marilyn refuses to open the freezer," Sid said. "Says she's conserving energy."

Jim laughed. "We already polished off all the Häagen-Dazs in there, Bernie. What else could be left?"

A few of the families were going to pool the contents of their refrigerators and have a barbecue, and the consensus was that an impromptu block party wasn't such a bad idea.

Michael rested the ax handle on his shoulder and started walking back with them in the general direction of his house. With David visiting his maternal grandparents, he hadn't bothered to shop for anything more substantial than a dozen eggs and some chocolate-covered doughnuts. In fact, if it hadn't been for the storm, he wouldn't have been on Long Island at all; he would have been in Upper Manhattan working on the gargoyle for the north side door of the cathedral.

This heavily mortgaged house on Harvest Drive was something he'd bought for David, and without his five-year-old son around it seemed echoingly empty.

"You're joining us, aren't you, Mike?" Sid asked.

The talk of franks and filet mignon was tempting, but not tempting enough to lure him into an evening of such concentrated conviviality.

"Not tonight." He stopped at the foot of his driveway and tossed the ax into the back of his battered four-wheel-drive. "I think I'm going to go out and do some exploring."

Bill shook his head. "You need counseling, friend. Anyone who ventures out farther than his own fireplace tonight is either a madman or—"

Sid Bernstein started to laugh. "Or a medievalist like our pal McKay."

It was an old joke, and one Michael was able to accept with good grace. For the three years he'd been there, he'd tried in vain to explain the difference between a medievalist and one who practiced a medieval trade.

To these men, rooted firmly in the next-to-last decade of the twentieth century, technology was king and speed the crown prince.

Why a man like Michael McKay would want to spend his life chipping away at two-ton blocks of stone with instruments his cave-dwelling ancestors would have found backward was beyond their comprehension.

How he could slave away at a project that wouldn't even be completed in his lifetime didn't bear contemplation.

"They barbecued in the Dark Ages," Jim Flannery was saying as he leaned against the fender of the Jeep. "In fact, if you happen upon a wild filet mignon out there, bring it back and we'll cook it."

Michael's baritone laugh rang out in the silence of his front yard. "You wouldn't know what to do with anything that wasn't wrapped in plastic and meant for the microwave. I can't wait to see what happens if Lilco doesn't get the power back on tonight."

"When the juice comes back on, you'll be the first one to turn to the Sports Channel, McKay. With the Yanks in the pennant race, you're not about to pretend they haven't invented the wheel yet."

Michael glanced up at the maze of cable-television wires that had been attached to his roof before Henry came along. "Can I blame the existence of all that paraphernalia on David?"

Jim Flannery snorted. "Hell, no. You were wired and watching long before you got custody of your kid."

Michael reached into the pocket of his pants and pulled out his car keys. "This place is worse than *Knot's Landing*," he said with a grin.

They all knew about his ex-wife's death and his ongoing custody battle with her parents; their quiet support had made the legal hassles more bearable.

"Abandoning ship, McKay?" asked Frank.

Michael climbed behind the wheel. "You got it."

"Coward." Jim ruffled the hair of his eldest daughter, who'd come out to tell everyone that the impromptu barbecue was ready. "Can't take ghost stories around the old campfire?"

"Not when the old campfire is on the deck of a three-hundred-thousand-dollar house, Flannery." The truck's engine roared to life. "Maybe I'll be back before you roast the marshmallows." He flicked on the headlights and backed slowly down the driveway.

"Guy's crazy." Jim's voice, tinged with curiosity and affection, floated down the street after him. "Doesn't know enough to come in out of a hurricane."

Maybe not, Michael thought as he steered around the split trunk of what had once been a beautiful weeping willow.

But there was one thing he did know: he'd rather be out there in the aftermath of a killer storm than back, safe and secure, in that empty house of his. He could protect himself against the elements; there was no protection against loneliness.

SHE HAD TO ADMIT it was one hell of a homecoming.

For six years Sandra Patterson had imagined how it would feel to return to New York in triumph, the city kid from the rough streets of Queens, with no advantages but a sharp brain and a lot of ambition, coming back with the keys to a new house on Long Island Sound in one hand, and the assistant-vice-president's job in the other.

Long Island had seemed like Shangri-la to kids from the New York City streets when she was growing up, and having a 516 area code had been the ultimate status symbol.

How great it would be to see the old crowd again, to know that at last she was their equal in every way. Oh, maybe she didn't have the husband and the children, but she'd managed to play the best hand possible with the cards she'd been dealt.

It had seemed as if the years of hard work and loneliness, the years of sacrificing things other women took for granted, were finally going to pay off.

Another gust of wind rocked the cliff house overlooking Eaton's Harbor. Sandra shivered, and for the hundredth time she imagined she heard footsteps along the driveway.

What a joke.

In the three weeks since she moved back, she'd discovered that the members of her old crowd had divorced and remarried, gone to jail, gone to seed, opened law offices and closed movie theaters. They'd gone into analysis and come out of the closet. Some of them had moved to Florida, others to Connecticut.

And the one she thought of late at night when her defenses were down had married and vanished to Virginia.

obviously forgetting his old dream to live on the Island one day.

He'd managed to forget her. Why should it surprise her that he'd forgotten his other dreams as well?

Not one thing had stayed the same—herself included.

She glanced at the huge stack of computer printouts on the makeshift desk in her family room. Thank God, assistant vice-presidents in charge of mortgage planning had precious little time to be lonely.

Sandra was used to hard work, but the degree of tension at this level was higher than she'd expected. It was as if Citi-National Bank were bound and determined to get its money's worth out of her, even if it got it in blood.

The latest bill for her mother's medical care caught her eye, and she shoved it farther under the pile of computer sheets. Anything she knew about self-reliance she'd learned from Elinor Patterson, the woman who had stopped dreaming so that her daughter could start.

Maybe she wasn't getting the ego boost out of her professional triumph that she'd anticipated, maybe there were nights when she wondered why it had seemed so damned important to come back home, but there was a deep satisfaction in knowing that the help her mother needed could be had—and that she could pay the price.

In a way, she was thankful for the demands Citi-National made on her time; it gave her less opportunity to think about the disease that was slowly but surely killing her mother.

So when Sandra heard the crunching sound beneath her window for the third time in ten minutes, she chalked it up to overwork and to the way the hurricane had jangled her nerves. She hated storms—she had hated them since childhood—and surviving Henry's brutal battering had obviously taken more out of her than she'd realized.

Then she heard it.

"She's in there." It was a man's voice, right beneath the side window. "I can hear her."

Sandra's pen clattered to the floor, and she gave up pretending that the footsteps she'd heard crunching along her gravel driveway were a trick of the wind blowing off the Sound.

"There are no lights on in there." A woman's voice this time. Equal-opportunity employment had apparently reached all sectors of the work force, the felons included.

"Idiot," said yet another woman. "We just had a hurricane. There are no lights anywhere."

A few hours ago, after the worst of Henry had passed, she'd thought spending a candlelit evening alone in her new house with only a stack of ledger sheets for company would be a rustic adventure, one of those experiences that would make for great cocktail conversation at Citi-National Bank networking sessions.

Somehow she hadn't bothered to factor in nightfall, or just how dark it could get out there in the heart of suburbia. Her neighbors were all tucked snugly away in their houses, probably telling ghost stories around their crackling fires, while she hid behind a pile of computer printouts and waited for a crazed ax-murderer and his accomplices to break into her house.

The footsteps crunched their way around to the other side of the house. She blew out the candles surrounding her desk with a burst of lung power that would have done her old aerobics instructor in Sioux Falls proud, and tried to ignore the blob of white wax that plopped onto the top ledger sheet.

Only a lunatic would worry about obliterating the 1985 foreign-interest figures while the Wild Bunch lurked outside her window, and while Sandra was a self-confessed workaholic, her obsession still managed to stay within the recognized legal bounds of sanity.

A tree limb brushed against the den window and her heart made a three-point landing in the pit of her stomach. So much for being rational: it was time to panic.

She stumbled across an unopened crate in the darkness and cursed out loud. Wouldn't *Newsday* love a story about a hometown girl who returned to Long Island in triumph, after surviving six years at Citi-National's billing center in South Dakota, only to die in her own hallway after tripping over a box of old Motown records?

If she could just find her flashlight and that baseball bat she used to keep in the back seat of her car, maybe she'd be able to—

"Open up, Patterson! We know you're in there." A woman's high-pitched voice echoed through the quiet house.

Sandra froze at the sound of her name, her back pressed against the wall to the left of the front door. Only the criminally insane would be out and about hours after the worst hurricane to hit Long Island in forty-five years. Only the criminally insane, or—

She flung open the front door and was nearly trampled as Ed Gregory, Carol Richter, and Ilene McGrath—three of her co-workers—swept into her house with the same subtlety shown by the storm.

"We aim to serve," Ed said, his arms laden with blankets and batteries and a bottle of Cinzano. "Your friendly corporate rescue squad comes prepared for any and all eventualities."

Carol turned her flashlight on the den and whistled. "Can you believe this?" She zeroed in on the scores of worksheets scattered about the desk. "She must have known we were coming. I mean, working by candlelight . . . ?"

"Good going, Sandra," Ilene chimed in. "Great way to impress the boss." Ilene cast a glance at Ed Gregory, who was in charge of the entire East Coast banking operation, and was also Sandra's mentor.

Sandra's promotion from the outback of Sioux Falls to second-in-command at corporate headquarters had engendered more than a little jealousy among her co-workers, and Sandra had been doing her best to ignore the slings and arrows fired in her direction. She'd worked damned hard to get where she was; no explanations should be necessary. People like her former fiancé, a conservative Sioux Falls attorney, and Ilene McGrath, however, made that stance difficult.

"Patterson's on the fast track," Ed said. "She's too busy to watch the clock. Something beyond your comprehension, McGrath."

This was dangerous territory. Sandra didn't need electricity to see jealousy in Ilene's eyes.

"You realize you people nearly sent me into cardiac arrest, don't you?" she asked, accepting the extra flashlight from Carol. "I was convinced you were a bunch of wild-eyed motorcycle maniacs hell-bent on pillaging my new house."

"Some thanks we get for risking our lives to free you from darkness," Ed said.

"The weather's still that bad out there?" Sandra asked.

"To hell with the weather," he said. "It's the people I'm worried about. Hijackers are lurking behind every felled maple tree, waiting to rob people idiotic enough to ride around with flashlights and batteries in plain sight."

Sandra turned to the women. "Please tell me he's exaggerating. He makes it sound like Dodge City out there."

Carol, already a full vice-president and therefore secure, laughed. "He's exaggerating, Sandra, but not by much. I heard on the radio that battery-operated televisions at Crazy Eddie's are going for just a little less than an Eldorado.''

"Maybe we're in the wrong business." She took the batteries from Ed and placed them on top of one of the packing crates near the door. "Maybe we should forget fixed-rate mortgages and start peddling appliances."

"Limited horizons," said Ed. "A boom market like this happens once every forty-five years. What do you do the rest of the time?"

Ilene's laugh was falsely hearty, and Sandra caught the look of disgust and pity on Carol's face.

Time to change the subject.

"Listen, I haven't unpacked my good china yet, but if you'll settle for paper cups and saltines with Cheez Whiz, you're welcome to sit around the fireplace and trade hurricane stories."

Ed brushed her suggestion aside. "Get your sweater, Patterson. We're going to dinner."

"Where? I thought old Hank managed to blitz everyone."

"One little strip over on Jericho Turnpike in Commack has lights," Carol said. "Everyone on the Island probably knows about it by now, but there's a Roy Rogers, a Burger King and a White Castle, all open for business."

"You don't mean White Castle with the little square hamburgers, do you?"

"The one and only," Ed said.

"I haven't had them in years," she said, thinking back to the scores of burgers she had devoured during her high school days. "I can't resist."

Ilene and Carol went out to the car to wait while Sandra found her sweater and locked up the house. Ed Gregory, however, stayed behind.

"So I've finally found Perfect Patterson's Achilles heel," he said as they carefully made their way over the fallen branches that littered her driveway. "You never look that happy when we go to Sitar or The Twelve Arches for dinner."

"Sitar doesn't have orange soda and fried onions."

"Orange soda and fried onions make you happy?"

"I'm a simple woman with simple tastes, Ed."

"I thought your tastes ran toward real pearls and BMWs."

"What can I say? Some tastes are ingrained in adolescence." She'd grown up in Queens, after all, not Sutton Place.

"I'd like to hear all about your adolescence, Patterson."

Sandra tried to control an involuntary shudder. "My adolescence was as boring as everyone else's, Ed. Typical teenage angst."

The whole long story of a fatherless childhood and a mother whose life revolved around her only daughter was not the stuff business legends were made of. She preferred to let her credentials, which included degrees from NYU and Harvard, speak for themselves.

"Hard to believe that after six years I still have a lot to learn about you, Patterson. I'm looking forward to it."

His remark went deeper than the obvious reference to food and drink and adolescent angst. Her engagement to Andrew Maxwell had managed to keep Ed's and her relationship purely platonic over the years.

Although she'd argued the point at the time, Andrew's assessment that her feelings for him had been more practical than romantic now seemed largely on target. Their engagement had made it possible for Sandra to keep her personal life exactly that—personal—during her six years of training in Sioux Falls.

Corporate ladder-climbing was difficult enough for a woman in the banking industry; she didn't need to add sexual politics to the already stacked deck.

Ed had recognized the boundaries Sandra's engagement drew and he respected them. Professionally they continued to work splendidly together, and they both managed to overlook the hum of sexual tension beneath the surface. However, now that she was no longer involved with Andrew their relationship was changing, and Sandra was doing her best to discourage Ed romantically.

Hurricane Henry, however, had provided him with the perfect opportunity. Ed had stopped next to a tangle of tree limbs and fallen wires, and was surveying the damage closely.

"How badly were you hit?" Ed asked as they scrambled over the maze of branches, taking care to avoid the wires.

"Fourteen trees—not including this one—and the roof on my living room. How about you?"

"That's one of the great things about living in a condo— fallen trees are someone else's problem."

Sandra made a face in the darkness. "Lucky you. Think of me tomorrow morning when I'm out here with a chain saw, trying to hack my way to the mailbox."

"I can help you, Patterson."

She hesitated. "That's a lot to ask of a friend and employer, Ed." And it could lead to all manner of complications, she thought.

"After bringing you back to Long Island just in time for Henry, it's the least I can do."

"There's a lot of work." It was hard to imagine the ever-impeccable Edward Gregory up to his ears in tree limbs, but apparently hurricanes brought out the pioneer spirit in everybody.

"What time do you want to start tomorrow morning, Patterson?"

He seemed serious. She thought about her wrecked front yard, her mutilated back yard and the gaping hole where her living-room ceiling had been, and gave in to temptation. "How does eight o'clock sound?"

"Disgusting, but I don't think Billy will mind."

"Billy?"

"My nephew," Ed said. "That kid will do anything for some spare cash."

Sandra laughed into the darkness. It wasn't hard to understand how Ed had risen to the ranks of the Citi-National biggies: anyone who could delegate responsibility the way Ed did and make it sound as if he was doing you a favor was definitely on the fast track.

There's a lot I can learn from you, Ed Gregory, she thought as he helped her into the car.

A hell of a lot.

MICHAEL HADN'T DRIVEN more than three miles beyond his neighborhood before he understood just how devastating the ridiculously named Hurricane Henry had been. Totaled Saabs and Toyotas and Chevy Cavaliers peeked out from under oaks and maples that had been saplings during the Revolutionary War. And the houses had fared no better; sheets and curtains were nailed in place where majestic picture windows had once provided a view of the Sound.

Despite everything, Long Island vibrated with a bizarre euphoria. Come morning, when daylight revealed the full extent of the damage, that euphoria was bound to wear off, but now, when they'd battled the worst that Mother Nature had to offer and come out the other side, a primitive sense of victory was everywhere.

So he was almost disappointed when he rounded a particularly sharp curve on Jericho Turnpike and saw ahead of him a strip of neon lights against the sky proclaiming Burger King and McDonald's and White Castle.

Almost, but not quite.

In all the years since high school, he'd yet to find a French restaurant or pasta palace that could please him the way a White Castle hamburger still could.

With apologies to the medievalists, he made a right into the crowded parking lot.

The twentieth century, after all, hadn't been a total washout.

NOTHING LOOKED the way Sandra remembered it.

The benign shopping malls, the innocuous housing developments with their three-bedroom houses and wide front lawns, even the A&P on the corner, took on an eerie, almost sinister quality without benefit of electricity. It was as if the world had ended and no one had bothered to tell her.

How on earth could everything change so totally in just twenty-four hours?

The pioneer spirit her neighbors and she had exhibited a few hours ago was well and good, when the pioneer spirit went hand-in-hand with central air conditioning and the security of your own four—or forty-four—walls. Out there in the middle of nowhere, it was a whole other experience.

She breathed a sigh of relief when the oasis of lights on Jericho Turnpike came into view and Ed angled his Lincoln Continental into the White Castle parking lot.

"If Thomas Alva Edison were here, I'd kiss his feet," she said as they walked into the lobby of the restaurant. "I've never been so happy to see fluorescent lights in my entire life."

Her sentiments were apparently shared by the other two hundred or so customers jammed into the place. Everywhere she looked, people—in various stages of post-hurricane disarray—laughed and joked and jockeyed for table space, thrilled to find both a hot meal and the chance to exchange war stories with other weary veterans.

Carol spotted a cousin of hers who was leaving, and they grabbed the tiny table he had just vacated near the rear door and sat down to decide what to order.

"I'm telling you, Patterson here brought the bad weather with her from Sioux Falls." They had no sooner sat down than Ed resumed the heavy-duty teasing he'd started in the car. "Think about it, everyone: Patterson's been here three weeks, and we've had an earthquake and a hurricane and another one threatening down around the Carolinas. I don't know about you two, but I'm thinking about moving to New Jersey."

"I can't take any more of this abuse," Sandra said with a laugh. "Give me your orders and I'll wait in line. Maybe that will give you beasts a chance to vent your hostilities on one another."

The line snaked its way through the restaurant and into the enclosed entrance near the parking lot, and despite the crowds and the noise and the work that awaited her at home, Sandra felt unexpectedly lighthearted and pleased that Ed and the others had decided to come and drag her out into the real world.

She'd known Ed since graduate school, when he'd come up to Harvard to scan the latest crop of MBAs and had plucked Sandra from the batch. His vision of her future had coincided with her own, and so far he'd kept her on the path to success with few detours.

Even the move to South Dakota as his ace assistant had proved to be as advantageous as he'd promised. Although

Sandra was a native New Yorker, she had adapted easily to the pace of small-town life, and her years in Sioux Falls had been a time to heal as well as a time to grow.

Ed had been promoted back to New York in her third year, and even without his presence she'd continued to advance. The only detour had been her engagement to Andrew Maxwell, and fate had taken care of that.

Fate, and Andrew's desire for the perfect wife.

But here she was back in New York, with Ed Gregory once again her mentor and friend. He and Carol and a few of the others at Citi-National had done a lot to make her transition a smooth one.

Showing up on her doorstep tonight and whisking her off to dinner was a perfect example.

While White Castle was hardly Lutèce, it still beat cold-pizza-for-one by a mile.

Besides, where else but a fast-food joint in Yuppie country could you eavesdrop on an argument concerning the relative nutritional benefits of White Castle and Burger King?

"Remember, there's lettuce and tomato at Burger King," the woman behind her was saying as Sandra tried to bite back a laugh. "Vitamin C."

"I still say the lower starch content at White Castle is highly preferable," the woman's companion shot back.

Sandra felt like saying, "Why don't you two bozos go home and graze on your front lawn?" when a tall man standing near the counter caught her eye.

He towered over everyone else. That alone would have made him worthy of notice. However, he had more going for him than height—a lot more. Despite the chilly mid-September evening, he wore only faded jeans and a black T-shirt that revealed biceps and forearms worthy of a Michelangelo sculpture. The fluorescent lighting overhead picked up threads of silver in his curly black hair. His head was turned, and she could see only a fraction of his profile, but the high cheekbones and the strong jawline were so familiar that her breath caught in her throat.

She was being a fool.

Michael McKay was probably balding and saddled with a potbelly by now, sagging into the beginnings of a sorry middle age. Just because her memories of him were of a man gloriously made, there was no reason to assume that his early promise had been realized.

And yet she couldn't stop watching the man ahead of her in line. How easy it was to fall into memory, to conjure up the heat of a summer day as it rose from the city pavement, to remember the heat of a summer night and the exquisite torture of passion denied.

Eavesdropping on the nutrition-conscious couple behind her paled by comparison.

The line snaked slowly along, and she lost sight of the man when she found herself trapped behind a Formica pillar. Then—damn the timing!—she was at the counter, and it was her turn to order.

"Order, please?"

"Two coffees, one hot chocolate, one orange—"

A movement to her left caught her eye, and she turned for a second, peering through the crowd behind her for one last glimpse of the dark-haired man.

"Hey, lady," the man behind her grumbled. "Other people are waiting, you know."

"Sorry." Chastened, she gave the rest of the order and reminded herself that she was thirty-five years old and beyond games as childish and fruitless as this one.

The last she'd heard, Michael McKay was married and living outside Arlington, Virginia, his adolescent dreams as forgotten as what they had once shared.

If her overactive imagination wanted to conjure up the past at every turn—well, she was just going to have to put a stop to that, and soon.

While the counter clerk assembled her order, Sandra glanced around the restaurant once again. A hell of a lot of men were tall and dark and handsome, but not one of them came close to the splendor of that man in the black T-shirt.

Just because that one perfect specimen had looked the way she'd imagined Michael would look now was no reason to ruin the rest of the evening with useless thoughts of the past. Thinking of the past never got you anything but a broken heart, and that was something she wasn't going to forget.

"Need some help?"

Her heart slammed into her rib cage and she turned to look into the concerned face of Ed Gregory. She hoped her disappointment didn't show.

"I guess so," she said, as the clerk loaded their order onto three trays. "Your timing is superb, Ed."

They were heading toward the condiment table for extra ketchup and paper napkins when she heard a man say, "Watch my seat, Tony. She forgot my fries," and a thousand nights of wanting rushed in at her with a force more violent than anything Hurricane Henry had to offer.

How could she think she'd forgotten his voice, that deep, smooth voice that had whispered secrets and dreams and promises in her ear back when she believed such things were possible.

A stupid, idiotic tremor rushed through her body and she felt seventeen again and on fire from within for the one, the only one, who had ever made her feel whole.

Chapter Two

Michael was halfway to the counter, his attention focused solely on his forgotten fries, when he saw her. Her hair was longer and a little blonder; there were hollows in her cheeks that hadn't been there the last time they'd been together; her body was still slender, but her breasts and hips were more rounded, more womanly than years ago.

And although the last time he'd seen her he had done his damnedest to hurt her the way she'd hurt him, he pushed his way through the crowded restaurant and did the first thing that came to mind: he pulled her into his arms.

"I can't believe it," he said, as her surprise turned to pleasure. "It's really you, isn't it?"

God, her laugh! How had he ever forgotten her laugh?

"Michael McKay," she said softly, touching his mustache with the tip of her index finger. "As I live and breathe."

The man next to her coughed discreetly. Sandy stiffened in Michael's arms, and something came over him, some wild crazy urge to stake a claim to all that there had been between them. He cradled her face in his hands and kissed her, long and slow and deep, kissed her for all the years they'd lost, all the things they'd said, all the times from here on in when he'd have to live with the thought of what might have been.

And if he'd ever really thought Sandy Patterson was a thing of the past, he found out in that moment just how wrong he'd been.

"I thought you were in Virginia," she said when he finally broke the kiss.

"I'm back." This wasn't the time for explanations. "I thought you were in Sioux Falls."

Her mouth, still full, still luscious, curved in the lopsided grin he'd always loved. "I'm back."

"You haven't changed," he said, meaning it. "You're still beautiful."

And she was still the woman against whom every woman he'd known since had been judged and found wanting.

Her laughter was embarrassed, yet pleased. She looked away for a moment and tugged at her sleek blond bangs. "Gray hairs," she said, looking up at him again. "Laugh lines. Oh, I've changed, Michael. Don't think I haven't."

"Not to me." *Never to me.*

The blond-haired man she was with backed away toward a table where two other women waited and watched in fascination.

She cast them a quick glance, then turned her back to them. "I've probably just committed professional suicide," she said. "This will be all over Citi-National by Monday morning."

He took a look at the three people who watched them. "They don't look too intimidating to me." Trendy sweat pants with color-coordinated headbands and leather-trimmed Reeboks didn't impress him.

"Don't let their clothes fool you. Ed's tops in his field; Carol's a full vice-president; and Ilene would like to have my job and send me back to Sioux Falls."

Suddenly the seven years since they'd seen each other yawned before him like the Grand Canyon, but there was no power in heaven or in hell that could have made him turn away from her now.

"So how's Elinor?" he asked. Despite Elinor's insistence that her daughter get a college degree and pursue the sort of life that circumstances had denied to her, Elinor Patterson had been one of Michael's favorite people.

And, strangely enough, he had been one of hers.

"Busy," Sandra said, her eyes darting back again toward her pals from Citi-National.

"Working?"

She shook her head. Her bangs shimmered with the movement. "Traveling."

"You're kidding! Elinor thought New York City was the focal point of the universe."

A funny look passed over Sandra's face, but disappeared before he could imprint it on his memory.

"She changed her mind a few years ago," she said.

"That's one hell of an about-face. What was it—early retirement?"

He knew he was getting sidetracked but the Elinor Patterson he'd known wouldn't have traveled farther than Atlantic City. Hell—she couldn't have afforded it.

Sandra coughed politely, as if to let him know the entire conversation was getting a bit tedious.

"She's worked hard enough all these years," she said, her voice strained. "Why not retire early?"

He raised a hand as if to defend himself. "Hey, listen—I wish I could do the same thing, Sandy."

Actually, early retirement was the last thing he wanted, but the conversation was taking such an odd turn that he was willing to say he drank radiator sealant instead of orange juice in the morning if it would help matters.

"Where is she now?" he asked instead.

"She's in—umm, I think she's in Zermatt."

"Zermatt, *Switzerland*?"

"There's another one?"

He whistled. "No wonder I lost touch with Elinor. She's been too busy jet-setting around."

Her glance was frankly curious. "I didn't know you and Mother had been in touch in order to lose touch."

"I always liked Elinor," he said, watching her carefully, wishing he could get past the barrier of caution on her beautiful face. "Just because it didn't work out for us was no reason to lose her friendship, was it?"

"Just when did you lose touch?"

He shrugged. "I don't know. Five, maybe six years ago...something like that."

She nodded, as if to say that made sense. "That's about when it—that's about when she retired."

A long, uncomfortable silence rose from the ground, separating them.

He searched around for some safe, neutral topic of conversation. "My folks have been on the move, too. They've gone down to Florida to be with Toni and her husband and kids."

Sandra looked surprised. "Toni's married?"

"Five years." He told her about Toni's daughters, and they spent a few minutes playing catch-up as he filled her in on the rest of his family. Brother in Ohio. Another brother in California and sister in Utah. Every single damned one of them solidly blue-collar. Living the life Sandra had predicted for him years ago.

The life she'd turned away from.

"So you're the only one left in New York?"

He nodded. He wanted to tell her where his life had taken him, but this was hardly the time—and definitely not the place. Another silence fell between them.

"How long have you been back?" he asked.

She stole another glance at her co-workers, and he noticed the small telltale twitch at the right corner of her mouth. What kind of life had she gotten herself into? What she did outside the office was her own damned business—or should be.

"Three weeks," she said with a groan. "I haven't even unpacked yet, and now I have a hurricane to clean up after."

He remembered the girl who'd been terrified of storms. "Still hate thunder and lightning?"

"Shh," she said, putting her index finger to her lips and looking around. "Not so loud. Bad for the corporate image." For a second he thought he caught a glimpse of her earlier vulnerability, but it disappeared before he could be sure.

"How bad did it get you?" He thanked the Fates for that damned hurricane. If Henry hadn't passed through, they probably wouldn't have one damned thing to talk about.

"A tree fell on my living room. If I ever get my phone service back, I can call a repairman." She angled herself away from her co-workers a fraction more. "How'd you make out?"

"Luckier than most. I lost a few trees. Nothing major."

They traded stories about where they'd been when the lights went out, and he laughed as she described the squirrel she'd found swinging from the philodendron in her caved-in living room. She was more sophisticated than when he'd last seen her; he was fumbling around, trying to keep from saying the things that were tearing up his insides, while she managed to keep their conversation as light and breezy as a summer day.

She might look the same as the girl he'd once known, but everything else about her had changed. Her rough city edges had smoothed themselves out; instead of her New York accent, there was the sound of Harvard in her voice. The insecurities she'd once had were obviously all safely under control. She might be wearing an old sweater and faded jeans, but she was executive material nevertheless.

The old angers began to resurface.

She must have felt the change in him, because she gestured toward the table where the friends he'd bumped into in line were sitting. "You're with some people," she said. "I should let you get back to them."

"They can wait, Sandy." She seemed to start at the sound of her name. "What's wrong?"

"You don't know how long it's been since I've been called Sandy."

"What the hell do your friends call you?" he asked. "Ms. Patterson?"

"Sandra," she said. "For years it's been Sandra."

"Sandra." He tried the name and didn't like it. Of course, it made no difference if he liked it or not. It was her name and her life, just the way he'd wanted it seven years ago.

"Well," she said, those shimmering blue eyes of hers meeting his, "it was terrific to see you again, Michael."

She extended her hand, and he hesitated. What he wanted to do was pull her back into his arms and kiss her until everything else disappeared, everything except the way she tasted and sounded and felt in his arms. He moved toward her.

"No," she said, closing her eyes for a second. "Please."

For a second he was tempted to override her wishes and pull her to him, but then she glanced again toward the man she was with, and reality hit him hard. They weren't seventeen any longer, nor twenty-two, nor twenty-eight. They were two thirty-five-year-old adults, with lives that extended far beyond the common memories they shared.

The choice had been made a long time ago, and nothing he could say or do in the middle of a crowded White Castle would change a damned thing, even if he wanted it to.

But it was still so hard to let her go.

"I really should get back to my friends, Michael."

"Listen," he said, wanting to keep her near him a little longer, "about that roof of yours. If you give me your number, I might be able to get some help out to you."

Her gaze flickered over his faded jeans and worn T-shirt. He knew what she was thinking, and it bothered him as much now as it had when he was younger.

"A friend already said he'd help out."

Michael gestured toward the banker-type in his spanking-clean running shoes and perspiration-free sweats. "I don't think he's much for repairs, Sandy."

She hesitated, and he was thinking he'd gone too far when that terrific grin resurfaced and his breathing started up again.

"You might be right," she said. From her canvas shoulder bag she pulled out a business card and scribbled a phone number and address on the back. "My home phone's out of order, but you can reach me at work on Monday."

He checked out the front of the card and whistled low. "Assistant vice-president. Making your old dreams come true, Sandy?"

Her cheeks reddened, and he wanted to call back his words. He'd wanted them to sound light and easy, but nothing between them had ever been light or easy. Why should this be any different?

"I'm trying," she said after an uncomfortable pause. "Maybe if you'd—"

"Hey, McKay! Invite her over!" Tony and his wife called out from their table by the window. "We're ready to eat the curtains!"

"I'd better—"

"You'd better—"

Michael inclined his head. "You first."

"It was good to see you, Michael. Take care."

Brief and to the point. She must be terrific in business. No wasted words, no phony sentiment, no prolonging the goodbyes. There was no point in talking about his marriage or her career or the tangled skeins of their common past. That was history.

She obviously wanted it to stay that way.

Sandy turned to go, and he reached out involuntarily and touched his forefinger to her right cheek in a gesture familiar to both of them.

"Michael?" There was a look akin to fear in her eyes, but he couldn't help himself.

"I'll call you, Sandy," he said quietly, knowing it could be no other way. "You can bet on it."

MICHAEL TURNED, and Sandra watched him walk away from her, watched that same beautiful line of shoulder and waist and leg that had once made her burn with a desire so intense that nothing she'd felt since even came close.

Don't call me, she thought. *Don't call me or write to me or think of me.*

The moment he walked that room and pulled her into his arms, she'd known that everything she'd ever felt for him— all the rage and desire and love—was still there, waiting to claim her once again.

The life of independence and security that she'd carved out for herself, inch by painful inch, had nearly been incinerated in the fire he'd ignited with just a kiss. He was as dangerous to her future now as he'd been years ago, and the pleasure she thought she'd take in besting him didn't seem to matter a damn.

How important was it to dazzle him with her hot-shot title and fancy house, when none of it would give Elinor back her health or make Sandra's nights any less lonely?

Seeing Michael had done nothing but awaken old longings, old dreams she had no business letting herself fall prey to.

She had responsibilities now, both to Elinor and to her job, responsibilities that gave her no time to pursue lost loves.

She had to remember her last encounter with Michael McKay if she was going to keep her balance.

She had to remember the pain and humiliation when he'd stroked and kissed and whispered to her, then abruptly walked out with the words, "Wish me luck, Sandy. I'm getting married next month."

She had to remember—

"You all right?" Ed Gregory appeared at her side. "You're looking a little rocky."

"I'm fine." She scooped up a handful of paper napkins and straws from the counter and followed him to their table, where Carol was talking about a co-worker's fiscal exploits. That simple act of stepping back into her normal self required all of her concentration.

"Michael is an old friend," Sandra said, although no one asked. "An old friend from high school."

Ilene twisted around in her chair and looked back toward Michael's table. "I don't know what you said to your old friend, Sandra, but he's leaving."

"What?"

"He put the tray down on the table, grabbed a few burgers, and he's going," Ed said, shooting Sandra a quizzical look. "Are you all right, Patterson? I still say you look a little green around the gills."

"Just tired," she said. "Nothing more serious than that." She was glad he was going. There was nothing more that could be said between them anyway. She pushed away the memories and turned to Carol Richter. "Now what were you saying about Dan Crivello in Accounting?"

Carol, God bless her, launched back into her story of corporate shenanigans, and for the next hour Sandra talked and laughed, and those good associates of hers never realized how hard it was to make idle conversation when your heart was laid bare for all the world to see.

HE COULDN'T STAY in there. He couldn't sit there and joke around with Tony and his family, knowing that Sandra Patterson was less than fifty feet away from him. The old crowd from St. Brendan's had kept up with one another, and the last he'd heard, Sandra had been engaged to a middle-aged trial attorney and living somewhere in Sioux Falls. For all he knew, she'd married him and had a commuter marriage. He hadn't thought to check for a wedding ring.

Her business card read "Patterson," but that didn't mean a hell of a lot—these days professional women often kept their maiden names in business. And the way Sandra had hung on to her independence years ago, he doubted she would have taken her husband's name, unless it were Rockefeller.

What the hell difference did it make, anyway? She was part of his past, a memory, like the first time he'd heard the Beatles or driven a car. Something you looked back on and smiled over, then promptly forgot.

Except that she was Sandra, the one he'd never been able to forget.

He jumped into his truck and roared out onto nearly-deserted Jericho Turnpike.

How many times had he wondered about her, asked their old friends about her, daydreamed about bumping into her on a Manhattan street and impressing the hell out of her with all he'd accomplished, all he'd become? The huge cathedral he was privileged to work on held so many of the hopes and dreams he'd wanted to share with her.

Not once had his fantasies included White Castle, or the beat-up pickup truck he used on the weekends, or a black T-shirt that looked like a reject from an old James Dean movie.

Of all the worst damn times to see her again, this was it.

All day long he'd rattled around that huge house of his, lonely as hell without his son, who was in Florida with Diana's parents. When he'd called earlier from the only working telephone in his neighborhood to speak with David and let him know he'd come through Hurricane Henry safe and sound, the Bentleys had made it sound as if David owed his very survival to their child-rearing expertise.

"Thank God, he was safe here," Margaret said, her voice still as identifiably midwestern as a field of corn. "I hate to think of what could have happened to him out there in the middle of nowhere."

"The middle of nowhere" was a fifty-year-old community adjacent to Stony Brook University where professors rubbed elbows with nuclear physicists, but since Diana's death there'd been no reasoning with either Margaret or Art.

They still saw Michael as they wanted to see him, as a rough and raw man who made a living with his hands and had never been good enough for their daughter.

The fact that he'd found their darling daughter in bed with his best friend while their infant son slept five feet away didn't seem to matter.

What Michael wanted to do was hop a plane to Florida, grab David and bring him back home where he belonged, but grandstand plays like that were the last thing he should be thinking of. David had had enough to deal with since he lost his mother and stepfather; stirring up the dissension between his former in-laws and himself would only hurt his son, and that kid had been hurt enough already.

Besides, he understood the Bentleys a hell of a lot better than they thought. They weren't going to be happy with the restricted visitation rights they'd been granted when Michael got custody after their daughter's death. Hell, they weren't going to be happy until they had that kid locked up in their pink stucco house, afraid to breathe, afraid to eat, afraid to dream.

Michael would kill before he let that happen to his son.

And if keeping his son meant living like the medieval monk his neighbors teased him about being—well, so be it.

But today, with David a thousand miles away and the storm raging out of control, Michael had felt agitated and helpless. His feelings had intensified with the hurricane, and by the time Henry had passed and the cleanup had begun, Michael was a six-foot-four-inch mainspring ready to snap. His emotions were frayed, his heart ached for something he couldn't define, his normal good humor had gone the way of the receding tide.

The friendly teasing of his friends and neighbors had gotten under his skin and pushed him closer to the edge.

When everyone adjourned to the communal dinner table for the impromptu barbecue, Michael would have braved the worst Henry had to offer in order to get the hell out of there.

He'd never felt lonelier in his life.

At least, not until he saw Sandra Patterson again, and seven years of wanting the chance to apologize—seven years of wondering what might have been—rushed in on him and showed him what a fool he'd been.

He turned onto Harvest Drive and pulled into his driveway, barely avoiding another fallen oak tree. He cut the engine, and let the stillness envelop him.

So, the worst had happened. He'd seen Sandra again, and the pain and the wanting were still there.

So what?

He had a good life now—a damned good life, with work he loved and a son he cherished. He didn't need the approval of an old high-school sweetheart any more than he needed the approval of his in-laws or the man in the moon.

The business card in his back pocket seemed to burn into his flesh. He reached back and pulled it out; without looking at it, he tore the card to pieces and tossed it to the wind, knowing it was already too late.

One-eighty-eight Corey Place, Eaton's Harbor.

The address was burned into his memory.

He was going to do his damnedest to forget it.

A COLD, MISERABLE RAIN was giving the windshield wipers a run for their money when Ed stopped his Lincoln in front of Sandra's house two hours later.

"The amenities are missing," she said, speaking over the drone of the news station on the car radio, "but you're all welcome to come in for a glass of wine."

"Too wet out there for me," Carol said. "Besides, I'm a news-aholic. It's physically impossible for me to turn off a radio until I hear the Dow-Jones average."

Ilene glanced out the window and shivered. "At least the car is heated," she said. "That's more than I have to look forward to at home."

Ed, to her surprise, took her up on the offer.

"Bad form, Gregory," she said a few minutes later after she'd lit some candles and poured him a glass of wine. "Ilene's suspicious enough about my promotion. You didn't need to throw fuel on the fire."

Ed swirled the wine around, then took a sip. "McGrath should worry about her own ass before she starts worrying about anyone else's."

Sandra made a face. "Vulgarly put, but effective." She poured herself a glass, and sat down behind her makeshift desk. "I am serious, though, Ed. I don't want any problems."

"I'll handle McGrath. You just worry about getting those ledger sheets done for Monday."

"You think we'll have the power back by Monday?"

"The end-of-the-month accounts are due Tuesday morning," he said, draining his glass and setting it on the edge of the table. "They'll get power back on Monday if they have to hook us up to five hundred hamsters on a treadmill."

"Let's write up a proposal and give it to Lilco," she said. "It beats the system they've got now."

He stayed a few minutes longer, outlining the agenda for the coming week and detailing how Sandra figured in it. She listened carefully, aware of the intimacy created by the darkness and thankful for the two women waiting for him outside.

At the door she shuddered at the bizarre tangle of fallen trees that blocked both her path and driveway.

"I think I'm going back to Sioux Falls," she muttered. "This mess will take me a month to clear up."

"Forget about the mess," Ed said, slipping his arms back into his jacket. "Worry about the ledger sheets."

"Easy for you to say. You live in a condo with a maintenance crew."

"You wound me, Patterson. I promised I'd get someone out here to dig you out, and I'm a man of my word. Just get to the damned ledger sheets and leave the rest to me."

She wandered around the house for a good half hour after the Lincoln eased its way back down her street, lighting candles and trying to banish the darkness.

Darkness was where old memories lived.

She'd give half of her Citi-National stock to be able to turn on all of the lamps and make the TV blare so that it reached every room of the house.

It was the only way she knew to keep the loneliness at bay.

She sat back down at her desk and gave it a valiant try, but the fiscal solvency of the mortgage department couldn't compete with the way Michael McKay had looked when he pulled her into his arms.

She poured herself another glass of wine and stretched out on the sofa. God knew, it wasn't a night to be alone with memories. The candlelight was too seductive, the sound of the rain lashing against her windows too reminiscent of old movies and the romantic fantasies of a simpler time.

A woman couldn't protect herself against the old heartaches on a night like this. She should get up and force herself back to her desk, to her work, to her own life. She could stop this rush back into memory with just the blink of an eye if she wanted to.

But, oh God, the way it had felt to be in his arms again...

IT IS A SUMMER'S NIGHT back in the days when birth control was hard to come by and the consequences of love were high.

A slender young blond girl and a lanky dark-haired boy are sprawled out on a faded yellow-and-white patchwork quilt on a small, precious patch of grassy park in the middle of New York City. Although they are in full view of anyone who might happen to pass by, at the moment they are completely, utterly alone.

She is lying on her back on the rumpled blanket, and sharp blades of grass tickle her ear; the smell of the damp earth and his breath delight her; all she can hear is the far-off city traffic and the quickened pounding of their hearts. Her white cotton blouse is open, her bra unhooked and pushed away. The night breeze against her breasts excites her, but it is nothing compared to the touch of his hand.

In two years, this is the first time they've managed to be so completely alone.

City kids of their generation seldom have cars, so privacy is hard to come by. Cars and drive-in movies are the sole property of rich kids on Long Island who don't understand subways and buses and necking in the balcony of the Elmwood Movie Theater away from the usher's treacherous flashlight.

All summer they've planned for this night, for they've outgrown the groping in the dark and the long kisses that once were enough. What they want is to take off all of their clothes, to feel the thrill of bare skin against bare skin, to see all that their imaginations had conjured up in the heat of a summer's night.

She lets her hands slide beneath his shirt and touch the muscles that are beginning to shape the body of a boy soon to be a man. He's on top of her, moving against her in a slow, insistent rhythm, and it takes all her willpower to keep her hips from answering that rhythm. It is getting harder to remember why the boundary lines were so important.

"Michael," she whispers as his hand slides down to her midriff and unsnaps the waistband of her Wranglers. "I'm scared. I'm afraid we won't stop in time..." Her voice trails off into a sigh as his hand slides under the elastic of her panties.

"I love you, Sandy." His fingers brush over the thick tangle of curls and begin to tease her. "I swear I'd never hurt you."

This is Michael who is speaking, Michael who has held her when she cried, who has seen her through braces and broken bones, the one person who knows all there is to know about her.

She knows he would never hurt her; he is incapable of hurting her. It is her own darker impulses that scare her; she is her mother's daughter, after all, and prone to making her mother's mistakes.

Elinor Patterson had believed a young man just like Michael eighteen years ago. A young man who had taken the first train out when, terrified and alone, she'd told him she was pregnant with their child.

Elinor's life had been changed forever by the baby forming inside her girl's body; her life had changed in ways that Sandra knew she herself could never survive.

The work. The worry. The unending, unyielding secrets and shame that had yet to become a part of a society's past.

Not for Sandra.

Never for Sandra.

But without his clothes Michael seems younger, more vulnerable, except for the part of him that terrifies and fascinates her and makes her want to throw caution to the four winds.

"Just close, Sandy," he whispers. "We won't do it, we'll just get as close as possible."

"What if I get pregnant?" Her voice is husky, not her voice at all. *"My mother would blame herself. I couldn't—"*

"I wouldn't run like your father did, Sandy." His fingers slip inside her, and she gasps with pleasure at this sudden, overpowering sensation. *"We would just get married sooner than we figured."*

"But my scholarship, your education... We couldn't—"

"We could," he says. *"We can do anything."*

But Sandra is old before her time, the daughter of a woman who had been made the same promise and believed it, only to be left with a child when she was little more than a child herself.

Michael believes they can handle anything life has to offer. They're invincible, he says, destined to see only the sweet side of fate. He's a product of the times, certain that everything they touch will turn to gold.

"Believe me," he says. *"Believe me."*

And this time she wants to believe, even though she knows she shouldn't.

She's yearning toward him, opening for him, forgetting her fears and ambitions and letting the one she loves more than life—

IT WAS THE LIGHTNING that did it.

One bolt of lightning with incredibly rotten timing hit a tree in Sandra's front yard and sent it crashing into the birdbath.

No matter how tightly she kept her eyes closed, how ardently she tried to recapture the dream, it was irretrievably gone.

She sat up on the sofa and let her surroundings come back into focus. The candles burning low on the end tables. The plush white carpeting. The lustrous mahogany furniture that had cost her a fortune.

The sound of a second hurricane approaching the Island.

No sultry summer night. No scent of wet grass and wild-flowers. No rumble of city traffic. And, oh God, no one to hold her, no one to love her, no one who understood one single thing about who she was and where she'd come from.

How ironic that, even in her dreams, she and Michael McKay hadn't quite managed to make things work out.

And how ironic that even now, more than fifteen years later, just the memory of his touch was enough to make her wonder why she'd ever said no.

Chapter Three

"Hurricane Iris is twenty miles south-southeast of Long Island and moving toward shore at..." The battery-operated radio faded, and Sandra gave it a sharp slap across its tinny face.

"Damn it," she muttered, glaring out the window at the dark gray sky. "Why couldn't you die during the baseball scores?"

She jiggled the dial and was rewarded with another bout of static, then: "National Weather Service predicts that Iris will hit storm-battered Long Island tonight with more force than..."

What a thoroughly rotten day.

First that painful, evocative dream last night, and now another hurricane bearing down on Long Island. Maybe Ed Gregory was right; she should have stayed in Sioux Falls.

They didn't have hurricanes in Sioux Falls.

And they didn't have Michael McKay.

Michael had filled her dreams the way he'd filled her life. Ridiculous that an idiotic teenage love affair—and one that had never even been consummated—could figure so prominently in her thoughts.

Sandra got up to boil water for coffee, then caught herself just as she was about to turn on the stove. So much for the modern, all-electric household; if Lilco didn't get the electricity back on soon, she'd end up having to use her furniture for firewood.

How many times in the last twenty-four hours had she flicked on a light switch, then cursed the darkness, or popped a tape into the VCR only to stare at a dead screen?

She opened the dark refrigerator instead, and pulled out a warm container of orange juice.

No wonder she was so jumpy and irritable. It had nothing to do with Michael and all those bittersweet memories filled with adolescent angst and forgotten dreams.

Who wouldn't be jumpy if they were suddenly plucked out of the twentieth century and plunged back into the Dark Ages?

She had a living room without a roof, a driveway completely blocked by fallen trees, a pile of paperwork that had to be done by Monday morning, and now that blasted weather report said another hurricane was about to send her house sailing toward Oz.

She took a sip of the warm orange juice, then poured it down the sink.

To hell with everything.

She was going back to bed.

THE SKY HAD BEEN DARK all morning, an evil, mean-spirited gray that was enough to depress the most stubborn of optimists.

When Michael awoke and saw it, he was pleased.

He welcomed the approaching storm. He wanted thunder and lightning and turbulence, because they matched the wild emotions he'd been struggling with since seeing Sandra the night before.

After calling David to let him know he was still all right and that the swing set in the yard was still standing, he pulled on a hooded sweatshirt and his old standby jeans with the hole in the left knee and went out to pitch in with the ongoing neighborhood cleanup.

The euphoria of the night before had disappeared with daylight as Michael had expected. Most of these men breathed fresh air only from the safety of their golf carts and redwood decks. They were upper-middle-class profession- als who had Lawn-Rite manicure their yards and kept the plumber on retainer. This return to nature was more than they could handle.

They kept up an easygoing banter while they worked, and it was almost enough to keep Michael's mind from straying toward thoughts of Sandy. Almost.

Around two o'clock the wind blew harder, the strong gusts held on longer. When the sky suddenly turned from gray to a peculiar mustard color, everyone stopped.

"She's on her way," Jim Flannery said, looking up at a nasty cloud formation that seemed to be settling in over the North Shore.

"It's going to be a bitch of a storm," said Sid Bernstein, shaking his head. "I hope the generator holds up." The hospital Sid was affiliated with was running on an auxiliary generator.

"We still haven't hacked our way out of Henry yet," said Frank, heaving a piece of a weeping willow onto the huge pile of firewood to the right of his driveway. "How much more can we take?"

"Not a hell of a lot," said Michael, glancing at the huge trees still left standing. "I think we'd better start battening down the hatches before it hits."

"Maybe it'll pass us by." Ever the psychologist, Bill made a practice of seeing the bright side of dark situations. "What are the odds on getting hit by back-to-back hurricanes?"

A blast of wind knocked them back on their heels.

"About even money." Michael rested the ax handle on his shoulder and turned toward the house. "You guys can stand out here and say hello to Iris. This time I'm going to tape up my windows."

"Don't think your luck will hold a second time, McKay?" Jim asked.

"Let's say I'm not going to take any chances."

An hour later all twenty-three windows were covered with giant masking tape X's in keeping with National Weather Service instructions. His house was as hurricane-proof as it was going to get, which was a good thing, since there was damned little doubt that Iris was on her way.

Despite the wind that seemed to intensify with every passing minute, an eerie stillness pervaded the neighborhood. Birds had disappeared; Jim Flannery's cat sat howling on the front step until Jim let her inside; Michael could see Sid's Labrador retriever racing in circles in the Bernstein's driveway.

He knew what the animals were feeling; he could sense the storm in his bones and in his muscles. His scalp fairly tingled with the electricity in the air. He welcomed it.

While he didn't wish any more destruction on the already badly battered Island, he wanted to drive down to the beach and stand out in the middle of the hurricane and let the wind and the rain and the lightning do their damnedest to wipe Sandra Patterson out of his mind.

He grabbed his car keys from the kitchen counter and was gone before any of his friends could tell him he had finally gone over the edge.

He didn't need to hear that.

He knew he already had.

SANDRA PATTERSON never cried.

At least not under normal circumstances.

However, being expected to survive two major hurricanes within as many days was certainly more than anyone—man or woman—should be expected to bear. Hurricane Henry hadn't been so terrible; it had been daylight, after all, and there was a certain novelty involved in spending a Friday morning watching all hell break loose right outside your living-room window.

Watching all hell break loose right outside your living-room window when you had no electricity, no running water, no heat and no telephone was another story entirely.

The thrill was gone.

Iris had conveniently managed to stall right off the Jersey Shore for a while that afternoon, building up force and giving day plenty of time to turn to night before she struck Long Island.

And strike Long Island she did.

Sandra had been so cavalier in refusing her neighbors' invitations yesterday that no one had bothered to reissue one today, and she regretted her haste. Pride was one thing, but survival was another. If her nearest neighbors weren't so damned far away, she would offer herself up on their doorstep and beg for shelter.

At least she knew her mother was all right. The storms had headed across the Sound and over Connecticut. New York's Westchester County hadn't been touched.

Another blast of wind rocked the house, and she burrowed further into her sweater. Any lingering urge to brave the elements disappeared in a burst of sanity. Only a lunatic would go out there, where trees snapped like matchsticks and picnic tables flew through the air as if they were made of papier-mâché.

For the thousandth time her mind returned to thoughts of Michael. He used to love storms, the brilliant flashes of lightning, the terrifying crack of thunder.

Once he had borrowed a friend's car and taken her out to Jones Beach, past the city and into the coveted suburbs of Long Island. He wanted to know how it felt to be in the eye of a storm, and she had crazily stood with him on the boardwalk as all hell broke loose around them and the Atlantic Ocean crashed at their feet.

His boyish sweetness had disappeared, and she had watched, mesmerized, as he seemed to gather strength from nature's violence and she glimpsed the man he was to be.

In her darker moments, it was a memory she returned to again and again.

The reality of Michael the man was not one that disappointed.

The radio crackled on again in a burst of Beethoven. She prayed for something rousing enough and beautiful enough to banish memory.

The reception, however, was horrible, a mass of tinny crackles and loud booms. She couldn't remember ever hearing that particular thump of percussion in that movement.

A piano interlude followed.

The thump recurred.

Sandra jumped up, spilling the apple juice she'd found in the pantry earlier. Someone was at the back door.

She knew full well that Ed Gregory would never risk his neck in a hurricane to keep her company, and for all her neighbors knew, she'd gone to stay with friends. The houses in the neighborhood were so far apart and so well-hidden by clever landscaping, that she could be held hostage for ten days and no one would even know.

The room was almost dark; one small candle burned on the end table. The thump turned into an insistent banging that matched the pounding of the pulse in her throat. She picked up the baseball bat she'd found earlier in one of the unpacked crates in the garage and headed for the front door.

"Who is it?"

A crack of thunder drowned out the voice.

"I can't hear you," she yelled. "Speak louder."

Wind and rain battled for dominance, but over it all she heard a man's voice. "Sandy?"

Michael?

She opened the door. He stood there on the top step, hands jammed into the pockets of his jeans, shoulders hunched against the rain. He wore a dark leather jacket with the collar turned up, and for a moment it could have been 1969 again, when they were just beginning to fall in love.

"What on earth are you doing here?"

"Are you going to invite me in, or wait for the hurricane to blow me in the door?"

She hesitated, unable to believe that after so many years he was once again on her doorstep.

He held his hands out, palms up, as a wicked blast of wind sent a flowerpot full of impatiens sailing across the front yard. "I'm unarmed, Sandy."

She snapped her mind back into gear and stepped aside so he could come into the foyer.

"Italian tiles," he said kneeling down to touch the mosaic pattern on the floor. "Donatelli outside of Milan?"

"Try Color Tile on Route 347." She closed and locked the door, then looked at him. "Donatelli outside of Milan?"

"Forget it. Just thinking out loud." He stood up and brushed the rain from his thick black hair. He took a step toward her, and she moved toward the kitchen.

"It's horrific out there," she said, tugging at the sleeves of her bulky sweater. "Only a lunatic would be out in that mess."

"You always said I was crazy."

She smiled at an old memory and caught the flash of his answering smile. "You were eighteen then, Michael. A certain degree of craziness comes with the territory."

He unzipped the front of his leather jacket, and she was struck by how powerful he seemed, how much more raw and male, than he had the night before in the bright lights of the White Castle.

"I'm not eighteen any longer, Sandy."

"I've noticed." She took a deep breath and extended her hand. "Let me hang up your jacket. You're dripping all over the floor."

He stayed in the foyer while she ducked into the bathroom and draped his jacket over the shower rod.

When she returned he was down on one knee again, inspecting a tile near the door to the living room with a flashlight.

"See this?"

She knelt down next to him and looked at the sandcolored octagonal tile. It looked like the 237 other sand-colored octagonal tiles in the foyer.

"So?"

"Look closer. There's a small cross carved into the upper left. That's Donatelli's signature."

"You know a lot about ceramic tiles." Not a brilliant rejoinder, but the subject had inherent limitations. She stood up and fiddled with the belt loop on her jeans. "I'd offer you some coffee, but . . ." She shrugged. "How about lukewarm apple juice instead?"

He looked up at her. "Sick of hearing about the tiles, are you?"

"I doubt if you came here to discuss my floor tiles, Michael." She kept her voice light, and tried to control the throb of emotion that threatened to give her away. "That is, unless you're in the ceramic-tile business."

He stood up and followed her into the den, where she lit two of the candles that rested on the mantelpiece.

"You should light a fire," he said. "Then you wouldn't have to walk around wearing a parka."

She looked down at her huge cable-knit sweater and laughed. "I'd love to, but I don't know how."

Surprise showed on his face. "How the hell long you been living here, anyway?"

"Three weeks. I can barely figure out how to work the timer on the stove."

"You never were mechanical, Sandy. Nothing's changed."

"Everything's changed, Michael. Everything."

He moved toward the fireplace, and she knew he was intent on getting it to work. He'd always been extraordinarily gifted in that way; anything he touched automatically sprang to life.

The analogy wasn't lost on her.

Michael opened the fire doors and was about to do something to the flue when she put her hand on his arm to stop him.

"Please, Michael." His head was down so she couldn't see his face. "Why are you here?"

"Would you believe I was heading down to the beach to watch the hurricane?"

"No."

She heard a click as he opened the flue.

"I was," he said. "Halfway there, I found myself turning the car around and heading toward Eaton's Harbor."

She said nothing. He turned and faced her, but his expression was difficult to read in the flickering candlelight.

"I remembered you were all alone. I thought you might need help."

A monstrous crash of thunder rocked the house, and she did her best to ignore it.

"I've been alone for a long time, Michael," she said softly. "This is nothing new."

Somewhere close by, a tree cracked, then hit the ground.

"Alone in a hurricane?"

"Try yesterday morning."

Another silence.

This isn't going to work, she thought. Too much time had passed, too much had happened, for them to be able to pretend they were nothing more than acquaintances catching up on old times.

He moved closer to her, and she backed away until her spine hit the edge of the entranceway to the den.

This was absurd.

She wasn't afraid of Michael McKay, no matter how menacing he might look at the moment with his savage dark looks complemented by the dimly lit room.

The last time they'd been together, seven years ago, he had made her cry, but Sandra was damn sure that wouldn't happen this time. She was too strong for that, and his power over her was seven years diminished.

He stopped within inches of her. The air crackled with more than the storm.

"I'll tell you why I'm here, Sandy."

Years of hiding her fears in the corporate battleground stood her in good stead. She met his eyes.

Before she could speak, she was in his arms and he was kissing her—not the exuberant, spontaneous kiss of the night before, but something deeper, more prolonged.

One of his hands cupped the back of her head, his fingers entwined in her hair. The other rested at the small of her back, and even through the layers of clothing she wore against the cold, the heat of his body came through. His body was larger and stronger than she'd remembered; the brief contact with him the previous night had only hinted at how well-muscled he'd become over the years.

No sorry decline into the beginnings of middle age here.

He was a man, plain and simple.

A man at the height of his powers.

His tongue teased her lips, and she parted them for him. His mustache was silky against her skin. The invasion was swift and painfully sweet.

She felt as if she'd been spun into some crazy kind of time warp, where her woman's body was being assaulted by the wild, unleashed emotions of a teenager on the verge of something beyond her understanding.

Years ago there had been a sweetly tentative side to Michael, but there was nothing tentative about him now, just as there was nothing uncertain about her response to him.

She wanted him.

More than her job, more than this house, more than security and safety and everything else she'd built her life around, she wanted Michael McKay.

"Tell me now, Sandy," he said, his breath warm and moist against her cheek. "If you're going to stop it, stop it now."

But it was going to happen; she couldn't stop it from happening any more than she could stop the hurricane outside. He moved against her in a way so powerfully sexual that she melted against him.

"Don't trust me, Michael," she whispered as his hands slid under her sweater and lit fires along the ridges of her spine. "Don't trust me."

The need for revenge was small and ugly and unmistakable.

"I don't trust you." He bent over and kissed the bare skin of her midriff where he'd pushed her sweater up.

She was finding it hard to think. He trailed his tongue across her rib cage, and a violent shudder buckled her knees. She had to grip him by the waist to keep from sagging to the floor.

"I've given you fair warning," she said as she pulled the zipper on his shirt and it fell open beneath her hands. "That's more than you did for me."

His chest was heavily matted with black curls. She bent her head, and as her tongue flicked against one of his flat nipples, she was struck once again by the changes the years apart had wrought.

He yanked his shirt off with a gesture almost savage in its urgency. Indeed, he looked almost savage with those fiery black eyes of his glowing in the candlelight.

The smell and the feel of him were familiar, but everything else had changed. There was a wildness to him that matched the storm raging outside—and the storm building within.

He was the fantasy lover of her darkest desires, the image she'd conjured up on the nights when her resistance to such things was at its lowest. He was the lure of danger when she knew she should stay safe.

His large hands were callused on the fingertips and palms, and her breasts tingled at their roughness against her skin.

Where had his life taken him that he should have hands like that?

Laborers had those hands: carpenters and masons and builders, not the boy who'd woven dreams so lofty, so ambitious that she'd almost been swept up in them herself.

But then he swept her up into arms as strong as the pounding of her heart, and she knew that no matter what the outcome, this was the night she'd been waiting for all her life.

For the first time in years, she was exactly where she wanted to be.

THE BEDROOM WAS at the end of the hallway, a large, high-ceilinged room with cartons lined up against one wall, and a huge brass bed against the other.

A quilt of some kind was tossed carelessly across the mattress, and he laid her upon it. The windows were wide and uncurtained, and he could see the trees in the backyard bending beneath the weight of the hurricane until their uppermost branches brushed the ground.

She lay against the quilt, her body falling into a line so inexpressibly lovely that he knew he would never be able to capture it in his lifetime.

He stood at the side of the bed and watched her, aware that this was a first—a first that quite possibly could be the last.

She raised herself up on one elbow. "Michael?" Uncertainty brought her alto to a higher range. "If you've—"

Her words stopped as he took her right ankle in his hand. His fingers encircled it with room to spare. She was watching him; he could feel the prickling, burning sensation of her intense gaze.

"Close your eyes," he said.

"No." She grew taut with apprehension.

"Do it, Sandy."

He wanted to say "Trust me," but words like trust had no place in this new alliance they were forming. Trust had disappeared that night seven years ago when he'd had her much as he had her now and had left her dry and wanting and humiliated.

He wouldn't do that again, but how in hell could she know that?

"I'm going to watch you, Michael." His hands were massaging her calf, behind her knee, the hollow of muscle where thigh met hip. Her voice betrayed her need. "I'm going to watch everything you do."

Her words were meant as a warning, but there was a challenge in them, too, and he rose, harder and hotter, to meet that challenge.

"Then watch me, Sandy. Watch me as I make love to you, because I'm through waiting."

They'd both waited long enough.

Chapter Four

For a moment, Sandra panicked.

Whatever she had once loved about Michael McKay, whatever they had once shared, belonged to the past, to the children they had been, to those innocent, adolescent dreamers whose realities had never quite managed to mesh.

It had little to do with this dark and dangerous man who stood at the foot of the bed and was slowly stripping her of her clothes.

This man was a stranger.

Oh, he called himself Michael McKay, all right, but she wasn't fooled. The Michael McKay she had known died that long-ago November night at the Plaza Hotel.

This man was a stranger she'd met for the first time the night before and had recklessly let into her house.

Mothers warned their daughters all the time about men like this; cautious women kept their doors locked and the chains on.

Some women, however, never learned.

Her clothes were off and draped over one of the boxes near the door before she could think of a reason to keep them on.

He was still standing at the foot of the bed, shirtless, his faded jeans just skimming his hips. His body language was loose, studiedly casual, but she sensed the restrained excitement thrumming just below the surface. She knew exactly what the sight of her naked was doing to him.

"Should I be afraid of you?" she asked, aware that she no longer was.

A low laugh was her answer.

She heard the rasp of metal on metal, then the sound of his jeans as they hit the wooden floor.

"This is the one place I thought I'd never be," he said as the bed sagged beneath his weight.

"It's not too late." The smell of his skin was disorienting her, knocking down the rest of her barriers. "You can get up and leave, Michael."

His hand covered her left breast, and her nipple rose to meet it.

"Not this time, Sandy." His dark head lowered until his lips found her and gently tugged the nipple even tauter. "Not this time."

"We have a history of stopping, you and I," she said, mesmerized by the sight of his thick dark hair as it fell across his forehead. A long, sad history of might-have-beens and rage and regret.

"We've made a hell of a lot of mistakes." He rested his hand on her belly, and the old angers, the old longings, were finally replaced by something new.

"I used to imagine this," she said as he opened his arms to her. "For years after we broke up, I'd try to imagine how it would have felt to lie in bed with you, naked beneath the covers, in a quiet, sunny room with all the time and privacy in the world."

In a world of complex dreams it seemed such a simple thing to wonder about, and yet it had been the one thing they'd never quite managed.

They'd made promises, Sandra and Michael, promises Sandra had found impossible to keep. He had represented the old way, the easy way, everything she had always wanted to escape. Sex was dangerous, her mother had told her, but what her mother hadn't understood was that pregnancy wasn't the only consequence.

By the time Sandra was in college, birth control was readily available and pregnancy no longer scared her; what did was the certainty that once she gave herself to Michael McKay, there'd be no escape.

His hold over her would be unbreakable.

"There were ways," he said now. "Even then. If you'd really wanted it, Sandy, we could have found a way."

Of course, he was right. She'd been so terrified of turning out like her mother, so frightened of finding her life over before it had even begun, that she'd turned away from the one thing she wanted more than anything: Michael.

Foolish little girl.

"I'm glad you're here," she whispered against his cheek. "Now I can stop wondering."

He gathered her to him and eased her over until his warm, solid body covered hers completely. There was something of destiny in her surrender. The thought that this wasn't just one night, that the actions of this night would change her life forever, couldn't stop her from moving beneath him in a way that told him she was ready, more ready than she'd ever been for any experience in her life.

Darkness made it easier.

She took his face in her hands, molding her fingers over the strong cheekbones, cupping her palm over the square, stubborn jaw. A two-day stubble tickled her skin as she brought her mouth to his. His mouth was wide, his lips soft, and she bit down gently on the lower one, savoring the taste of him with the tip of her tongue.

She was voracious in her need to know all of him, to experience everything she'd once denied herself before she remembered the thousand reasons why this should never be.

"Love me, Michael," she said. "We've waited so long for this moment."

Love me so we can finally say goodbye.

THEIR MOVEMENTS WERE simple. The combination of discovery and reunion blended in a way that made control impossible. Just the act of sliding into her warm and willing body was enough to take him over the edge. The fact that he was able to hold off long enough to take her with him was a testament to the triumph of experience over youth.

That was one trip he wasn't going to make alone.

She kept her face buried between his chest and arm long after it was over. At one point he thought he felt tears against his skin, but perhaps it was his imagination.

He didn't question her.

This coming together after so long left him beyond words. Two lifetimes of shared and separate histories were in that bed, and seven years of silence and regret.

Soon enough it would be time for questions, time for letting the normal pattern of his life pull him back within its familiar boundaries.

Right now, he had a lot to make up for.

MICHAEL HAD SPOTTED HER the moment she entered the church that morning seven years ago.

He had just turned to say hello to Clint and his wife Bonnie when he caught a flash of movement at the door and a low rumble of male voices punctuated by a husky, wonderful female laugh.

She was standing in the vestibule talking to the father of the bride. Her silky dark blond hair was pinned up, and long tendrils brushed against her neck. The sharp, clear November sunshine fell across her shoulders like a mantle, and he was struck again by just how beautiful she was.

Mr. Callahan said something, and she reached out and put her hand on his forearm. Michael felt her touch clear across the church.

It was four years since he'd last seen her. Four years since the last time they'd tried to bridge the gap that kept them so far apart. He'd been struggling against her memory of him as a kid with no direction, no goals—the child of a bricklayer and a supermarket cashier, who would probably amount to nothing. He'd been bumming around since getting out of the service, searching for something to channel his intense energy into, something beyond the sphere of a union and a weekly wage.

He'd found it in London in the person of Wallingford, the master builder, premier stone carver of the twentieth century. At twenty-three, Michael had finally found what he was meant to do. His hands were made for the ancient craft; his soul soared with the opportunity to create a beauty that could transcend time.

Finally—*finally*—he had something tangible to lay at her feet, some offering fine enough to make her see that there could be a future for them.

When she said no, he didn't see it coming.

She wanted security; she wanted to set down roots, have CDs and Money Markets and all the other trappings of American prosperity in the latter half of the twentieth century. She wanted a man in a three-piece suit who carried a briefcase and had a string of initials after his name.

He never had a chance to lay his dreams at her feet.

So on that November afternoon when he saw her standing in the sunlight in her expensive dress and her expensive pearls, laughing the laugh that had belonged only to him, he hated himself for wanting her.

He had no business wanting her.

He was engaged now to a woman he cared for, determined to build himself a life that didn't include Sandra Patterson. He told himself he was happy with the career he'd chosen, with the path his life had taken.

But there was always Sandra Patterson he wanted to impress, Sandra's approval he wanted to gain.

He looked up at her as she searched for a seat. She hesitated, obviously thinking of their last meeting. He smiled and made room for her.

She sat down next to him, and the air around him blossomed with the scent of French perfume. Suddenly he knew that if he ever wanted to be free of Sandra, first he would have to seduce her.

His need for her was out of all proportion. He'd had many women through the years, and there had been few surprises. Memory and imagination had played a trick on him and turned this one woman into something no woman could possibly be. If his upcoming marriage was ever to have a chance to succeed, he was going to have to exorcise Sandra Patterson from his life, once and for all.

And there was but one way to do that.

Of course, it didn't work out exactly as he'd planned.

Holding her as they danced had set off hundreds of tiny brushfires inside him, making it hard to think clearly. Kissing her in the darkened corner of the hotel ballroom proved to be as powerful an experience now as it had been years ago.

She was softer than he remembered, more yielding, and when he suggested taking a room she put her hand in his in a manner so trusting that he recalled a time when she would have trusted him with her life.

Through high school and college she'd managed to steer clear of this ultimate involvement with him, and now, when he wanted to hurt her, she came to him willingly.

This wouldn't be seduction, the fiery mindless coupling he'd wanted. This would be a communion, the sacred coming together of two people who'd loved each other for a very long time.

Soft lighting bathed the room and brought out the pale gold highlights in her hair. She looked younger, more nervous, more eager than he'd expected—not the harried businesswoman who'd told him her expectations went beyond what he could give her.

He leaned against the mantelpiece and lit a cigarette in a blatant ploy for time and noticed that her hands shook as she unpinned her hair.

That should have pleased him.

Somehow it didn't.

She sat on the edge of the bed and slipped off her high heels, then walked over to where he stood and rested her head against his chest. He threw the cigarette into the fireplace, then touched her hair, her cheek. She lifted her face to his, and he brought his lips down to meet hers and found himself drowning in the sight and smell and sound of her.

As they fell upon the bed, he knew it would never work, knew he'd been a damn fool to think it would. Nothing on earth could break the connection between himself and Sandra—he knew that now beyond any doubt. If he had any decency left inside him, he'd stop before he hurt her any more than he already had.

He'd stop while his impending marriage still had a chance.

She lay diagonally across the bed, her champagne-colored slip tangled around her hips, the lacy cups of her bra as delicate as angel's wings against her skin. Leaving her would be the hardest thing he ever did—and the finest.

He pushed away from her and stood over the bed. His shirt was open to the waist; his chest heaved as he tried to slow his breathing.

Say it, damn it. Just say it and get the hell out of here.

He buttoned his shirt and tucked it into his pants, ignoring the way they strained against his body.

"Wish me luck, Sandy," he said, his words like razors ripping his throat. The hazy glow of passion was beginning to fade as she realized something terrible was about to happen. "Wish me luck, because I'm getting married next month."

He was out of there before he had a chance to change his mind.

SO NOW, seven years later, as he lay in bed next to her, watching her sleep, lost in the wonder of this unexpected splendor, he wondered if the magic they'd finally shared was the beginning or the end.

SANDRA'S FIRST SHOCK the next morning was the brilliant sunshine streaming through her uncurtained bedroom window. She'd been deep in a dream that was unconscionably erotic, and she'd buried her head in her pillow to hang on to those glorious sensations just a little longer, but the bright light awakened her as effectively as any alarm clock.

Not that her alarm clock was working. She opened one eye and peered at the small Panasonic on her nightstand. It still read 11:42 a.m., Friday.

The day Hurricane Henry had come to visit.

The day she bumped into Michael McKay in White Castle.

The day—

Good God.

She opened her other eye.

It wasn't her pillow she'd been nuzzling; it was Michael's chest. She raised up on one elbow and noted a slight soreness in her thighs and upper arms. If the luxurious, well-used feel of her muscles was any indication, those erotic sensations had been no dream.

What on earth had she done?

Next to her, Michael cleared his throat. "It's about time," he said, looking up at her. A shock of thick black hair fell across one brow, and he pushed it away with the back of his hand.

Even with the harsh, uncompromising sun shining directly on him, he looked wonderful. The random strands of silver, the laugh lines encircling those dark eyes—on him, they were terrific.

"I didn't know you were awake," she said, pulling the sheet up around her breasts. Daylight was proving to be a hell of a lot tougher than darkness had been.

"I've been awake a long time," he said. "I had a lot to think about."

He sat up and rested his back against the headboard. The sheet fell down around his waist, and her gaze followed it. He grinned and shrugged.

"It happens," he said. "Watching you sleep wasn't easy."

Sandra Patterson, noted for her quick wit, had absolutely nothing to say.

He reached out and took her right hand. "Come back here, Sandy," he said, his voice low and full of promise. "Let me see the woman I loved last night." He seemed so relaxed, so casual, as if what had happened between them was no more earthshaking than watching the evening news.

Tears stung her eyelids, and she pulled away from him and stood up, wrapping the pale yellow sheet around her body as she did.

"It's no use," she said, fumbling with the two ends of the sheet as she tried to tie them together. "I can't make small talk with you, Michael. I can't banter. I can't flirt. This never should have happened."

The stupid sheet refused to cooperate with her and she awkwardly tried wrapping it up and around her torso so that she could flee.

Michael, totally nude, got up from the bed and approached her. He was so long, so lean, so incredibly well-proportioned, that her hands stopped fumbling as she watched him. He seemed unaware that he was fully aroused, but she couldn't imagine how he could ignore that fact.

She certainly couldn't.

"Don't run again, Sandy."

"I'm not running anywhere."

"You're trying to."

She tugged at the ends of the sheet. "All I'm trying to do is tie this damned thing around me."

"Let me."

His hands covered hers, and she began to tremble. "Please, Michael. Don't."

How could she sound like that, so soft, so yielding, when all she wanted to do was forget this had ever happened?

His large fingers brushed against her breasts as he took the ends of the sheet from her. Her breasts seemed to be swelling to meet his hand, her body yearning toward him in a way she couldn't control.

If he touched her she was lost.

She held her breath to minimize the chances of contact.

"Breathe, damn it," he muttered, fumbling around just as she had. "The phones don't work, and I don't know

CPR." He threw the left corner of the sheet over her right shoulder and shrugged. "Maybe you should cut a hole in the middle and stick your head through it."

That did it.

The nervous tension, the embarrassment, the sharp edge of desire exploded into a laugh. A real laugh. The first laugh they'd shared in a thousand years.

She sat down on the edge of the bed. "I didn't want any of this, Michael," she said as the laughter faded. "This is the last thing I ever imagined happening to me at this point in my life."

He didn't need to know how many times she'd wondered about him, fantasized about him, dreamed about him. No man had the right to know secrets like that.

"You think this was part of my master plan, Sandy?" He sat down next to her, and she had to resist the urge to ask him if he wanted to borrow part of her sheet.

"You're the one who showed up at my door. Obviously you had a plan of some kind."

That wonderful, tough-street-kid grin of his was back. "Sure I had a plan, but it was all in the interest of being a concerned neighbor."

"You're not my neighbor."

"A concerned friend."

She looked away. "You're not my friend," she said softly. "You haven't been my friend for years."

"You're wrong." The seductive sound of his voice drew her gaze back to his. "Despite everything, we've always been friends. No one knows as much about me as you do, Sandy. No one ever will." He stroked her hair gently, and memories of hot summer nights and lazy afternoons and a thousand impossible dreams filled the room around them. "We were friends long before we became lovers."

She shook her head. "We stopped being friends the night Kathy and Tom got married."

"I'd waited for so damned long to get back at you," he said, "but when it came down to it—" He shook his head. "I couldn't."

She remembered the way he'd walked out on her, leaving her on that rented bed, feeling more vulnerable and used than if they'd actually made love. "You mean you didn't plan it that way?"

Believing he had planned it that way was the one thing that had kept her pain at bay and fueled her anger.

"No, Sandy. What I'd planned to do was make love to you, *then* walk out." He smiled, but his eyes betrayed him. "I found out I wasn't as big a bastard as I thought."

"I suppose I should thank you for that?"

"Why not?"

She turned away for a moment and looked out the window. His words had changed the balance between them and, if possible, made her even more vulnerable than making love with him had.

The bed tilted as he swung his legs over the side. "Look, I admit I was rotten to even think of something like that, but give me a break, Sandy. I stopped before I really hurt you." There was a long silence. "That's more than you did for me."

God, how enraged he'd been the night before she left for college. Her sensitive, understanding Michael had towered over her with all the fury of a jilted almost-lover.

Her scholarship—the miracle that had somehow dropped into her lap at the eleventh hour—had opened up a world she had only dreamed about. A world of opportunity that had never been possible for her mother was now hers for the taking.

The chance to matter, to hold her future in her own hands, to shape it and mold it into something that could make her valuable, keep her secure—Michael had wanted her to toss all of that away because he simply couldn't wait.

He was the product of a working-class family who lived from paycheck to paycheck and never planned beyond the next union raise. Sure, Michael had his dreams—romantic, foolish dreams of happily-ever-after that had nothing to do with reality as Sandra saw it. A reality based on a need for security and independence that had been ingrained since childhood.

Now she understood the terror of a young man up against the unknown that threatened to rob him of the girl he loved, but that was little comfort to the children they had once been.

"More than anyone, you should have understood," she said, picking at a loose thread at the top hem of her sheet. "You knew what I was up against, Michael. You knew how important it was for me to go to school."

"What about the other times we tried, after you had your degree? What the hell were the reasons then?"

"I was a fool," she said quietly. "How's that for a reason?"

Sandra had loved the man but hated what he was. He'd seemed aimless, without ambition, always running off to Rome or London like some ridiculous overage hippie. So much had rested on her shoulders back then—both her mother's expectations and her own—that she hadn't understood what was of real importance.

Her own insecurities had forced her away from the one thing she honestly wanted: Michael McKay.

He didn't say anything. Who could blame him? Years after the fact, most of this didn't matter a damn.

"Not much of an excuse, was it?" No matter how many time-travel movies Hollywood turned out these days, a woman still couldn't go back and set the past to rights.

He stood up abruptly, reached for his jeans, which were on the floor near the window and slipped them on.

"I was in love with you, Sandy." He bent his knees slightly and zipped the fly. "You were everything in the world to me." When he looked down at her, she saw clearly the shadow of the boy he'd been, and her heart ached for all the mistakes they'd made. "I would've worked my tail off for you, to keep you safe, to send you to school. You never gave me the chance."

I don't need this, she thought, fighting down the waves of aching memory his words called up. She'd come so far since those early days that she didn't need his old angers and fears to pull her back down. Not when so much now depended on her success.

She stood up, straightened the sheet around her and headed for the door. "I usually eat a huge breakfast," she said, as their eyes met across the room, "but since there's no electricity and no food and no—"

"Forget it," he said, brushing past her in order to grab his shirt from atop the wardrobe carton. "I've got a lot of work waiting for me at home."

"I'm not trying to hustle you out of here, Michael." Her voice quavered slightly, and she hoped he didn't notice. "I just wanted you to know that—"

He slid his arms into the sweatshirt, and she watched as he inched the zipper up over that incredible torso of his. The feel of those muscles beneath her fingers, against her mouth, her thighs, was burned permanently into her sensory memory.

"I know exactly what you're trying to do, Sandy. You're still as transparent as hell."

"You don't know anything about me. I'm not the same little girl who used to wait for your call and live for your smile."

He crossed his arms over his chest and leaned against the mahogany armoire in the corner. "Your memory's more selective than I thought. I remember doing my share of waiting on you."

"This isn't getting us anywhere. I'm going to see if I have any more juice in the pantry." She swept the end of the sheet over her left shoulder in as elegant a manner as she could manage, and turned to leave.

"You're scared, Patterson."

She turned back. "What?"

"I say you're scared."

"I say you're crazy."

"You've always been afraid of letting people see through that shell of yours."

"And, of course, you think you can see through it?"

"I'll bet I've come closer than anyone else in years."

Sandra had always been remarkably adept at side-stepping personal questions by bouncing them back with a neat little verbal topspin that stopped her questioners cold. As a little girl, it had been necessary to shield her illegitimacy.

As an adult, it was part of her nature. Her high-visibility work performance, coupled with her low-profile personal life, had taken her far.

As the years went on, her illegitimacy no longer mattered. In some ways the world had changed for the better, but too late to change the woman she was.

"I don't hear you denying it, Sandy."

"You know what *was*, Michael. You don't know what *is*."

He gestured toward the rumpled bed in the center of the room. "We've made a start."

He was moving too fast for her to get her defenses back in place.

"What happened, happened. It was wonderful, but there won't be a second time." She was older now and wiser; she understood who and what he was and why it would never work.

Besides, there was too much at stake. It was no longer just her career, her future, her life; it was her mother's as well, and that was a burden few men wanted to share.

She'd learned that from Andrew Maxwell.

He followed her into the kitchen.

"You're not married, are you, Sandy?"

She shook her head. "Took you long enough to get around to asking me, McKay."

"I had other things on my mind." He leaned against the doorjamb. "Grapevine said you were engaged."

She lifted her chin slightly. "Did the grapevine also say I broke the engagement?"

That wicked grin of his made a reappearance. "They must've missed that part."

"Don't look so pleased, McKay. That doesn't change one damned thing." She pulled the last can of juice off the pantry shelf, then looked for two clean glasses. A horrible thought formed. "Last thing I heard, my sources told me you were a married man."

"Better update your sources. I've been divorced almost four years."

She offered him a glass of juice, but he shook his head. Instead, he waited for her to pour one for herself, then took a long swig straight from the can. She tried to picture Ed Gregory from Citi-National doing such a thing, but Ed probably traveled with a portable wineglass in his glove compartment.

Michael was watching her steadily. "I'm flattered you've been asking about me."

"I didn't have to ask," she lied. "You know the old crowd. They love to spread the word on the two who got away."

Of the old group, only Sandra and Michael had left Queens and built lives that ran counter to the lives of their friends. Although, judging by the calluses on Michael's hands, she wondered if he'd just traded the subway for the Long Island Rail Road, and his old dreams for a newer, harsher reality.

"And you say you've never wondered about me, Sandy? All these years, you never once wondered?"

She hesitated long enough for him to take her into his arms.

"You never wondered where I was or what I was doing or who I was doing it with?"

"Never. I stopped thinking about you seven years ago."

"You're a lousy liar."

A smile twitched at the corners of her mouth. "I'm a wonderful liar. How do you think I manage to survive in the corporate jungle?"

"Maybe they don't know you the way I do, Patterson. When you lie, your eyes get bluer."

"Ridiculous. Eyes don't change color with emotion."

"The hell they don't."

"That's not logical, Michael."

"I don't give a damn if it's logical or not. When you lie, your eyes get bluer. They also get bluer when—"

His jet-black eyes picked up an unholy twinkle and she braced herself.

"Go ahead," she said. "I can take it."

"They also get bluer when you make love."

"The room was dark. How could you know that?"

"I watched you by the light of the storm. I watched it all happen."

Her body trembled, and she leaned her forehead against his shoulder. "You're making this difficult."

"It shouldn't be. This should be the easiest thing that's ever happened to us." He stroked her hair in a way that made the intervening years disappear behind a scrim of smoke. "We've been preparing for it long enough."

"I've missed you so much." Her voice was low; it cracked on the last word. "Each step along the way, I wondered how it would have felt if I'd had you to share it with me. When we saw each other again at Tom and Kathy's wedding, I thought, 'Oh, God, here's my chance. Here's my chance to make up for my mistakes.'" She shook her head. "You know how well that turned out."

"Yeah," he said slowly. "I know how well that turned out."

"I hated you for a long time after that," she said, meeting his eyes. "I used to lie awake at night and think of all the rotten things I should have done to you."

"Such as?"

"Murder."

"Murder?"

"I considered it, Michael."

"If it's any consolation, retribution wasn't all it was cracked up to be."

"And if it's any consolation to you, I understand why you had to do it." What they'd shared had been so deep, so all-encompassing, that his act of passion and anger had been inevitable.

"I'd take it back if I could, Sandy." He held her tight. "It didn't help either one of us, did it?"

"It helped us to make the break," she said, blinking back her tears. "At the time, that seemed pretty damned important."

He pulled away from her slightly and tilted her chin so she could do nothing other than look into his eyes. "And here we are again. We can't seem to get away from each other, can we?"

"Doesn't seem that way." Her heart was pounding so violently that she could feel it at the base of her throat. "Long Island's a big place," she managed. "I think there's room enough here for both of us."

He released her from his embrace. His eyes glittered like chunks of onyx, and like onyx, they were unreadable. She wanted to step back into the protective circle of his arms, but he had closed himself off to her.

"This time it's up to you, Sandy." He scribbled two phone numbers on the chalkboard that hung over her kitchen counter. One was local; the other, a New York City exchange. "I took the first step. The second one's up to you."

He turned and walked out the door, and Sandra wondered what Ed would say if she told him she wanted to transfer back to Sioux Falls.

Blizzards, tornadoes and a forest of fallen trees suddenly seemed a whole lot safer than living anywhere near Michael McKay.

ONE GREAT THING about living in a neighborhood with a world-class surgeon and a famous attorney was how quickly things get done.

By the time Michael got back to his house Sunday afternoon, not only had the power been restored, but his phone service was back as well.

There was a message from Annie Gage, one of his friends from work, two messages from neighbors asking if he wanted to come over for dinner and one terse request to call his former in-laws in Florida. Just the sound of Art Bentley's voice was enough to set Michael's nerves on edge.

He knew David had the right to be with his grandparents—life had already dealt the kid a tougher blow than most five-year-olds should have to deal with—but, hell, Michael hated the thought of his son learning to be afraid of his own shadow, to be as suspicious and narrow-minded and lost as the Bentleys were.

He flipped off the machine. He didn't want to think about Art, or dinner, or even his job at the cathedral. What he wanted to do was get into his car and head back to Eaton's Harbor and drag Sandra Patterson back into bed.

What the hell was wrong with them that pride was always getting in the way of passion? Hadn't growing older—and supposedly wiser—done them any good at all?

Once again he'd made a grand macho-man exit. Stuff like that was terrific in the movies, but it was hell in real life.

He looked out the window, and the sight of Jim Flannery clearing his walkway of hurricane debris caught his eye.

Maybe he couldn't jump back into his car and sweep her off her feet again, but there was one promise he'd made that he could do something about.

It wasn't much, but damn it, it was a start.

AFTER TWO HOURS of trying to make sense of both her emotions and her account ledgers, Sandra finally gave up and went to get dressed. She was tugging on her favorite old jeans when she heard the noise in the yard.

Two young men in work shirts and sweatpants were stretching a huge canvas tarpaulin out on the lawn, while a third was dragging an aluminum ladder up the driveway.

She pulled her sweater on and hurried out the back door.

"Are you here about the roof?" she asked, squinting into the sun.

"Yeah," the tallest of the three answered. "Your pal's got a lotta pull, lady. We had to move back four other jobs to do yours."

The wind was biting, and she wrapped her arms around her chest. Ed Gregory might not be the most physical of men, but when it came to getting a job done, he had no equal.

"Do me a favor," she said. "If you see Mr. Gregory to-night, tell him thanks."

"Gregory?" the young man asked. "Who's Gregory?" He pulled out a pile of crumpled work tickets from his back pocket and sifted through them. "Some big shot named Mike McKay put in the order."

"A big shot named Mike McKay, hmm?"

"Yeah. You want we should thank him for you?"

"No," she said. "Just tell him I'll call him tomorrow." As if she'd ever had a choice in the matter.

One thing about Mike McKay was, he never did play fair.

It was nice to know some things never changed.

Chapter Five

The Cathedral of St. Matthew the Divine dominated the skyline of upper Manhattan, no mean feat in a city famous for buildings that soared higher than most people dreamed.

Not even the Monday-morning traffic—a hideous, Byzantine maze of tangled vehicles and snarling drivers—could dim the rush of sheer joy Michael experienced each time he saw the church.

That morning, it was almost enough to wipe away the bone-crushing fatigue caused by a sleepless night spent waiting for the damned phone to ring. He'd considered staying home from work and doing some hurricane repairs, but he knew it was useless.

He knew that every time a phone within a five-block radius rang, his stupid adrenaline would start flowing hot and fast, and he was afraid that sooner or later some innocent person soliciting for the American Heart Association would be sent into a coronary by his uncensored language.

No, it was better that he went in to work. He needed something bigger than himself, larger than his own chaotic world, to think about.

The Cathedral of St. Matthew the Divine was certainly that.

Except for a thirty-five year break after the Second World War, the cathedral had been under construction for more than a hundred years, and would still be under construction well into the twenty-first century. In an age when ecclesiastical projects ran a distant second to MTV and Cablevision, funding for a project of such scope and duration was difficult to come by.

They were currently coming to the end of a major piece of funding, and the cathedral staff was beginning to wonder if construction would continue much past the first of the year.

Michael was the master stonecutter on the project, a position of honor inherited from George Wallingford, the genius behind the renewal of interest in the medieval art. Just when it had seemed that stonecutting had gone the way of the dinosaur, Wallingford had finished work on the cathedral in Liverpool, England, and had come to America at his own expense to teach a new generation.

Michael knew Wallingford from his own days as an apprentice in Rome and Liverpool, back when he was just beginning to understand how much this work meant to him. Being asked to join Wallingford at St. Matthew's was the second best thing that had ever happened to him. Wallingford had wanted to bring in apprentices from abroad to work on the north tower and the finials and the gargoyles and everything else that had yet to be done, but Michael had surprised himself by voting that idea down.

There was something unsettling about the notion of investing millions of dollars in a work of art that rose amid the painful poverty of the New York streets, streets that not so long ago had been his own home. A hundred years ago, when the cathedral's foundation had been laid, this part of Manhattan had been farmland, pastoral and lovely.

Times had changed.

The city had sprawled northward; the church now rose above tenements and street-corner hustlers hawking their games of three-card monte.

It hadn't been hard for Michael to figure that resentment, ugly and dangerous, could halt the progress of the cathedral as surely as a lack of funds.

The strange and wonderful craft that had captured Michael's soul had, oddly enough, proved financially lucrative, and Michael, who'd never given much thought to the power of money, found himself with more than he'd ever dreamed. He wasn't rich, but he was a hell of a lot better off than the street punks who hung out on the corners looking for a way out.

It occurred to Michael that he could provide it.

So, after wheeling and dealing and bucking up against the system for three dead-end months, he managed to convince the powers-that-be that the best place to find apprentices for the stonecutting work was right there in front of them.

Slowly the neighborhood was beginning to come back to life.

It didn't matter to Michael that the cathedral was unfinished; it didn't even matter that the cathedral wouldn't be finished in his lifetime—or even during the lifetime of his son.

The completion of the Cathedral of St. Matthew the Divine was a project larger than Michael, or Wallingford, or any of the hundreds of other craftspeople who would leave their mark in the stone. What they were building would still stand a thousand years from now.

What they did—and who they were—mattered.

St. Matthew, with its spires and turrets and two missing towers, was a testament to faith in the future, and for the first time in ages, Michael was beginning to think his future might include the one thing that had eluded him all these years.

Love.

There was no denying that he and Sandy were still on shaky ground; no two people with as rocky a history as theirs could possibly come together after eight years and expect clear sailing.

Providence, in all its divine wisdom, had seen fit to bless their reunion with the worst hurricane to come sweeping up the Atlantic coast in the last seventy-two years.

Make that the worst two hurricanes.

And somehow it had seemed fitting.

There had been anger in their reunion—anger, and rage, and a bone-shaking sense of rightness that had taken the simple movements of sex and transformed them into something as magnificent as a piece of marble in the hands of an artist.

If she didn't call him by that night, he *was* going to go back to that house of hers by the water and—

A messenger whizzed past him on a sleek Italian bike and Michael slammed on the brakes, then turned onto Amsterdam Avenue and whipped into the vacant lot the construction crew used for parking. The parking area was the corner of what was by Manhattan standards a huge piece of property that currently did triple duty as a parking lot, storage area and baseball diamond.

Five years ago, when he had first begun piecing together his crew, it had seemed that every low-life sleazebag in Upper Manhattan would find his way to that corner lot, and Monday mornings the ground would be littered with used hypodermic needles, razor blades and other weapons of self-destruction. Michael still had to navigate through a mine field of beer bottles on occasion, but the change was happening. It was real.

And the work going on at St. Matthew's was largely responsible for it.

On those mean streets, it was miracle enough to turn one life around. The apprentice program he'd initiated had managed to turn thirty young lives around.

If a miracle like that were possible, was he crazy to begin to wonder if maybe, just maybe, he and Sandy might make it over the long haul?

Leon's mock-up of a gargoyle for the western turret was propped up on top of the gate, a snarling, fanged demon adorned with Michael's unmistakable head of hair and ever-present Walkman. When it came to gargoyles, each stonecutter was given free rein, and it wasn't unusual to see a lot of fire-breathing demons with the McKay look about them.

The soaring sound of Marvin Gaye rang out from the construction shed near the employees' door to the cathedral proper, and Michael grinned.

Oh, he understood all about artistic integrity and freedom of expression within the boundaries of his medieval craft, but when it came to music, he was one mean mother.

If it wasn't Smokey or Marvin or the Four Tops, with their sweet, sweet harmonies about love and longing, it just didn't play. Michael wasn't a man given to philosophical musings, but he knew that the songs you grew up with, the music you cut your sexual teeth on, was the music you turned to when life was good—and especially when it wasn't.

He was whistling "Shop Around" when he swung open the door to Altar Ego, the cathedral's design workshop, which was run by Annie Gage.

As usual, Altar Ego was a whirl of motion and sound and riotous color. He stepped around a bolt of fabric waiting to be silk-screened with the workshop's logo, dodged a Hispanic boy and a black girl who were setting up an enormous loom, then peered around the partition shielding the potters.

Rap music and Madonna vied with Placido Domingo and Vivaldi, and he upped the volume on his whistle. He was preparing to launch into a rousing version of "Ain't Too Proud To Beg" when a raucous laugh rose over the din.

"What are you doing here, McKay?" Annie Gage's distinctive voice floated across the room. She was a small, delicately made brunette whose stature belied her strength. "I thought you suburbanites were still digging out after the hurricanes."

He walked over to where she was supervising a trainee on the intricacies of silk-screening.

"I have the fastest shovel in the east. Besides, I lucked out. Not too much damage to my property." He told her about the severe damage to most of Long Island, which still included loss of electricity.

"I told you not to move out there east of no-man's-land," Annie said. "No civilized person moves to the other side of the East River."

"I was born on the other side of the East River. As far as I know, Queens is still part of New York City, Gage."

"Barely." She adjusted the screen, then gave her trainee the sign to start work. "I think you were crazy to leave Manhattan."

"You've been telling me that for three years now."

She brushed her hands on the side of her khaki pants and led him toward her office, where the seemingly bottomless coffeepot awaited. "It bears repeating," she said as she grabbed their mugs from the shelf over the refrigerator and handed him his. "Sooner or later, you'll come to your senses."

It was old territory, but since they both enjoyed a good argument, he plunged right in. "I came to my senses the day I moved out of the city."

Annie grunted her thanks as he poured the coffee. "Interest rates are good right now. I bet you could turn a decent profit on that barn of yours."

"What about that shoe box you call home?" he asked, taking a gulp of pure caffeine. "Why don't you put it on the block and find out what it's like to have some land to call your own?"

Her narrow shoulders shuddered in horror. "Wash your mouth out, McKay!"

He lifted his coffee mug. "Can I use this?"

Annie took a sip, made a face, then added sugar to her cup. "Do I seem the type to spend my Saturdays pushing a lawn mower around the south forty?"

"Live dangerously, Gage," he said, settling himself in the swivel chair behind her desk and putting his feet on the windowsill. "You might find you like the great outdoors."

"No chance," she said, perching on the edge of the rusty lateral file cabinet adjacent to the refrigerator. "I only like the great outdoors when there's a picture window keeping it away from me."

"I'll be damned. You're a coward."

She shot him as fierce a look as a woman who barely topped five feet could muster. "I brave the IRT every night, McKay, while you're on your way home to your own private Stepford. You tell me who's the coward!"

He reached for one of the bagels stacked on a chipped blue plate that rested atop the lateral file. Amenities like cream cheese were too good for the cathedral staff.

He made a production out of biting off a chunk. "Stale."

"So get your butt in earlier and *you* can pick them up at Bagel Master."

"I'm a commuter," he said. "That gives me certain inalienable rights. You city dwellers have to do the donkey work."

"I must say you're in a disgustingly easygoing mood for a Monday morning. David must be home."

"Almost," Michael said. "His plane gets into Newark at three."

"Hmm," she said, narrowing her eyes. "Is that happiness I see, or relief?"

"Both. Art is beginning to talk about longer visitation rights again." He stopped. Talking about it would make his vague fears seem too real.

She put her hand on his forearm for a second. "Listen, McKay, you've already been nicer to them than they deserve. David is *your* son. Another man might not have given them any visitation rights at all."

Michael's sympathy for the Bentleys had vanished not long after Diana's death, when they had suddenly refused to part with David and started talking about a custody fight.

"Believe me, Gage, I'm doing it for Davey, not Art and Margaret." His son's world had been shattered twice: first by divorce, then by the death of his mother and stepfather. Michael was going to move heaven and hell to make sure it didn't happen a third time.

"How do you think he'd feel about trying his hand at the potter's wheel?" she asked, pulling a cigarette out of the pocket of her lab coat and lighting it. "You could bring him here from the airport. I promised him he could the last time he was here, but Dominica was working under a deadline. I tried to explain that to him, but..." She shrugged her shoulders in a gesture of defeat.

Michael laughed. "Yeah, and you were more disappointed than Davey was." He went to cadge a cigarette off Annie, then caught himself, remembering his vow to quit.

"If you've got the time, Gage—and the patience—he's yours."

Annie was one of those rare people who were instantly comfortable with children without being patronizing or distant. His mother's death had made David quiet and cautious when it came to forming ties with new people; Annie had instantly been able to get past his defenses and make the little boy laugh.

It was hard to imagine Sandy with his son.

Michael liked Annie; he respected her talent and admired her determination. Her offbeat, unpretentious sense of humor appealed to him. She was bright, sexy, great with kids and—on more than one occasion—had made it known to Michael that she wouldn't mind sharing more than morning coffee and after-dinner drinks with him.

Because he sensed it would mean more to her than he wanted it to, he'd never taken her up on it. It was a rough world out there, and friendship was too important to screw up.

"I have an idea," Annie said, stubbing out her cigarette with two quick jabs. "The two of you could come back to my apartment later and I'll fix tacos. If my memory serves me, tacos are a big thing with the Sesame Street set."

"Anything that drips down your arms and ruins your clothes is a big deal with the Sesame Street set."

Annie's quirky smile lit up her face. "So, we're on." She stood up and straightened the nonexistent creases on her khaki pants. It was no wonder David was crazy about her; she had a child's lack of concern with minor details like hemlines and creases. "We'll take your Jeep, McKay, and pick up the groceries at that store on Tenth Avenue with the four-alarm salsa."

He swung his feet to the ground and polished off the rest of his coffee. "I thought you loved the IRT."

"I'll make an exception tonight for Davey's sake." Her laugh made her shiny black hair swirl around her face in a way that would once have delighted him.

"Annie."

"Uh-oh. Whenever you say 'Annie' in that tone of voice, I know something's up."

"I don't think tonight's such a good idea."

Annie was obviously having trouble keeping her smile in place, but there was no help for it. They'd prided themselves on their honesty, and he wasn't about to start making exceptions.

"You think Davey will be too tired?"

He shook his head. "It's not that."

The smile faltered badly. "You'll be too tired—hurricane cleanup and all that?"

He pushed his hair back off his forehead and cursed his terminally lousy timing. "I wish it were that simple."

She leaned against the file cabinet and fiddled with her earring. "Why do I get the feeling this is something more serious than hating Mexican food?"

He touched her arm for an instant, but pulled away when he saw the open, vulnerable look in her eyes. "You know me too well, Gage. You always have."

Annie looked out the window for a moment, watching Angel and Raul move a block of limestone away from the door of the construction shed. "If you tell me you met her when Hurricane Henry deposited her house in your front yard, I'll knock your block off. I have a notoriously low tolerance for bull, McKay."

"That's one of the things I like about you."

"So what's the story?" she asked, pulling another cigarette out of her pocket and lighting it. "And don't pull any punches. I'm a big girl."

He thought of Sandra, and the strange turn of events that had brought them to a place they'd never been before. What had happened between them was something he himself couldn't understand, much less explain to someone else.

"Damned if I know what the story is," he said, fighting the urge to grab her cigarette out of her hand and give in to a full-fledged nicotine attack. He briefly outlined their chance meeting at the White Castle, and offered a few choice highlights of their common history.

"So far, the only thing I like about her is the fact she works for Citi-National." Annie's words were as blunt as her demeanor. "Bring her around. We could use some new funding for the arts project."

"She doesn't even know I work here."

Her feathery dark brows lifted. "A grand reunion after seven years and you don't exchange work information? Highly suspect, McKay."

The last thing he needed was to tell Annie everything. "The hurricane was Topic A, Gage."

"I'll take your word for that," she said, her voice suddenly soft, "because, frankly, I don't think I'm ready for the truth."

"Don't go reading anything into this. For all I know, I'll never see her again." His grand gesture of sending the cleanup crew to her house the day before had gone unacknowledged.

Michael didn't want to speculate on what that meant. Annie might like honesty; he wasn't altogether sure that he felt the same way.

"She must have been surprised when you told her about Davey."

He froze.

"She doesn't know you have a son?"

"We didn't have that much time to talk, Gage," he said, trying to skirt the issue. The past had loomed so large between them that the present had been pushed aside.

"How much time does it take to say, 'By the way, I have a son'?"

"Get off my back, will you, Annie?" As usual, she had him dead to rights. He hadn't brought up David or the cathedral or Diana's death, because for that one night, he had wanted there to be nothing but Sandra.

It made him feel like a bastard, but there it was: the pure, unvarnished truth.

She sighed, and he reluctantly met her eyes across her office. "You got it bad, pal," she said softly. "Damn you."

He had it bad, all right, and he couldn't help but wonder if he wasn't damned at that. Damned to keep finding the right woman at the wrong time.

It was too bad he couldn't share that thought with Annie, because he had a feeling she'd understand.

As it turned out, Citi-National hadn't managed to get the power back on by Monday morning, so Sandra found herself with another unscheduled day off.

Ed had dropped by early to pick up the ledger sheets for the Connecticut job, and he had mentioned that he fully intended to have the office operational by three that afternoon.

Although he didn't say it—you didn't talk that way to an assistant vice-president, after all—Sandra knew she was expected to be at her desk later on, electricity or no electricity.

Sunday night had been a long one. She'd struggled for hours with her feelings for Michael, reliving that first incredible moment when they'd been naked and together and she'd known it was going to happen, really going to happen, *finally* going to happen after so many years of waiting.

The notion that making love with him could be an isolated experience, one of those wonderful interludes that have no place in the scheme of your life, had disappeared with the dawn.

If she called Michael McKay, she'd be acknowledging the one fact she'd been trying all night to deny: she was still in love with him.

She wandered through her house, barely noticing the countless boxes and crates still waiting to be unpacked. More than anything, she needed someone to talk to, someone who understood the girl she'd been and the woman she'd become.

TWO AND A HALF HOURS LATER, Sandra approached the nursing station at Fair Oaks.

"Well, Ms. Patterson, hello! I never expected to see you here today." The day nurse looked up from her paperwork and smiled at Sandra. "What with that terrible hurricane and all, I thought you folks were all busy keeping body and soul together."

Sandra swallowed. She hated the hospital, and it took every ounce of her formidable willpower to return the nurse's smile.

"I was lucky, Nancy. I had some help digging out from under, and since we still have no electricity, I figured I'd drive up and see how my mother is today."

Please tell me she's fine, Sandra thought. *Let this be one of her good days.*

More than anything, she needed to talk to someone who would understand.

"Elinor is doing splendidly today. As a matter of fact, she's in the solarium."

If there was one thing Sandra had learned in the last six years, it was that these minor triumphs were always followed by major setbacks. That was the nature of ALS, to play on that damned this-time-it'll-be-different optimism that most victims and their families seemed to share.

Sandra knew better.

Her mother knew better.

Everyone in the hospital ward knew better.

And yet it was still impossible not to feel a surge of excitement each and every time it happened.

Amyotrophic lateral sclerosis was an insidious disease that attacked the spinal cord, the brain stem and the cortex in a way so gradual, so unpredictable, that its inevitable result often surprised even the most knowledgeable. Throughout the entire process, however, the patient's mind remained clear and the senses intact, which made the final progress of ALS doubly tragic.

So they took their triumphs wherever they found them and saved their questions for later on, when there would be plenty of time to ask why.

Nancy wrote out a visitor's pass and handed it to Sandra.

"The east solarium by the new wing?" Sandra asked.

"That's the one. It has the best view in the house, and with the leaves beginning to change color, we've had to add a few more chairs."

Sandra chuckled and headed down the corridor, trying her best to ignore the subtle scent of controlled fear that seemed to permeate every hospital she'd ever been in.

From the road, though, Fair Oaks looked more like a resort than a hospital. Set on a hill overlooking the Hudson Valley, it was nestled at the edge of a forest that was now tinged with splashes of gold and crimson and rust that would soon spread and set the grounds ablaze with autumn color.

Her heart usually started to beat faster as soon as she turned off the Major Deegan Expressway and began to thread her way along the back roads toward the hospital. No matter how many mental tricks she tried to play on herself—counting the number of mansions set back from the road, promising herself to stop at the antique shops that seemed to pop up around every bend—it was impossible to pretend that this was a leisurely drive and that her destination was just some country inn along the route.

Country inns didn't have oxygen tents and respirators and hideous tangles of wire and tubing designed to trap bodies that yearned to finally be set free.

Country inns didn't have her beautiful, bright, fifty-two-year-old mother sitting in a wheelchair by the picture window with her hands draped gracefully—uselessly—on her lap.

The solarium was as crowded as the day nurse had said it was. Patients in pastel bathrobes and fuzzy slippers perched politely on leather couches that squeaked each time they changed position. Visitors chatted with one another, their lips stretched tightly over mouths that had forgotten how to smile naturally.

Sandra thanked God for the modeling she'd done while in college. She'd thoroughly hated the mindless job of being a human coat hanger, but the trick of smiling on command had come in handy over the years.

How many CEOs and bank presidents had she smiled at while they made long, dull presentations that sent many of her co-workers into temporary comas?

And how many times since her mother's diagnosis had she stood outside hospital rooms from Baltimore to Chicago to upstate New York and tried to summon up a smile to brighten Elinor's day?

So what was one more time?

She straightened the hem of her sweater, tossed her hair off her face, dug up her best smile, then walked into the solarium.

Larry, an octogenarian with the attitude of a teenager, let loose with a wolf whistle that rattled the rafters. "Will you look at our Sandra all decked out in that red sweater of hers? Now if that ain't a sight to warm a man's heart, I don't know what is."

Sandra bent down and planted a kiss on top of his bald head. "I wore it just for you," she said, playfully ignoring the ribald laughter of the man's three cohorts. She pointed toward the splashes of emerald and turquoise on the pockets. "I even managed to work in your two other favorite colors."

The teasing escalated, and she was reminded how human nature remained the same however much the packaging changed. Larry was being treated for a debilitating hip problem, but he was fortunate enough to be ambulatory most of the time. He and Sandra had met near the water fountain, and had instantly formed a friendship that included Elinor and some of the other patients on the floor.

While the nursing staff at Fair Oaks was superb, Sandra took comfort from the fact that Larry Munson kept a sharp eye out for Elinor's well-being and didn't hesitate to call Sandra if there was something he thought she should know.

"We were all watching the TV last night," Larry said, "and wondering how you made out. Didn't old Henry and Iris hit right on the North Shore?"

Sandra groaned. "Not only did they hit right on the North Shore, Larry, they hit right in my back yard. I don't think we'll have electricity back until Christmastime. Lilco isn't exactly known for its efficiency.''

Mention of Long Island's utility company started a no-holds-barred comparison of the tri-state area's power sources. The language was bluer than the skies outside the solarium, and Sandra used the distraction to slip away.

Elinor was dozing by the large bay window that looked out over the rear grounds of the hospital. Her wheelchair rested in an oval of sunshine that made her pale blond hair glitter. She looked pampered, elegant, a woman born to privilege with the elegant bed jacket of champagne-colored silk and the cashmere lap robe tucked around her.

On her good days, she and Sandra shared a private joke over that one.

Lucie, the personal nurse Sandra had hired for her mother, was settled in an overstuffed chair adjacent to the window, knitting one of her famous Aran sweaters. The last time Sandra had been in, Lucie had managed to hug her three times, and while the woman was known for being de-monstrative, Sandra's suspicions had been confirmed when she'd seen a cloth tape measure poking out of the pocket of Lucie's uniform.

The metallic clicking of the needles stopped as soon as Sandra approached.

''Well, will you look who's here? We weren't expecting you until next weekend, lovey.''

''I had an unscheduled day off thanks to Henry and Iris, and I couldn't think of a better place to spend it,'' she said, giving the woman a hug. ''Besides, I had to check up on how my sweater's coming along, didn't I?''

Lucie's dark brown eyes were wide and innocent. ''Your sweater? What on earth are you talking about?''

Sandra ran a hand lightly over the intricately knitted cables and grinned. "I think we'll both find out what I'm talking about on my birthday, don't you?"

Elinor sighed softly and moved her right shoulder as she napped. It was one of the few voluntary movements that ALS hadn't already stripped from her.

Sandra cleared her throat and brought her gaze back to Lucie. "Nancy says Mother is having a good day today."

"One of her best days in ages." The professional in Lucie surfaced, all talk of knitting and birthdays forgotten. "She was able to eat solids. Her speech was clear, and some of her motor abilities are sharper than we've seen since the last setback."

"Has Dr. Gardstein been in to see her today?"

Lucie nodded. "In fact, he ran a few tests yesterday. She's holding her own better than anyone expected."

"Do you think she's up to a walk on the grounds when she wakes up?"

Lucie started to answer, but a familiar voice interrupted her.

"Just you try to get away without one, honey. The day is too beautiful to spend indoors."

Elinor's speech was halting, her voice low and a little raspy, but to Sandra it was the most beautiful sound on earth.

"You're looking wonderful, Mom." Sandra knelt down in front of her mother and gave her a hug. Each time she saw her mother it seemed as if her body had grown smaller, her bones more fragile, as the disease gained another foothold.

These visits were the source of great pleasure for Sandra—and exquisite pain.

"What brings you here today, honey? I thought you were coming next Saturday."

Sandra explained about her unexpected day off.

"I thought I'd take advantage of it and come to see you."

Elinor's gentle features rearranged themselves into a smile, as each tiny movement fell into place slowly, individually.

"And?"

"And what?"

"I think there's more to it."

Sandra looked over at Lucie, who nodded her approval. She unlocked the wheels on the chair and began to push Elinor toward the door.

"You're too suspicious, Mom," she said, easing the wheelchair down the incline toward the ramp that led outside. "I can't come for a visit without an ulterior motive?"

The disease had done nothing to dull her mother's mind. She caught on to her daughter's ruse in a second.

"Stop this second, Sandra Elizabeth Patterson!"

Sandra broke stride, but didn't stop.

"This chair has an electronic alarm switch, and I won't hesitate to use it."

Elinor Patterson had never been a woman to make idle threats, and there was no reason to believe she'd changed. Sandra came to a stop next to a wooden bench that overlooked the duck pond.

"Great view," she said, avoiding her mother's eyes. "You can see the old field house over that rise."

"Sit down."

Sandra laughed nervously. "You're sounding awfully dictatorial, Mother."

"We just saw each other five days ago, honey. You came all this way for a reason. Now out with it. I'm a busy woman; I don't have all day." Her laughter mingled with the sounds of the wind in the trees.

Sandra sat down on the bench. "I bumped into an old friend the night after Hurricane Henry." She fought the urge to look down at her feet like a shy and backward child.

Elinor said nothing; she just watched. Normally the expression in her cornflower-blue eyes was easy for Sandra to read. This time her mother's face remained totally impassive.

"Aren't you going to ask me who I met?"

"You'll tell me in your own good time."

"That's not what you said a minute ago, when you almost threatened me if I didn't spill the beans."

Elinor changed the angle of her head slightly, and Sandra slipped the neck pillow back into position for her. "A minute ago I didn't know it was this serious."

"You know who it was, don't you?"

Her mother's eyes closed for a second. "I think I have a pretty good idea."

"You're not going to be happy, Mom."

"You may be surprised."

And so Sandra told her mother about meeting Michael McKay again—the same Michael McKay Elinor had loved but had never felt was right for her daughter. She gave her mother an expurgated version of their meeting seven years ago, and of the inexplicable pull that still existed between them, despite the anger and the pain.

"And so I told the workmen to tell him I'd call."

Elinor's gaze never once wandered from her daughter. Sandra understood the enormous physical effort that required, and the love that made it possible.

"And have you called him?" Elinor asked.

"Not yet."

"Will you?"

Sandra laughed, but it sounded nervous and breathy and embarrassingly hopeful. "You're the mother," she said. "I thought you would have all the answers."

"If I recall, my answers haven't always been the wisest."

"I don't know what to do."

"I think you do, honey."

Sandra arched an eyebrow. "Do you know something I don't?"

Elinor said nothing, but Sandra noticed the fine beads of sweat breaking out along her mother's hairline. At times, the effort required for her mother to coordinate her thought processes with the muscles necessary for coherent speech was as taxing as running a marathon would have been for someone else.

"I know you," Elinor said finally, "and I knew Michael."

"Meaning?"

"Meaning maybe this time you should follow your heart, not your intellect."

"This from the woman who taught me the way to happiness was through a 4.0 grade point average?"

Thank God nothing had yet been able to extinguish the fire of life in her mother's eyes.

"Mothers don't always know everything, Sandy."

Sandra pulled in her breath sharply. "That's the second time someone has called me Sandy in the past four days."

"Michael?"

She nodded. "Michael."

"Call him, honey. Don't make the same mistakes I made."

For a second Sandra was confused.

"My situation's nothing like yours, Mom. I'm not a teenager. I'm in no danger of getting pregnant, and I don't have the damnedest idea if I'll ever see him again."

Elinor closed her eyes for a second. "You will."

"You don't sound happy about it."

"I love Michael," Elinor said. "I always did. Sometimes I wonder if I should have just let you two kids run off to Maryland and get married."

Her mother's words shook Sandra more than the weekend's twin hurricanes had.

"I'm glad you didn't," she said, forcing a laugh. "I'd probably be a divorced mother of four by now."

"No," Elinor said slowly. "I don't think so."

"This whole conversation is making me feel odd, Mom."

"That's because you know I'm right."

"I don't know any such thing."

"In your heart you do."

She pushed her bangs off her forehead and shifted around on the bench.

"What's the point to all of this?" she asked her mother finally. "It's over. We can't change the past, can we?"

"Maybe not, but you have your future ahead of you."

"Exactly," said Sandra. "And Citi-National owns it. You're getting forgetful, Mom."

Elinor's pithy four-letter response shocked Sandra into silence.

"My body may be withering, Sandra, but my mind isn't. Don't ever forget that."

How could she? That was the hideous reality of ALS, and the hardest thing of all to bear.

"No company owns you, honey," Elinor continued. "No job is worth your life's blood. You deserve more. *I* want you to have more."

"I'm sorry," Sandra said finally. "I wanted to change the subject, and that seemed the best way."

"Give yourselves a chance, honey. Fate brought you two together for a reason. Find out what that reason is."

She tried to ignore the odd tug of emotion her mother's words conjured up. "What I'd really like to know is why you never told me you and Michael kept in touch."

"You never asked."

"Don't play games, Mom."

Elinor sighed. "Think back ten years. Would you really have wanted to know I was consorting with the enemy?"

"I suppose not," Sandra said grudgingly. "But I have to say it came as one hell of a surprise when he told me."

"He told you about our letters and phone calls?"

"Yes. He said you both fell out of touch a few years back and he never understood why. That was when you became sick, wasn't it?"

Elinor managed a nod. "Yes."

"Why didn't you tell him?"

"Why would I?" her mother countered. "The fact that I'm dying isn't something you work into a casual conversation."

"I don't think there was ever anything casual about either one of you. He was always like a son to you, and God knows he loved you. You should have told him."

Elinor looked at Sandra, her blue eyes huge. Her long eyelashes cast shadows against her cheekbones. "You didn't, did you?"

Sandra shook her head. "When I realized he had no idea what happened, I thought I should speak with you first."

Her mother nodded, her eyes drooping shut with relief.

"What did you tell him?"

"The first thing I could think of—that you were traveling."

"Good."

Sandra cleared her throat. "I'd like to bring him by, Mom. I'd like you to see him again."

"No!" Elinor's voice was vehement, stronger than Sandra had heard it in the last few months. "I refuse. You wouldn't do that to me, Sandra."

Sandra stared at her mother. "But I—"

"No!" The word was louder this time, more forceful. "Not like this." She gestured clumsily toward the wheelchair. "Let him remember the way I was."

"He cares for you, Mom. He'd want to know." *I need for him to know.* Andrew Maxwell's reaction to Elinor's condition was never far from her mind these past few days.

"Respect my wishes on this, Sandra. Don't humiliate me. If you love me, you'll do this one thing for me."

But before she could question her mother further, Lucie popped up, all smiles and apologies. She was not about to let one of Elinor's good days go by without her obligatory bout of physical therapy.

The moment for explanations disappeared.

Sandra walked back into the building with Elinor and Lucie, her mind only half on Lucie's nonstop monologue on hurricane trivia gleaned from the *Daily News*. They stopped in front of the door to the PT room. Lucie, her knitting needles poking out of her pocket, gave Sandra a quick hug, then slipped inside to ready the equipment for Elinor.

"Give 'em hell," Sandra said, bending down to kiss her mother. "Remember: no pain, no gain."

"Honey," Elinor said, "maybe you're the one who should remember that."

IT HAD BEEN ROUGH GOING for a while, but Elinor had pulled it off.

Elinor had smiled at Sandra until the doors swung shut behind her, then had closed her eyes and willed her heartbeat to slow down to a rate that wouldn't send Lucie and the rest of the PT staff into a panic.

Back in the early stages of her disease, she had been embarrassed by her lack of physical dexterity. Her body's unwillingness to cooperate with her brain had made her uncomfortable around people, and she had withdrawn from her old friends and sought to disappear.

Thanks to the staff at Fair Oaks, she had finally grown to accept her condition and allow herself the luxury of friendship.

But when Sandra had mentioned bringing Michael McKay to see her, she had let those old fears out of hiding and had used them shamelessly to manipulate her daughter.

Elinor would have moved heaven and earth to keep Sandra from making the biggest mistake of her life.

The breakup with Andrew Maxwell had been more difficult than Sandra had ever let on. Elinor had seen the dark circles beneath her daughter's lovely eyes, had noticed the way she had thrown herself into work with even more determination than usual in an effort to battle down the fears Andrew had brought to light.

No matter how often Sandra denied it, Elinor knew that her illness, her dependency, had been the root cause of the breakup, and she would be damned if the same thing happened again.

She'd already done enough to hurt her daughter. The scholarship she'd begged and borrowed and stolen for had changed Sandra's life in ways that went far beyond education. That opportunity had broken apart her daughter's relationship with Michael McKay, exactly as Elinor had hoped it would.

At the time, it had seemed the kindest thing she could do for both of them. There was a world out there waiting to be discovered, and those two kids could never discover it if they were saddled with children and bills and the numbing realities of adult life.

If what they had was real, it would survive; and if it didn't—well, better to find out now.

Now she wondered how she could ever have believed she could play God with something as precious as love.

Sandra was truly her mother's daughter. The blood that ran in Sandra's veins was so purely her mother's that it sometimes terrified Elinor when she thought of her own mistakes.

Elinor had loved once, and had never loved again.

A ridiculous fact, but a fact nevertheless.

All of the love that Frank Ryan had refused had been channeled into the daughter he never knew.

For Sandra, it was Michael McKay. Elinor didn't need to hear Sandra say those words to know it was true.

Now that he was back in her life, now that there was a chance for them to find the happiness they both deserved, Elinor would be damned if her daughter lost the man she loved because of the illness that was taking her life.

Let Sandra think her vain. Let Sandra think her foolish and sad.

Elinor didn't care.

All she wanted was to give her daughter this one last gift: a second chance with the man she loved.

SANDRA LINGERED for a while after her mother disappeared into the therapy room.

Elinor wasn't a woman given to elliptical statements; she was normally as blunt as Sandra had been before she turned herself into a rising corporate star schooled by Harvard Business to talk a great deal while saying damned little.

Once she poked her head into the therapy room to see how Elinor was progressing, but the intensity of the workout, and the breadth of her mother's pain, had her hurrying back to the solarium to say her goodbyes to Larry and the others.

"Next time you come up, we'll have that game of draw poker you keep promising me," she said to Larry. "I've been practicing keeping that poker face you showed me."

Larry's laugh started at his toes, rumbled its way up through his bony body, then erupted in a loud guffaw that was so outrageous everyone else in the room burst out laughing.

"Just you keep that face you got," he said, patting her hand. "And while you're at it, find yourself a nice young man to bring up here for Thanksgiving dinner. You'd make your mama's day."

"She said that?" Elinor had never married, and she had raised her only child to be an independent woman. "That hardly sounds like my mother, Larry."

Larry looked genuinely puzzled. "Don't all mothers want to see their children happy and settled?"

Sandra forced a laugh and stood up to leave. "I'm very happy, and I'll be settled as soon as I get all those blasted boxes unpacked."

"Don't tell me," Larry said. "Tell your mama. She's the one who worries."

She pulled her car keys out of her pocket and practiced her poker face on him. "Well, next time you two talk, you tell her for me, okay?"

She hurried down the corridor at a near-run, but, damn it, she couldn't outdistance the feeling that in four short days her entire life had been turned upside down.

Hurricanes Henry and Iris might have spared her house, but they'd done a number on her heart.

When her mother had refused to let Michael know about her condition, a sudden wave of relief had weakened Sandra's knees. Now the memory of it shamed her, but it didn't lessen the sense of being given a reprieve.

She stopped in front of the pay phone in the hospital lobby.

Why not?

Wasn't it time to stop playing games?

Michael's phone number just happened to be in her wallet and, God knew, her telephone credit-card number was committed to memory.

Her hand was shaking as she reached up to pop off her huge button earrings, and her stomach was twisted into sailor's knots. How on earth had men managed this as a steady diet in the days before women's liberation?

The telephone looked about as inviting as a women-eating Venus flytrap.

"Coward," she muttered to herself.

The whole point of this visit to see her mother was to be forced to sort out her feelings, and now that she had begun to make sense of them she was ready to turn tail and head for the hills.

The truth was painfully simple: she had finally managed to take him into her bed, but she was afraid to let him into her life.

The concept of no pain, no gain suddenly acquired a new dimension.

Life had been a lot easier back in 1969. All a woman had to do back then was own a telephone and have a vast reservoir of patience. The burden of decision used to rest squarely on the man's shoulders, where she was beginning to suspect it belonged.

Well, it wasn't 1969 anymore, and she wasn't seventeen and women no longer sat by the phone waiting for it to ring.

Gloria Steinem had changed the rules forever.

Sandra picked up the phone, dialed Michael's number and, when it started to ring, made a mental note to cancel her subscription to *Ms.* magazine.

Chapter Six

The hawk was in there, and Michael was going to find it.

He moved his chisel another fraction of an inch and brought the hammer down again and again, the rhythm of his tapping in synch with the music blasting through his Walkman.

The fifth time his hammer struck the chisel, the curved beak of a raptor emerged; on the tenth blow, the angle of its head.

"All right," he muttered, pushing his hair back with the back of his arm. He had the son of a bitch in his sights, and now he was going in for the kill.

He rocked back on his heels in order to get a better angle. His thigh muscles ached from the squatting position he'd been in the last hour. No wonder Gary Carter, the Mets' catcher, was bowlegged. Who wouldn't be, squatting down for nine innings 162 days a year?

The chisel was in place; he raised the hammer, and was about to strike when Leon Williams, in his ever-present red leather bomber jacket popped up at his side.

"...on the phone."

Michael looked at him. "What?"

Leon shot him one of his best former tough-kid looks and yanked the Walkman off Michael's head.

"Hey, man, if you wanna hear, you gotta take off the machinery."

"The only thing between you and death right now, Williams, is the fact that I'm too tired to kill you." The hawk was disappearing back into the limestone and, damn it, he wasn't sure he could recapture it. He glared at the young man next to him. "This'd better be good."

"Phone for you, boss man." The tough-kid look slid into a wicked grin. "It's a woman. A fine-sounding woman."

Bobby, Julio and Ray looked up from the template they were positioning on a virgin slab of limestone.

"A lady's callin' the boss man?" Julio let loose with a howl. "We gotta hear about this."

"Get back to work on that piece of rock, guys, or you'll be hearing about it on the unemployment line."

He tossed his Walkman down on his workbench and headed toward the phone in the anteroom.

"Must be serious."

"He don't get no calls at work *ever*."

"What about that fine fox down in the art place?"

"You think maybe he—"

Michael shut the door on his four speculating apprentices, and picked up the receiver balanced on the windowsill.

"McKay here."

There was a laugh, throaty and feminine, then, "Not very cordial, Michael."

He leaned against the door. Just the sound of her voice was enough to send his blood shooting south.

"I wasn't expecting to hear from you, Sandy." There was nothing in their past to make him think she would ever take the initiative.

"The workmen came by yesterday afternoon."

She paused a moment, but he couldn't think of anything to say, clever or otherwise.

She cleared her throat. "You'll be happy to hear I can now use my driveway for its intended purpose."

"Great." *Say something, damn you.* He could usually shoot his mouth off with the best of them. Why was he suddenly finding it hard to come up with words of more than one syllable?

"If this is what it's like calling someone for a date, it's no wonder males have such a high incidence of stomach ulcers."

Tension loosened its hold on his vocal cords. "Beginning to feel sorry for the enemy, are you, Sandy?"

Her laugh had always done wonderful things to him, and time hadn't changed one damned thing.

"I never thought you were the enemy, Michael."

He looked out the window, at the parking lot littered with cars and trucks and eight-ton slabs of Indiana limestone. Four fat and ornery pigeons pecked at the wrapper from a Milky Way bar and ignored the apple core not twenty feet away from them.

"What am I then, Sandy? What the hell are we?"

"You're making this awfully difficult, McKay." The hesitation was gone from her voice, and he detected an undercurrent of amusement. "I just might hang up on you."

His old self-confidence made a reappearance. "Come on, Assistant Vice-President. You must have called for a reason."

"I called to thank you for sending the workers."

"The hell you did."

"I called to see how you were doing."

"Don't kid yourself, Sandy."

"I called to tell you to go to hell."

"Getting closer."

"Damn you, Michael. I'm beginning to wish I hadn't called at all."

Everything they'd said and done and imagined throughout that long and wonderful night swept over him, sending caution up in flames.

"Too late. This time there's no turning back, Sandra. You knew that when you picked up the phone."

He wanted all of her, or nothing at all.

"Are you trying to scare me?"

"Have I?" he countered.

"Sorry to disappoint you, McKay, but I don't scare easily."

"We have a lot of years to catch up on," he said, thinking of his marriage, his son. "You may be surprised."

Again that wonderful laugh. "So might you, friend."

That gave him pause.

They made plans for Wednesday night. He needed time to get David settled in, and he needed time to figure out how to tell Sandra he was a father.

He had no idea how she felt about children; she might turn around and walk out of his life the second he broke the news.

Sure, she'd talked about a family back in the days when they'd both been young and full of dreams, but that was more than fifteen years ago now. And even then she'd been cautious, hiding behind "someday."

Who knew how she felt now?

If he had half a brain, he'd be worried.

Pulling a rabbit out of a hat was nothing compared to pulling a full-grown five-year-old out of thin air.

But he still felt so good, so hopeful.

His future stretched out before him like the flat part of the Expressway in front of a '69 Camaro.

It didn't even matter that he wasn't a kid anymore, or that his Camaro had given way to a Jeep—or even that at the center of his future was a five-year-old boy Sandra didn't even know existed.

She'd said, "I don't scare easily."

Good thing she didn't, because he was starting to sweat bullets.

MICHAEL WENT BACK into the studio and resumed work on the hawk. Apparently his mysterious phone call was still the prime topic of conversation, and Julio and Bobby kept up a steady stream of low-grade teasing that normally would have driven him up the walls.

That afternoon he just grinned and continued to chip away at the limestone, paying no attention to the sly look on Leon's face as he carved a valentine heart on the left ear of one of his McKay gargoyle specials.

The head of the hawk was fully articulated by the time he had to leave for the airport. His fingers itched to free the shoulders and the curve of the wings, but if he hit any traffic going through the tunnel, he'd be late meeting David's flight.

His heart felt as if it had been embedded in a chunk of rock just like the hawk, and Sandra's phone call had set it free.

Wouldn't Leon and the others have a field day with that? But, damn, he was fired up with excitement. His body hummed with the need to work, to create, to try to express some of the wild feelings that were racing through him.

Maybe he *would* bring Davey back to the cathedral. While his son was learning to toss a pot with Annie, he could sneak back into the construction shed and try to work off some of this manic energy.

He grabbed his jacket from the hook behind his work table; it was a plain black-leather job that Annie and her crew had transformed with their oil paints into a walking advertisement for Altar Ego and the cathedral. Designer jeans did nothing for him, but this was something else again.

"Catch you later," he said, rapping his knuckles on Leon's table as he headed for the door. "I'm picking up my kid in Newark."

Traffic was light, and he made it to the airport with time to spare. He grabbed a cup of coffee at one of the self-service cafeterias, then watched two inept baggage handlers try to figure out how to stuff some poor sucker's Italian suits back into his busted Vuitton suitcase.

Finally Flight 826 from Tampa–St. Pete rolled up to the jetway, and the passengers disembarked. Old men in pastel leisure suits paraded next to second wives with diamonds the size of walnuts, and brains to match. Businessmen in three-piece suits trooped out, clutching their pagers and their *Wall Street Journal*s.

Servicemen.

Girl Scouts.

Tourists.

Everything but a little blond kid in a Yankees T-shirt who somehow managed to make Michael feel he must have done one thing right in his life to deserve him.

Finally the plane was empty. Panic began to do ugly things inside his belly, and he collared a ticket agent near the gate counter.

"Flight 826," he said, aware of how he must look to her with his ecclesiastical-Hell's-Angels jacket and his wild Irish hair. "Is that everyone?"

She took a long look at him, as if sizing him up for potential terrorist tendencies. "Are you waiting for someone from that flight, sir?"

No. I get my kicks watching people come in from Tampa. "My son was supposed to be on that flight."

She flashed him a professional smile and brought the passenger list up on the computer screen. "Name?"

He hoped she didn't see the cold sweat breaking out around his forehead. "David. David McKay. He's five years old, about this high, probably wearing a T-shirt, though knowing his grandparents he—"

Shut up, jackass.

The agent had quit listening to him as soon as he gave David's name. He sounded like the worst kind of overprotective parent, and he knew it, but in a world where missing kids stared out at you every morning from the back of a milk carton, how could any sane parent not panic?

She looked up from the screen. "I'm sorry, sir, but there's no David McKay on the passenger list."

He didn't know whether to laugh or cry. "You're sure? It's McKay, M-C-K-A-Y."

Her professional manner softened. "I'm positive, sir. Perhaps you'd like to check with my supervisor. She might be able to help you further."

She gave him directions to the main office on the second level, but he barely heard her. He felt as if he were trapped in one of those monstrous wind tunnels, surrounded by the scream of engines and waves of heat.

Maybe he had the flight number wrong. Maybe he'd misunderstood Margaret's flat twang, and Davey was coming in at La Guardia. Damn it, the kid could be standing there in the middle of that insanity, wondering where his father was.

He turned to race back to ask the agent to look into it for him. Then he thought he heard his name over the loudspeaker.

He stopped and waited. Crowds of people, yammering in French and Spanish and Italian and a thousand Chinese dialects, flooded past him. Then he heard it again.

"Would Mr. Michael McKay please dial one? Michael McKay, please dial one."

"What the hell—"

He lurched toward the nearest red wall phone. His mind seemed to be freezing over, brain cell by brain cell. By the time he'd dialed one, he was wondering if he'd even be able to talk.

"Can I help you?"

"I'm Michael McKay."

"Ah, yes. You're to please call Arthur Bentley in Tampa. His number is—"

"I know his number." He hung up the telephone and stared at the wall in front of him.

If he'd been scared before, he was terrified now. The invisible chain of love that linked a parent and child tightened around his chest and made it hard to breathe.

Mysterious illnesses, out-of-control cars, the stranger on the street corner—every nighttime fear there was bore down on him.

He dialed the right number on his third try. His former father-in-law answered the phone, his voice beautifully modulated, carefully controlled. The perfect Dale Carnegie graduate.

"Where's David?" Michael roared into the phone. "Is he all right?"

There was a pause. His right hand began to shake. Why had he ever given up smoking?

"Is that you, Michael?"

Who the hell else? "Yes," Michael managed, fighting to control his sudden anger. "I'm at the airport. What in hell happened to David?"

Art's genteel chuckle made Michael's left hand curl into a fist. "You sound upset, Michael. Good Lord, Margaret and I never meant to alarm you this way."

"I'll ask you one more time, Art. Where is my son?" He put the emphasis on the last two words and hoped they'd find their target.

Art's voice was a shade cooler. "Why, he's at the Baxter boy's birthday party."

Michael sagged against the Plexiglas ledge. "He's okay?"

"Of course he is."

"Then why the hell wasn't he on that plane?"

Another well-rehearsed chuckle from Art Bentley. "Funny thing. Margaret was just packing up David's valise when Connie Baxter came by to borrow some birthday candles and, well, one thing just led to another."

"Meaning?"

"Meaning he's at the party. Lord knows, the poor boy hasn't had a great deal of pleasure of late, Michael. Surely you don't begrudge him the opportunity to play with children his own age."

Take it slow. There's more going on here than just a birthday party.

"School reopens tomorrow, Art. I think that's more important than a party." *What do you really want, you bastard?*

"You sound angry, Michael." Somehow it seemed more a taunt than a statement.

"I'm not angry at all, Art. I know you and Margaret are concerned about David, and I appreciate it. But I'm his father, and his schooling comes first."

"Our mistake, my boy." Art's affability was back in place. "It never occurred to us that the schools would reopen so soon after those dangerous killer hurricanes."

Michael's fist connected with the phone book that was dangling from a metal chain attached to the ledge. "They were dangerous," he said, "but they weren't killers. You underestimate Long Islanders, Art. We're a tough group."

"Point well taken, Michael." Another pause. "We're planning to send David home Thursday morning."

"No good. He'll miss too much school."

"He's five years old, Michael. Certainly he'd be better off with his grandparents than in some cold, impersonal day-care center."

"David is enrolled in a fully accredited kindergarten, Art, not a day-care center." Damn it. Explanations shouldn't be necessary, no matter which his son was in. "I want him home tomorrow."

"We made an appointment with the optometrist for him tomorrow."

"His eyes are fine, Art. I had them checked before he registered for school."

"Margaret and I are only trying to help you, Michael. After all, you are a single parent with a demanding job, and—"

"Tomorrow," Michael broke in. "There's a 9 a.m. flight out of Tampa–St. Pete that goes straight to La Guardia. I want David to be on it."

"I don't care for that tone of voice, Michael."

"Then we're even, because I don't care for the game you're playing, Art."

"We're only thinking of David. He needs friends."

"He has friends," Michael said. "At school."

"We can't work something out? A few more days in the sunshine would certainly be good for the boy."

"A few more days at school will be even better. Tomorrow, Art." Michael made no attempt this time to disguise his anger. "I mean it."

"Margaret told me you wouldn't be flexible about sharing David with us, but I was so sure you would." A low, melodramatic sigh eased through the wires. "You disappoint me, Michael. I had hoped we could be civilized about this."

The hairs on the back of his neck rose. "Is that a threat?"

Art laughed. "Still the same Irish temper. You do jump to conclusions, my boy. All I'm saying is that I had hoped you would be more flexible when it came to visitation rights."

"Visitation isn't your right, Art, it's a privilege. If you remember, I have full custody of my son."

Art suddenly dropped his Toastmaster-of-the-Year demeanor. "He's our only link to Diana. We'll do anything we have to in order to preserve that."

"Meaning what?"

"Meaning we're not afraid to fight for David."

"You'll lose," Michael said slowly. "That's the one thing you can be sure of, Art."

"We'll see about that. Margaret and I can offer David much more than you realize, Michael. A judge may find that difficult to ignore."

"Flight 22, 9 a.m." Michael's words were as sharp as gunfire, and as deadly. "He'd better be on it."

Inside Michael McKay was the same streetfighting kid from the streets of New York who hadn't been quite good enough for the Bentleys' darling daughter.

If Art and Margaret were looking for a battle, they would get more than they bargained on.

He hung up the phone. His blood pounded in his ears as if he'd just finished an eight-mile run on a hot day. The terminal was too noisy, too crowded; the walls seemed to be closing in on him.

He elbowed his way past a crowd of college kids waiting for a flight up to Harvard, maneuvered around a cluster of nuns near the Delta Airlines counter, then sprinted for the exit.

What he needed was to surround himself with the other things that were important to him. He needed to ground himself, he needed to be in the place that made him happiest.

But this time it wasn't the workshop at St. Matthew's that he sought.

He drove past the cathedral, past the place and people that had kept him going all these months, and headed toward Long Island and Sandra Patterson.

It was time she knew about David, and it was time she knew he still loved her.

"SNAP TO, PATTERSON."

Sandra jumped at the sound of Ed Gregory's voice, and spilled her coffee across the mortgage memorandum she was drafting.

"Damn it, Ed! Are you trying to scare the life out of me?" She blotted up the brown liquid with a paper napkin, and frowned at the pale brown stain creeping across the top page.

"I've been talking to you for the last five minutes, Patterson. Where've you been?"

"Sorry." She passed her hand across her eyes. Fluorescent lights always gave her a headache; she had to remember to get a lamp for her office. "What were you saying?"

"Those damned hurricanes really set us back. We're going to have to put in a lot of hours around here if we're going to make the regional review next month." He leaned over her desk and glanced at the curled length of adding-machine tape that wound its way across the top of a pile of ledger sheets. "You do good work, Patterson." He gave her one of his best smiles. "Now if you can just keep doing it eighteen hours a day until the review, we've got it made."

Sandra stifled a yawn. She'd come to work directly from visiting her mother, and had worked straight through dinner. The office was quiet except for the sound of Ilene McGrath's printer clacking away three doors down.

Everyone with half a brain had called it quits for the night.

It was painfully obvious where that left her.

She pushed her eyeglasses to the top of her head and stood up.

"That's it, Ed. It's late, I'm exhausted, and if you don't move fast, I just might eat your tie for supper."

He grabbed her wrist and checked her watch. "Nine-thirty," he said. "You couldn't push it another hour? We could finish the Andersen acquisition."

"Forget it."

Ed's eyes widened. "You don't sound like yourself, Patterson."

Her laugh was shaky with fatigue. For the last few days she'd been living on the edge of her emotions, and it had finally taken its toll.

"I don't feel like myself, Ed. I'm wiped out. What I need is a Lean Cuisine and a date with my Sealy Posturepedic."

"Is that an invitation?"

"Somehow I can't imagine you being happy with a Lean Cuisine, Ed. You've always been more the steak-and-potatoes type to me."

"What about the Sealy?" His tone was light, but Sandra sensed he meant every word.

She shook her head. "I've always been a believer in that old chestnut about mixing business with pleasure. It never works out."

"Times are changing, Patterson. The workplace is where people get to know one another. It sure beats happy hour at Howard Johnson's."

"Sorry, Ed. I like you too much as a boss to take chances."

He sat on the edge of her desk, arms crossed over his chest. "You know, I've never really understood you, Patterson. You're not like any other woman I've worked with."

She picked up her sweater from the coatrack near the window. "Should I take that as a compliment?"

"I haven't decided yet. I've known you almost nine years, and I still don't know one damned thing about you."

This was turning out to be the strangest day. Ed Gregory had never expressed the slightest interest in knowing anything about her private life despite his occasional half-hearted overture.

"What do you want to know?" she asked, slipping her arms into her sweater. "My résumé is an open book."

An odd look passed across his face. "You've come a hell of a long way, Patterson," he said, his voice gruffer than usual. "Don't go screwing up on me now."

The muscles across her shoulders and back stiffened. She took a deep breath in an effort to control her anxiety.

"If you're dissatisfied with my work, Ed, tell me. I don't want any surprises later on."

"Your work's been great, Patterson. That's not the problem."

"Then what is?"

His right forefinger disappeared into his thatch of brown hair as he scratched his scalp. "Damned if I can explain it, but I have the feeling those hurricanes did more than cave in your roof."

Sandra wasn't a fool. Ed was talking about Michael McKay, and they both knew it.

She forced a calm, professional smile. "Everything's under control, Ed."

"Glad to hear it. You're on your way, Patterson. I'd hate to see you get sidetracked by any unnecessary home improvements."

It was a low blow, but since they were speaking elliptically she had to let it pass. He had already glimpsed more of her personal life than she would have liked, including her mother's illness.

"Don't worry, Ed. You'll get your eighteen hours a day."

She couldn't control the edge of anger in her voice, and Ed apparently felt its sting.

"Did I sound like that big a bastard?" he asked.

"Yes," she said, looping her pocketbook over her shoulder. "Citi-National would be proud of you."

"There are big things ahead of you, Patterson. This transfer is just the beginning."

She drew in her breath sharply. "I'm in line for something else?" *Not now. Oh, God, please, not now.*

For so many reasons, she finally wanted to stay put.

"Have dinner with me, and I'll fill you in on the latest developments."

She shook her head and headed toward the door. "Maybe when the power's back on. I'm afraid you've already tipped your hand tonight, Ed."

He stepped into the doorway, blocking her exit. "Not even White Castle?"

She looked sharply at him. "A little White Castle goes a long way, Ed. I thought you knew that." *Not this time, Gregory. This is something that belongs only to me.*

"That's what I like to hear, Patterson."

He moved out of her way, and she walked down the hall, conscious of the fact that he watched her until she rounded the corner and disappeared from view.

Whatever happened between her and Michael, it was going to happen without an audience.

Citi-National already had most of her life. She'd be damned if they got it all.

Once again her mother's words came back to her, and she wondered just how much Elinor really knew.

SANDRA'S FRONT PORCH LIGHT was on, so Michael knew the power was back on. The workmen he'd hired had obviously cleared her driveway, but her car was nowhere in sight. Huge piles of broken tree limbs and split branches were stacked haphazardly all over the front and side yards, waiting to be split into firewood.

For a long while he sat on the top step of her redwood deck, listening to a symphony of chain saws from nearby yards and letting the salt breeze from the Sound blow over him. He'd come to Sandra's house in a state of high emotion, a powerful mixture of need and anger and hope that had his adrenaline pumping hard and fast.

He glanced again at the pile of tree limbs. Maybe he was the crazy medievalist his neighbors said he was, because right now what he needed was to let off steam in the most basic way he could think of.

To hell with chain saws.

He got up to get his ax.

THE FIRST THING Sandra noticed when she pulled into her driveway forty-five minutes later was the fact that the streetlights were working.

The second thing she noticed was the fact that the shoulder-high stacks of tree limbs the handymen had left in front of her garage were missing.

She cut her Mazda's engine, then got out. A brisk wind was blowing off the Sound; the smell of salt and wet earth surrounded her as she searched around the front of her property.

With the thousands of felled trees on Long Island there was enough free tinder simply for the asking. It didn't seem likely that anyone would bother to steal this particular cache of firewood.

She thought about her earlier conversation with Michael. She'd told him about the huge pile of tree limbs the handymen had left neatly stacked in the middle of her driveway. Maybe he'd called them back out to cart the wood into her back yard so she could at least use her garage.

She followed the flagstone path around the side of the house, and was about to enter the moonswept yard when she saw him.

There, stripped to the waist, his torso gleaming in the luminous silver light, was Michael.

Hidden by the bare lilac bush, she watched him.

He raised the ax, its blade poised for one heartstopping moment over his head, then brought it down in a sweeping arc until the glittering blade buried itself deep within the fragrant wood of a fallen pine tree.

She drank in the way his torso rippled with lean muscle; she reveled in the shadow formed by the inward curve of his abdomen, the way his jeans dipped low across his hips. His body and the ax were one unit, the motion as fluid and beautiful as anything she'd ever seen.

She couldn't imagine any of the other men she knew taking such obvious pleasure in physical action for its own sake. No Reeboks, no treadmill, no Nautilus, no incline bench. He didn't monitor his pulse rate every five minutes or balance his upper-body workout with his lower.

He used his body for the sheer joy of it, the same way he had used his body to bring her more pleasure than she had ever imagined possible.

He brought the ax down again in a wide, sweeping arc, and she felt as if it were her own resistance to the future being split in two. For a long time she'd recognized the empty spaces in her life that her career could never fill.

Her engagement to Andrew Maxwell had been an attempt to let go of all that had come before, to embrace the future, uncertain as the future might be. When her mother's illness had suddenly taken hold, she'd turned to Andrew for emotional support, only to find that Andrew had none to give.

He had his ex-wife to contend with, his three children, mortgage payments and an upscale career. Sandra would be a welcome addition to his life, an asset to him. He hadn't banked on a mother-in-law who needed round-the-clock nurses and oxygen tanks and wheelchairs, or on the slim, but real, chance that it might happen to Sandra, too.

And so Sandra had finally discovered how tenuous their connection really was, a connection born of dinners and late-night talks and shared political viewpoints. She hadn't expected him to understand the responsibility she felt toward Elinor, and, true to form, he hadn't.

She was willing to shoulder that responsibility on her own and keep her marriage to Andrew separate.

He had his children to worry about, both the ones already born and the ones he'd thought to have with Sandra.

He couldn't risk anything less than perfection.

Andrew was a decent man, but the past meant nothing to him. He had loved the woman Sandra presented to him, the beautiful, brilliant package; he hadn't given a damn about the girl who'd shaped that woman.

But with Michael it could be different. He'd sat next to her in first grade. He'd given her her first kiss.

He was her first love, the only person she'd ever trusted with her heart.

The years had made her cynical, but maybe, just maybe, he'd be able to understand the forces that drove her, the bittersweet responsibilities that had shaped the woman she'd become.

And as she watched him working in her back yard, with the moonlight spilling over him like a benediction, she knew she'd traveled nearly twenty years simply to return to the place where she belonged.

In Michael McKay's arms.

Chapter Seven

Michael had heard her car crunching its way up the gravel driveway. He had listened to the sound of her footsteps against the wet leaves as she came around the side of the house, and his whole body had been aware of her gaze on him as he wielded the ax.

It would have been a simple matter to acknowledge her presence, but being the object of her scrutiny turned out to be so powerfully erotic that he found himself slowing down his movements, drawing out the moment of discovery as long as he could. His blood was beginning to gather in all the familiar places, a downward rushing of heat and anticipation that made him want to pull her out from the shadows and make love to her right there in the moonlight.

Finally she stepped out from her hiding place.

"Hi," she said, her voice drifting over to him on the salty night air. "If you do windows, you've got yourself a job."

He leaned against the ax handle and casually hooked a thumb into the belt loop of his jeans, as if the sound of her voice hadn't sent a violent surge of desire rocketing through his body.

"What kind of job you got for me, lady?"

She walked toward him, a wonderful slow walk that could only belong to a woman approaching her prime.

She stopped about ten feet away from him. The scent of her perfume mingled with the smell of the Sound, and called to mind sex in all its infinite varieties.

"Do you do windows?"

"I don't do windows."

A smile flickered across her face.

"Do you do floors?"

The ax toppled to the ground with a soft thud.

"Sorry."

"Walls?"

"No way."

"Carpets?" Her smile widened.

"Wouldn't be caught dead." He took a step forward, closing the distance between them.

She met him halfway. "Not good for much, are you, mister?"

He ran his hands down the sides of her arms, then wrapped his fingers around her narrow wrists. "Invite me inside, lady, and we'll see."

The look she gave him was long and slow and hot. "Why is it I feel as if I've been set up?"

He had no answer for that, but then she hadn't expected one.

She was in his arms before the door closed behind them.

SANDRA LEANED ACROSS Michael and grabbed another handful of popcorn from the huge bowl propped up on his side of the bed.

"Okay," he said, grinning as she tossed a kernel in the air and caught it in her mouth, "so now you're in South Dakota. What happened next?"

For the past two hours, they'd been playing catchup, filling each other in on the parts of their lives their mutual friends had neglected to mention.

It was still Sandra's turn, and she felt as if she'd been trapped in a time tunnel. The occasional modeling jobs, the miserable year at Harvard when she went for her MBA, the long hard climb up the ladder at Citi-National: amazing how much detail she could remember.

She took a sip of Beaujolais from the glass they were sharing.

"You know what happens next. I worked very hard, performed brilliantly, and was transported back to New York in a blaze of glory." She licked some salt off her fingers. "It's your turn."

He took her right hand and drew his tongue across the palm, over the tips of her fingers.

"Oh, no!" She laughed as a ripple of pleasure went through her. "I'm too old to try for the Guinness Book of Records."

"You're thirty-five," he said. "I think you have a few good years left."

She shot him a look. "How are we going to work this out? It's impossible to lie about your age when the man you love sat next to you in grade school."

"I have a short memory. If you can ignore it when I turn forty, I'll ignore it when you do."

"Will we be together?" Her voice was soft. "The odds aren't exactly in our favor, Michael."

He pulled her close, and she let the warm, familiar smell of his body fill her senses.

"What were the odds that we'd find each other again, Sandy?" he asked, stroking her hair. "If we managed this, we can manage anything."

"I used to daydream about seeing you again," she whispered. "I would be rich and successful and married, and you'd hate yourself for ever letting me go."

"I didn't let you go, Sandy. You pushed me away."

"I was seventeen," she said. "I had to find my own way."

If Sandra had learned anything watching Elinor struggle to keep food on their table, it was that good men didn't always stick around when the going got rough.

If a woman couldn't support herself, she'd always walk three steps behind.

"I would have helped you find your way, Sandy."

"You hadn't even found your own way, Michael. You were still in love beads and bell-bottoms when I was going for my MBA." She propped herself up on one elbow and kissed the cleft in his chin. "For all I know, you still burn incense and draft cards for old times' sake."

"What if I told you I was CEO of a Fortune 500 company?"

"Not with those hands of yours. CEOs have paper cuts, not calluses."

"Do you still have something against blue-collar workers, Sandy?"

"Are my old prejudices coming back to haunt me?"

"You haven't answered my question." His eyes were riveted to hers.

She took a deep breath; it wasn't hard to figure that they were venturing out onto thin ice.

"I never had anything against blue-collar workers," she said. "I hated what they represented."

"Which was?"

She made a face. "Elmhurst," she said. "Queens. The subway. The dirt, the noise." *The feeling of being dead-ended.* "Everything I hated about New York City."

"You know I never quite believed it was that simple, don't you?" His hand rested against the small of her back. The roughness of his fingertips was in strange contrast to the gentleness of his touch. "You hated yourself too, Sandy."

She said nothing; his words had hit too close to home. She'd hated the softness she felt every time she looked at him; she'd hated the deep, yearning feeling that crept into her heart when he held her; she'd hated the way she wanted just to let go, give in, turn her life over to him and hope for a happy ending.

Her mother had been trapped by love, first by loving a man, then by loving the small daughter he left behind.

Michael had represented everything dangerous, everything that could take a woman's dreams and turn them into an endless chain of love that held her back.

But, God, it had been a seductive trap. Turning away had been the most difficult thing she'd ever done.

"I've learned a lot since then," she said finally. "I might be slow, but I finally caught on."

"So how do you feel about blue-collar workers now?" His dark eyes twinkled, but she sensed his underlying anxiety.

She drew her finger lightly across his chest. "Depends on the blue-collar worker."

"I don't wear a suit to work every day, Sandy. I don't carry a briefcase or read the *Wall Street Journal*. Can you handle that?"

She met his eyes. "I don't care, Michael. None of that is important to me anymore." Success came in different guises; it had taken a long time, but she finally understood that. "I don't give a damn if you dig ditches for a living, as long as you're happy."

She waited for his smile, but it didn't come. Her right eyelid began to twitch.

"I don't dig ditches," he said, watching her closely, "but I am happy."

"I'm glad for you."

"I work in Manhattan." He paused. "At the Cathedral of St. Matthew the Divine."

"That huge church off Amsterdam Avenue?" There'd been a few items on her desk lately about fund-raising events. "The one that needs money?"

He laughed, and some of the tension in the room broke up. "That's the one. I'm working on the construction crew."

She fought down the last vestige of white-collar snobbery left in her. "That's great."

"But I have another job besides that one, Sandra."

"Part-time?"

"Not exactly." He sat up against the headboard. "Actually, this job's more important."

Maybe he was back in school, or building a new home for himself. A sign of growth, not failure. "What is it?"

His chest rose as he drew in a deep breath before answering. "I'm a father."

She sat up straight and stared at him. "You're what?"

"I'm a father," he repeated. "I have a five-year-old son."

What on earth was the matter with her? His words tumbled over themselves inside her head like Scrabble tiles. "You have a son?"

"David," he said. "He loves chocolate-chip cookies, *Fraggle Rock* and the New York Yankees." He took a quick gulp of wine from the glass on the nightstand. Her heart twisted as she saw the way his expression softened. "Not necessarily in that order, you understand."

No, she didn't understand.

She was finding it hard to understand anything at all.

Accepting the fact that he'd been married had been relatively easy. Why hadn't it occurred to her that a child would be the natural result?

"Well." She took the glass from him and polished off the rest of the wine. "I suppose he lives with your ex-wife?"

He reached for the bottle on the nightstand and refilled the glass. It didn't seem like a good sign.

"Diana and her husband died in a plane crash last year," he said. "David lives with me."

"My God, Michael, you spent the night with me Saturday. Where was Donald—"

"David."

"Where was he?"

"Down in Florida with Diana's parents. It was the first anniversary of her death, and..." His voice trailed off, and he shrugged. "They said they needed David there to give them strength."

"When does he come home?" It amazed her that she was able to hold up her part of the conversation, because her mind was numb with surprise.

Time hadn't stood still for Michael, and she'd been a damned fool to think that it might have.

"He was due home this afternoon, but Art Bentley pulled one of his cute tricks on me."

"Cute tricks?"

"Custody stuff," he said, swinging his legs off the bed and rummaging through the nightstand. "Don't you have any cigarettes in this place?"

"I don't smoke anymore," she said. "And don't change the subject. Do you have custody of David?"

"Of course I do. It's just that they're beginning to get ideas." He pulled out a half-empty pack of Virginia Slims. "Where're the matches?"

She grabbed the cigarettes from him and threw them across the room. "Talk to me, Michael. Please."

He sagged back onto the bed. "Damn it. Can't we keep real life out of here a little longer?"

She thought about her mother and her own responsibilities. "Maybe not."

What had happened to the free-spirited man she had once known? Was nothing the way she imagined it to be?

He bunched the pillows behind his back and drew her close to him. "They want my son," he said, his voice harder than she'd ever heard it. "And I'm beginning to get the feeling they'll do anything to get him."

"But you have custody," she said, pushing away the thought of how much simpler their relationship would be without the child. "You're a decent, hardworking sort—at least I think you are." She forced a smile. "What can they do to you?"

He told her about what had happened that afternoon at Newark Airport.

"A power play," she said, snapping her fingers. "Simply to get under your skin. I wouldn't worry."

"You don't know the Bentleys," he said. "It's part of a plan." His hand curled into a fist on top of the blanket. "I should've caught on a hell of a lot earlier."

A tremendous feeling of loss washed over her. The past few days had been filled with the most powerful emotions she'd ever experienced. This unexpected renewal of love, this coming back to the place where she belonged, had given Sandra a sense of the future that shattered all the careful, cautious plans she'd settled on.

Even her mother's illness, terrible as it was, could be dealt with if she had Michael in her life.

Michael McKay, with his rough hands and gentle touch.

Michael McKay, with his hopes and dreams.

Michael McKay, with his five-year-old son.

Why on earth did she feel as if she'd been betrayed?

"You're quiet," he said after a while. "You can't be that surprised about David. People do have kids, Sandy."

She pushed away from him and pulled the covers over her shoulders. The room seemed to be growing colder by the second.

"Sandra?"

"I don't know what to say, Michael. Every damned thing I can think of sounds so incredibly selfish, so horrible, that—" She stopped, horrified to find herself close to tears.

"I love that kid," he said, gently brushing a lock of hair off her forehead. "He's the only good thing to come out of that lousy, stinking marriage of mine."

"It's ridiculous, and I know it, but somehow I never thought of you as having a child."

"We didn't plan on David," he said. "We'd been talking about divorce, and Diana had stopped taking the pill—hell, I don't have to explain to you how these things happen."

"No," she said, her tone suddenly sharp. "That's one thing you don't have to explain to me." Her own existence was the end result of just such a slipup.

"Damn it, Sandy. Don't take everything so hard. This is as tough on me as it is on you."

She said nothing. What could she say? Nothing would change the facts.

"I take it you're not crazy about kids."

"How would I know?" she asked honestly. "You don't meet too many of them in the boardroom at Citi-National."

"You must have had a social life out there in South Dakota. Didn't any of those people have kids?"

"I suppose so," she said. "I was too busy working to find out."

His expression was an odd mixture of pity and curiosity. "What the hell have you been doing all these years, Sandy? What kind of life have you been leading?"

"Boring," she answered. "Single-minded."

Arid.

Lonely.

Empty.

Pick one.

"I'd like you to meet David."

She closed her eyes for a second. "Yes," she said. "I'd like that, too." It would be interesting to see if she could look at Michael's son and not feel a stab of jealousy so intense that it took her breath away.

"He's had it rough since his mother died," he said, picking his words the way a soldier picks his way through a mine field. "I'm not going to let him get hurt."

She stiffened. "Meaning?"

"Meaning I don't want you to get too close to him, Sandy. Not unless you're going to stick around for the long haul."

She let out a long, shuddering breath. "You don't beat around the bush, do you, McKay?"

"I can't. Not when it comes to David. There's too much at stake."

She thought about Michael's in-laws, the custody threat, the terrifying pain of losing a parent.

"That's a lot for a child to go through," she said. "I understand why you worry about him."

He leaned toward her, his dark eyes guarded but hopeful. "He's a great kid. Smart as hell. He's having trouble believing I'm not going to leave him the way his mother did."

Who could blame him? Seeing the dark side of life so young made a mockery of childhood. It was something Sandra could well understand.

"Maybe we should skip the meeting for the time being," she said, wishing she could blink away this whole conversation and start again. "Your son has had enough traumas to last him awhile."

"Spell it out," Michael said. "Are you telling me this is going to be a short-term arrangement?"

"I'm not telling you anything." She felt like the target in a shooting gallery. "Who knows what's going to happen? I'm just thinking of David." Wasn't that what this whole conversation had been about?

His two-syllable Anglo-Saxon curse brought her up short. "I can't change the fact that I'm a father, Sandy."

"I wouldn't want you to."

He gave her a measuring look. "Then why do I get the feeling you wish David would disappear?"

"Because you're paranoid?" Her tone was flippant. She hoped it masked her surprise at just how close he'd come to the ugly truth of the matter. A living, breathing reminder of the years she'd let slip away would be difficult to deal with.

"Because I know you."

"The hell you do. I'm not seventeen years old any longer, Michael. You can't read my mind."

"Level with me, Sandy. Spell it out. If you don't, we're not going to have a chance in hell of making this work."

Emotions she couldn't name, much less control, broke free, and she smashed her fist into the pillow bunched against the headboard.

"I hate this," she said, hot angry tears sliding down her cheeks. "I know it's lousy and reprehensible and every other rotten adjective you can come up with, but I'm so damned jealous right now that I'm seeing red."

"Of David?" He was looking at her as if she were an escapee from a rest home, and she almost laughed.

"Of course not. I'm jealous of Diana. I'm—"

"You're jealous of Diana? It was a bad marriage. A rebound thing. I was trying to get back at you, and I ended up hurting a lot of other people instead."

"Damn it, Michael. It's not your marriage that bothers me." She'd had relationships; she'd even been engaged. But no other man had come close to reaching the secret, hidden part of her that Michael had, and she felt certain the same was true for him.

At least she'd been certain up until now.

"I don't get it," he said.

She brushed away the tears with the heel of her hand and wished she'd had the foresight to keep a box of Kleenex by the bed.

"For all that you say your marriage was terrible, one pretty important fact comes through loud and clear: Diana gave you a son." A strangled laugh rose up in her throat. "That's one hell of a tough act to follow, Michael."

"Damn you, Sandra." He pulled her into his arms, gripping her so tightly that she knew his fingers would leave marks on her skin. "I never figured you for a coward."

Their faces were just inches apart, and she had to force herself to meet his anger head-on.

"I wanted everything like it was, Michael. I didn't want shadows following us around."

"Too bad, lady." His words were like sharp, spiny rocks beneath the surface of a lake. "Too bad you can't always get what you want."

She tried to look away, but he turned her face back to him.

"I hate you," she whispered.

"I almost wish you did. Life would be a hell of a lot easier." Although he still gripped her tightly, she sensed a subtle shift in the emotion behind the touch, and—damn it—her body began to respond. "I love you, Sandra Patterson. I never stopped loving you. The only thing that kept me from making love to you that night at the Plaza was the fact that

I loved you too much to hurt you any more than I already had."

"You don't know how much I wanted you," she said, her voice husky with both sorrow and desire. "I burned for you, Michael. I wanted you more at that moment than my career, than my degree, than anything on earth. When you walked out that door, I wanted to die."

"But you didn't," he said. "I knew that. You're a survivor, Sandy. You always were. You always will be."

It was that same deeply rooted will to survive that made the ultimate giving of herself so difficult. So terrifying.

"Even with Diana, I never managed to break free of you. I'd take her to bed and feel your breasts beneath my hands. I'd kiss her, and it would be your mouth I'd taste. Even the sounds she made were the sounds I imagined you would make when I moved inside of you. You were in my brain, Sandra, like a fever I couldn't shake."

She was trembling uncontrollably. His words had reached deep inside her, and they clawed at her heart.

How could she tell him about the nights with Andrew, nights when she'd prayed to feel something—anything—when he touched her?

How could she tell him about the bone-deep loneliness that had driven her into a relationship as practical as a money-market account, and about as warm?

But she'd needed something of her own. She had finally reached a point in her career where she felt secure, and some of her mother's old dreams for her no longer seemed so foolish. She'd believed Michael was lost to her forever.

Had it been so terrible to want a family of her own? To want to give birth to a baby, to create a child who could receive the love waiting inside her?

Was it so awful to want someone to share both the joys and the sorrows?

Why was she finding it so difficult to understand Michael's needs?

The truth was more complicated than simple jealousy.

She already had the overwhelming responsibility of her mother's medical care. The thought of taking on the added responsibility of a child scared the hell out of her.

The realization that Michael just might say goodbye when he heard about Elinor terrified her. The same ugly feeling of relief that had washed over her when Elinor swore her to secrecy came back again.

God forgive her, but she would honor her mother's wishes.

So now there was just one way out. Take what she could, while she could, and try not to look too far ahead.

Maybe reality could be held at bay.

"Let's take it slow," she said finally. "Why can't we see where we stand before we bring David into this?"

"Spell it out for me, Sandy."

"An affair," she said bluntly. "Don't tell me you've brought every woman in your life home to meet your son?"

There was a long silence. "There haven't been any other women in my life since I got custody of David."

It was her turn to be silent. "Why is it I believe you?"

"Because we've come too far for lies, Sandy. We're thirty-five years old, and if we're ever going to have a life together, we'd better get started."

"You make thirty-five sound like we're ready for Social Security."

"How quickly did the last fifteen years disappear? We don't have time for any more false starts. We've been given another chance." He put his finger under her chin and tilted her face up to his. "Let's give it our best shot."

He was right, and she knew it.

They had this one last opportunity for happiness together; she'd be a fool to let it slip through her fingers.

She swallowed hard. "When did you say your son was coming home?"

"Tomorrow," he said, watching her. "You could meet him tomorrow night."

"He might hate me." She forced a smile. "I used to think *Sesame Street* was a cooking show. David may find me too ignorant to talk to."

"He'll love you."

"Don't be so sure. The last kids' show I watched was *Leave It To Beaver* and that was in 1961."

Michael laughed. "Then you'll have a lot in common. That's David's favorite show."

"I didn't know the reruns were back on the air."

"Where have you been, Patterson? The Beav is back on the tube."

"A forty-year-old Beaver Cleaver? Now you've gone too far, McKay." Next thing he'd be telling her that Eddie Haskell was a civil servant.

"Brace yourself, Patterson. Theodore Cleaver is divorced with two kids."

She threw herself back against the pillow and groaned. "You've ruined my night. Are the Mouseketeers grandparents by now?"

"A few times over," he said grinning.

"I feel a thousand years old."

"Wait until after a day with David."

"Maybe we should put this off."

"Forget it."

"A clandestine affair has its charm, Michael." There was something to be said for pretending reality didn't exist.

Especially a five-year-old reality whose existence could spell the end to their second chance.

"Not for us, Sandra." He pulled the sheet away from her torso, and she felt herself melting beneath his eyes like a quick-burning candle. He cupped her left breast gently in his palm, and her heart almost leaped through her skin.

She couldn't speak. With him watching her like that, as if he knew every corner of her heart, she couldn't even breathe.

He bent down and flicked the tip of her breast with the point of his tongue. When he looked up, his eyes glittered with a light that seemed both savage and tender.

"Make no mistake about it: I want your body, but lady, I'm not going to rest until I claim your soul."

Chapter Eight

"...Oust two hundred and fifty clericals from Sioux Falls before we can begin to balance—are we boring you, Patterson?"

Sandra's head popped up, and she met the angry eyes of Ed Gregory.

"Sorry." She flipped her notes to the appropriate page. "I had a rough night."

"We've all had it rough since the hurricanes," Ed said, his voice ominously low and controlled. "Lousy excuse."

Her face burned, but she managed to keep her expression neutral. "It's the best excuse I can come up with, Ed."

It was certainly a hell of a lot better than telling him his presentation could have cured the most hard-core insomniac.

Carol Richter shot her a quizzical look and Ilene McGrath scribbled something on a ledger sheet and passed it to one of the other assistant vice-presidents at the conference table.

Ed picked up his speech where he'd left off—some incredibly dull point about balancing the South Dakota budget with the New York budget—and Sandra tried her best to keep from sneaking a peek at the time.

Her mentor's flash point was pretty low, and she knew he was already halfway to murder. If he caught her clock-watching, he'd probably stuff her Seiko down her throat and bury her with an unbalanced budget at her breast.

She was meeting Michael and his son at the Cathedral of St. Matthew the Divine at six o'clock, which meant maneuvering the god-awful Long Island Expressway right at the height of the rush hour.

Her plan to slip away from work early was obviously not going to work now; if she knew Ed, he'd monitor her desk until closing time.

Damn.

She looked over at Carol, who was turning to yet another page in the mega-report in front of her. Everyone else was doing the same.

Sandra caught a glimpse of the page number and forced her attention back to the work at hand.

If she could just hang in a little longer . . .

An hour and a half later, after the meeting had broken up in a flurry of company spirit fostered by a catered late, late lunch complete with rolling bar, Sandra slipped back to her office to get something accomplished.

She had just finished making notations on the morning's meeting and was about to dive into the monthly forecast for international property rates when Ed tapped on the fiber-glass partition that surrounded her work area.

"I thought you liked Beef Stroganoff, Patterson."

She ignored him and started to read the monthly forecast.

He stepped into the cubicle and sat on the edge of her desk.

"I made sure they were generous with the sour cream."

"Thanks." She continued with her reading.

"The vultures are making short work of everything," he said. "If you don't move your butt, you'll be out of luck."

She glanced up at him over the top of her glasses. "I'll take my chances."

"Come on, Patterson." She could hear the sarcastic edge to his voice, and it immediately got under her skin. "Can't take some constructive criticism?"

She tossed her pen down. It hit the edge of her blotter and bounced to the floor.

"Constructive criticism is great, Ed. Public criticism is something else entirely."

"Don't go getting sensitive on me," he said. "You were out of line."

"You could have saved the hurricane remark for after the meeting."

"Judgment call. I made a bad one. Are you going to sulk the rest of the day?"

"I won't dignify that with an answer."

"What the hell's the matter with you, Patterson? What happened to your pleasant personality?"

"Did you hire me for my personality or my work habits?"

He threw his head back and laughed, and Sandra had to plunge her fists into her jacket pockets to keep from knocking him flat.

"I wouldn't pursue that line of questioning today if I were you, Patterson. You're not doing too well on either count."

"Terrific." She stood up and reached for her briefcase and pocketbook. "Then you won't miss me if I take the rest of the day off."

For a woman who had always prided herself on her professionalism, she was behaving in a way that horrified her.

But there was no hope for it. Her emotions were at the surface, and there was nothing she could do to stop herself.

"Hold on a minute." Ed blocked her exit. He looked as surprised by her outburst as she was. "What gives, Sandra? Exactly how rough a night did you have?"

She regretted having said anything.

"Forget it," she said.

"Like hell. You're strung tighter than a piano wire. What gives?"

She'd already said more than enough; she sure as hell wasn't going to tell Ed she'd spent the night worrying about meeting a five-year-old boy.

"I told you. Digging out after Henry and Iris was tougher than I expected."

"Damn it!" Ed sagged against the side of the cubicle. "I promised to get someone out there for you, didn't I?"

She nodded. Ed was always filled with good intentions that rarely amounted to anything.

He reached for the phone. "Let me get my nephew on it. If you can hold out, I'm certain he can get that roof done by the weekend."

She took the receiver from him and put it back in the cradle. "No need. It's been done."

He stared at her. "It's what?"

"It's done."

Damn. This whole thing was getting more ridiculous by the second.

"For someone who's been back in town less than a month, you're better-connected than I figured. Who do you know? Good help is harder to find than dock space on the Sound."

"He's not for hire." She tried to control the edge in her voice. "It was a favor."

Ed narrowed his eyes. "You're not talking about that black-haired monolith you bumped into at Burger King Friday night, are you?"

"It was White Castle, and yes, that is who I mean." Her words were clipped and tight. There was something else going on here besides interest in her house repairs.

"He did the repairs himself?"

"What is this, Ed? Twenty Questions?"

"Just curious, Patterson. I may need a repairman someday."

"You have a town house, remember? Call the maintenance crew. That's what you pay them for."

She went to push past him, but he held his ground. More than anything, she wanted to avoid the confrontation she seemed to be heading toward.

"We begin putting together the end-of-the-year reports in a week or two, Patterson. Things are going to get pretty hairy around here."

"The end-of-the-year reports are legendary, Ed. I've been upping my vitamin B-12 intake in preparation."

A brief smile flickered across his face, then died. "It seems to me you have enough to worry about as it is."

He'd had to initial some changes in her health-insurance coverage when Elinor was stricken, so he knew full well what was going on and one of the reasons why career stability was so important to Sandra.

This was the first time that he'd ever alluded to the situation, however. "Maybe you should think twice before you take on anything else," he said.

She forced a smile. "Are you planning on giving me an extra two weeks' paid vacation?"

"The hell I am. If I could get you in here seven days a week, I would."

He moved aside so he was no longer blocking the door, but Sandra knew he wasn't through.

Not yet.

"If you have something to say, Ed, then say it, damn it. I'm not in the mood for games."

"You want it straight?"

"Yes."

He looked so serious, so angry, that suddenly she was no longer sure she wanted to hear it.

"We've been working together a long time, Patterson. I've seen you through some tough spots and watched you turn into one of the best financial analysts around."

He paused. She'd seen Ed operate before; she knew the routine.

First the praise.

Then the bomb.

She cleared her throat. "And?"

"I put myself out on a limb to bring you back here to headquarters, Sandra. If you fail, I take the heat." He met her eyes. "I don't like taking the heat for anybody. Not even you."

"And I don't like to fail, Ed. You should know that."

Her mother's medical bills made money more of an issue than ever before, but Sandra's need for a career went far beyond that. She liked what she did; a part of her self-esteem was defined by it, and always would be. That part of her emotional makeup had been decided in childhood, and wasn't likely to change.

But she was beginning to let herself understand that there were other, stronger needs she had long ignored.

Needs that Michael McKay had awakened in her once again.

"Then keep on track," Ed said, his voice sharp. "A few more rough nights and you might find yourself trapped here permanently."

"Would that be so terrible? This is headquarters, isn't it?"

"I have bigger plans for you." He dropped the names of three of their most prestigious European branches. "Don't let your social life hold you back."

"What happens when I leave here is my business, Ed, not Citi-National's."

"When it affects your work, it *is* Citi's business."

"I'll keep that in mind."

Ed stepped out into the hallway. "I'm not trying to run your life, Patterson. I just want to make sure you stay on track. You've come too far to blow it all now."

"Meaning?"

"Your friend. That unexpected reunion might be the worst thing to ever happen to you. I—"

She raised her hand. "Uh-uh, Ed. No more. You've gone as far as I'm going to let you."

"You're changing, Patterson. I don't know if I like it."

She slung her pocketbook over her shoulder and switched off the office light. "I like it," she said, meeting his eyes straight on. "For the moment, that's all I care about."

She turned and headed toward the elevator. Ed fell into step with her, his heavy wing-tip shoes thudding against the polished tiles. She pushed the button and looked over at him.

His brows were drawn together in a scowl, and for a moment she didn't know whether to laugh or cry. Meeting Michael again had been like flinging open a door to a forgotten room; not even for Ed could she close that door again.

"Keep your nose to the grindstone, Patterson," he grumbled as the elevator doors creaked open. "Just because I trained you doesn't mean I won't fire you if you get out of line.''

"Ah, Ed," she said, as she stepped into the elevator and pressed the button for the ground floor. "How could I live without your sweet talk?"

The doors closed after the first two words of what promised to be a particularly inventive description of a physical impossibility.

A soft laugh of relief escaped Sandra as she sagged against the rear wall, the wooden handrail pressing against the upper curve of her derriere. Ed Gregory wasn't about to fire his star protégée; that much she knew.

His warning, however, was something else.

Corporations stole as much from an employee as the employee cared to have stolen. For too long she'd been willing to hand over her life on a silver platter, contenting herself with the bones that remained after Citi-National was through picking over them.

Even her engagement had been arranged around her career. Of course, that type of careful planning had been something Andrew understood; his own social calendar was constructed around his law career.

She'd cared for Andrew Maxwell, and would have made him a good wife had they married; but he had never made her feel that what they would create together was greater than anything she could create alone.

Their marriage would have been a merger, like any of the mergers she'd handled on her job.

Precise. Legal. Faultlessly constructed on a firm foundation of logic and respect. But so lacking in passion, so devoid of real commitment that the breakup had left her feeling relieved that it had happened before their wedding, saving them the legal hassle of filing for divorce.

Heartbreak had never even occurred to her.

The elevator opened at the ground floor. She hurried through the marble-and-gilt lobby, then pushed her way out into the early October sunshine. The air was crisp, impossibly clean, filled with autumnal promise. She almost hated the thought of being cooped up in her car on the drive into Manhattan.

But the thought of seeing Michael again was too seductive, the need to meet his son too imperative to ignore.

If she and Michael should ever come together permanently, Elinor would remain Sandra's problem; her medical bills, Sandra's worry. If she'd learned anything from the breakup of her engagement, it was that.

She climbed into her car and started the engine.

David, however, was another story. Everything he did, everything he said and thought and dreamed, would become part and parcel of her life if she and Michael decided to marry. That one small boy held the key to her future in a hand used to carrying nothing more important than a baseball or a comic book.

If he didn't like her, the chances for happily-ever-after for her and Michael would be pretty slim.

If she didn't like him—

She shuddered.

What kind of woman could dislike a five-year-old boy?

But Sandra knew her life had taken her away from the mainstream lives of most women.

Children were foreign creatures to her: small, exotic beings who inhabited a world with places like *Sesame Street* and *Mr. Rogers' Neighborhood*, and robots that could transform themselves in the blink of an eye.

In the best of circumstances, she found talking to them more difficult than understanding the new tax laws.

Talking to the living, breathing proof that the man she loved had taken another woman to wife was going to be almost impossible.

She turned to back out of the parking spot and noticed the beeper resting on the passenger seat. She'd always sworn she would never, ever use the damned thing, but she was about to make an exception.

If there were a fiscal emergency, a sudden worldwide rush for mortgage information, it was her duty as a responsible employee, a card-carrying assistant vice-president, to be on call for the hierarchy at Citi-National.

Any hardworking executive would do the same thing.

As she pulled out of the parking lot and headed toward the Expressway, she glimpsed herself in the rearview mirror and sighed.

"Get real, Patterson," she said to her reflection.

At the moment, she didn't give a damn if Citi-National went bankrupt or was bought out by a handful of power-mad Arab sheikhs who planned to turn the mortgage division into their own private harem.

The beeper was the modern equivalent of a safety net. If the going got too rough, she could always sneak out to a pay phone and have herself paged.

Emergency. You're in over your head. The boy hates you. Return to the safety of your old life before his father ends up hating you too.

"The age of technology," she muttered as she pulled onto the highway. "Is it great or what?"

MICHAEL PULLED THE TELEPHONE into his cramped office in the construction shed and kicked the door shut.

"Would you repeat that again, Arthur? I didn't catch what you said."

And what he had caught didn't set too well with him.

Arthur Bentley's cultured tones eased their way through the telephone wires. "I said, the morning flight was canceled. David will be coming in at three o'clock."

"Why was the flight canceled?" Make up a good one, Bentley.

"Thunderstorm," Arthur said calmly. "It knocked out four of our power stations. We're just getting back on line now."

Michael ran his ringers through his hair and tried to control his anger. "I know all about power failures," he managed.

He'd had a long talk with Jim Flannery that morning about Arthur's veiled and not-so-veiled threats to launch a battle for David. Jim had been patient, thorough, and brutally honest. He didn't feel the Bentleys had much of a case, but he had pointed out that reason and logic rarely entered into custody fights.

"Rein in your temper, Mike," Jim had warned. "Give in on the small things and save yourself a big heartache later on."

The implication had been that, if pushed, the Bentleys were still emotionally fragile enough simply to take the boy and run.

Michael thought he'd managed to cover every parental fear in the book. He'd been wrong. Jim Flannery's sober warning lay upon his shoulders like the eight-ton blocks of Indiana limestone outside the workshed.

"David has been riding the Andersen child's bicycle while he's been down here," Arthur was saying. "I hope you don't mind, but Margaret and I have taken the liberty of buying him his own. We're shipping it up for his birthday."

"David already has a bicycle."

"This one is an Italian racing bicycle. Gunn Andersen says it's the finest one on the market."

"David's Schwinn can make it another couple of years."
An Italian racing bicycle for a five-year-old who still needed
training wheels? Bentley was off his rocker. Michael wanted
to tell him so, but the memory of Flannery's warning
stopped him. "Listen, why don't you keep it down there,
Arthur? That way David can use it when he visits."

"Margaret had her heart set on giving David a reminder
of us. We see him so little, you realize, Michael." A pause
for effect. "Since we lost Diana, he's all we have."

The Bentleys were suffering; no matter what Michael
thought of them, he would never minimize their grief. Their
loss had shattered them. It was up to Michael to make sure
their loss didn't shatter his son's chances of having a normal childhood.

"Why don't you send David a photo of the two of you to
keep on his nightstand? An Italian racing bike makes more
sense on those flat Florida roads."

It also made more sense in the hands of a world-class
athlete, Michael thought, but he managed to hold his
tongue. Jim Flannery would have been proud of him.

He headed inside and found Annie Gage waiting for him
in the workroom.

"You look like hell," she said. "Another delay with David's homecoming?"

He nodded and put the phone back on the ledge. "What
else? He comes in at three."

Annie made a face. "Well, at least this time you found
out before you left for the airport. That's an improve-
ment."

"He's up to something," Michael said, taking the mug of
coffee she'd extended to him. "I don't know what, but
Bentley's cooking something up." He took a long sip of
coffee, let it sit in his mouth a moment before he swallowed. "I don't like it."

"My coffee?"

He shuddered as the thick liquid slid down his throat. "That's a given. I'm talking about Bentley's threats."

"Is he trying to trade on Diana's death again?"

Michael shook his head. "Not at the moment. This time he's concentrating on the importance of the nuclear family, how David needs a full-time mother."

"A full-time mother is a luxury few kids have these days," Annie said, her dark eyes thoughtful. "They still seem to be doing okay. Why should David be the exception?"

"You want to call Art and tell him that? I didn't get too far with the same line of reasoning."

Annie just grinned, and poured herself some more coffee from the huge urn near where Leon and Angel were working. "Why don't you tell him you're getting married?"

Michael stared at her. "What?"

"Tell him you're getting married. Tell him you're providing your son with a full-time mother yourself."

She was joking. The twinkle in her eye, the laugh in her voice, were easy enough to recognize. Why, then, was he finding it impossible to summon up an answering wisecrack?

"Don't look so nervous, McKay. That wasn't a proposal of marriage."

"That's not nerves you see, Annie. That was shock. And here I thought you cared—"

Annie put down her coffee cup and looked him straight in the eye. "I do care," she said slowly. "I just have the funny feeling the time is never going to be right for us."

"We're friends," he said. "Nothing is going to change that."

"That's not exactly what I wanted to hear. I could be more specific, but I'm afraid you aren't ready for it."

He thought of Sandra, of the dreams she had brought to life within him, and he shook his head. "And I'm afraid you're right, Annie. Just this once, I have to play it by the book."

Anything less wouldn't be fair to any of them, himself included.

Annie tossed her hair back over her left shoulder with a quick gesture and smiled at him. "Does playing it by the book preclude bringing David by for tacos tonight?"

He hesitated, trying to think of the easiest way to say no.

"Other plans?" she asked.

"Afraid so, Annie."

"I won't even ask you if it's your old friend."

"Thanks," he said, finishing his coffee. "I owe you one for that."

He grabbed his car keys from his work bench and was heading for the door when Annie reached for his hand.

"If it doesn't work out, call me," she said. "I think the three of us could make it work."

Damn it, he thought as he jogged across the vacant lot to his car. *She's probably right.*

Annie was warm and loving and talented, and probably dynamite in bed. She could cook and paint and tell dirty jokes and fairy tales with equal flair. She was a great friend to him, and would probably make a great mother for his son.

But there was one big problem.

She wasn't Sandra Patterson.

Chapter Nine

Sandra hadn't been in the city for more than five minutes before everything she despised about her old hometown came flooding back in vivid detail.

The thick layer of smog hovering over the skyscrapers. The crazed cab drivers playing leapfrog with two-ton taxis as they tried to cop a fare. Bearded wonders wearing necklaces made of empty tuna cans, proclaiming the end of socialism and pay toilets.

The noise, the crowds, the feeling of being at the edge of civilization and about to teeter over into mass hysteria.

New York was a microcosm of everything, both good and bad, that America had to offer.

Except a parking space.

Sandra circled the Cathedral of St. Matthew the Divine for the fourth time. A slight young man in a tweed blazer was standing by the driver's door of a Renault chatting with a woman in a tight red dress with a thigh-high slit.

She considered double-parking and waiting while they concluded their business deal, but three cabs and a city bus were bearing down on her, and not even a parking spot was worth dismemberment.

She'd noticed a vacant lot near the rear of the church where two vans, an MGB and a Cadillac with a harried-

looking businessman sitting in it were parked near a construction shed.

Why not?

If she didn't find some place to leave her car soon, she
might as well turn around and drive back home again.

That, of course, was the coward's way.

She hadn't driven all this way to back out now. Meeting
Michael's son was the logical, inevitable next step in their
relationship, and as far as she could tell, there would never
be a perfect time to do it.

So she went around the block one last time, then whipped
into the vacant lot, wincing as her poor Mazda bounced its
way through ruts and over pieces of unidentifiable gar-
bage.

The place was quiet except for the traffic noise from
Amsterdam Avenue. She'd expected rumbling jackham-
mers and sweaty workers, the usual hubbub associated with
construction.

This silence was positively unnerving.

She parked the car and locked it; then she took a good
hard look around at the alleyways and toppled fences ring-
ing the lot, and double-checked the doors.

Not even the Almighty could protect a fully-equipped
Mazda 626 in New York City.

It was hard to imagine Michael sweating and straining
here in this broken-down neighborhood where dreams came
to die. Even the huge Gothic church—beautiful despite its
missing spires—seemed almost obscene, a testament to the
worst kind of ecclesiastical excess imaginable, in a city where
people lived on the street, shielded by cardboard boxes and
old newspapers.

Surely the money spent on this construction project could
have been put to better use than this.

But none of that had anything to do with Michael, did it?

He'd said he was part of the construction crew, not on the planning board or the funding committee. The moral responsibilities inherent in the project had nothing to do with him.

It was a job—and most likely a good job—and in this age of economic uncertainty he was probably damned glad to have it.

Of course, to be fair, working as a paid slave for Citi-National probably didn't look all that wonderful to him either. Except for the fact that she worked in an office and worked up a sweat only in the exalted presence of a Jane Fonda video, how did the way she made a living differ from his?

Both worked because it was necessary, because they knew no other way.

Neither of them had been a child of privilege. Working for a living had been a given since they had been old enough to stand on their own.

She had managed to come to terms with the fact that not all of her old dreams were going to come true.

Why, then, was it so hard for her to accept that the same was true for Michael?

She stopped at the door to the huge construction shed near the back entrance to the church. The windows were clouded over with city grime and iron bars. She couldn't see inside, but figured it was probably the construction equivalent of an employees' lounge.

Male laughter rumbled through the metal door, mixed with the sounds of the Temptations.

A warm, sweet feeling washed over her, then crept inside her heart.

No doubt about it: Michael McKay worked here.

She knocked sharply on the door, but the racket inside was so loud that no one heard her.

Normally she would just have opened the door and stepped inside, but the possibility of walking in on a score of naked construction workers snapping towels at one another's derrieres was something to consider, and she hesitated.

Sandra stopped hesitating when she heard a scream too close for comfort, followed by the quick footsteps of someone either running away from or running toward something Sandra had no business being in on.

She flung open the door and stared, dumbfounded.

It wasn't a locker room or a lunch room or any of the hundred and one run-of-the-mill things she'd imagined the shed to be.

It was a dance hall.

There, in the center of what seemed to be ten tons of uncut rock, a black girl and a Hispanic boy were doing a crazy parody of one of the old Sixties' dances—which had probably come and gone long before either of them was born, much to Sandra's dismay—while a crowd of laughing cohorts egged them on.

How on earth did Michael figure in this?

She stood there in the doorway, too stunned to do anything but watch. Finally the song ended.

"Hey, Leon," a tall skinny guy lounging in the corner to Sandra's right called out, "the man ain't here. Why don't we play some *real* music?" He was wearing a Run-DMC sweatshirt and dark glasses.

The black girl who had been dancing turned and made a face at him. "This stuff may be old, Redbone, but it's hot! Why don't you—"

The girl stopped as she caught sight of Sandra standing in the doorway. Sandra watched the girl's large dark brown eyes widen with surprise, and the construction shed grew as quiet as the adjacent cathedral.

She was being sized up by twenty curious pairs of eyes, and she felt old and out-of-place in her idiotic dark blue suit with the de rigueur white blouse and tie.

Where were the miracles when you really needed them?

She'd have given a month's salary to be back in her car and trapped in traffic rather than facing this type of scrutiny.

Okay, Ms. Big Business, she thought. *Show them your stuff.*

"Excuse me," she said, managing her best professional smile. "Is Michael McKay around?"

The silence deepened. She forced her smile a fraction wider and waited. A young man with skin the color of toasted almonds finally stepped forward and faced her. His hair was dark and curly with an incongruous purple streak over his left ear, and she had trouble not staring at the well-muscled forearms exposed by his rolled-up shirt-sleeves.

"You're lookin' for the man."

It was a statement, not a question.

"I'm looking for Michael McKay." She paused. "I think he qualifies."

A few chuckles broke the silence.

"Michael McKay *is* the man," the guy with the purple streak said. "Around here he is the *only* man."

Since ninety-five percent of the people in that room seemed to be of the male gender, that left only one interpretation of the word *man.*

The boss.

Their curiosity was so open and—she suddenly realized—so friendly, that her anxiety eased somewhat.

"Is he around? We have an appointment."

That did it. The room broke up into raucous laughter, complete with a lot of nudging, high-fives and wolf whistles.

"Come on, guys," she said, walking into the workroom with a bravery born of insanity. "Why don't you let me in on the joke?"

The guy with the purple streak—she'd heard him called Leon—grinned at her. "We know all about you, lady."

"Yeah," said the girl who'd been dancing when Sandra first opened the door. "We've been wonderin' when you'd finally show up."

"I didn't know he talked so much," Sandra muttered.

"He doesn't."

Sandra spun around at the sound of a new voice in the doorway and found herself face-to-face with one of the most exotically attractive women she'd ever seen. She was tiny, with yards of curly black hair that tumbled around a triangular face blessed with clear, ivory-colored skin. Her eyes were huge, a burnished gold and frighteningly direct.

Sandra felt an odd, queasy sensation in the pit of her stomach.

"He doesn't what?" she finally managed.

"McKay doesn't talk that much," the tiny woman with the lushly curved body said as she came into the room. She smelled of pottery clay, turpentine and Obsession. "At least not to the kids." She circled Sandra once, then stopped in front of her, her hands deep in the pockets of her black jumpsuit. "And sure as hell not about you."

"Does everyone in this damned place talk in riddles?"

"Whoo-eee," hooted one of the workers in the far corner of the workshop. "The lady's got a temper! Wonder what the man thinks about that?"

"Mind your own business, Bobby!" The small woman wheeled around, instantly back to business. "Don't you people have anything better to do than eavesdrop? If Michael comes back and the finials on the east portico aren't started—'' She shrugged and let them fill in the rest of the horror story themselves.

Then she turned her attention back to Sandra.

Sandra willed herself to stand perfectly still while the woman blatantly checked her out.

"Do I meet your approval?" Sandra finally snapped. "I feel like I'm up on the auction block and you're not sure I'll bring full price."

The woman grinned up at her, and Sandra had to restrain herself from trying to knock her block off.

"It's the nose," the dark-haired woman said, tapping her booted foot against the cement floor. "It should be a shade thinner at the bridge."

Sandra glared at her. "I'll make an appointment with the plastic surgeon tomorrow."

Did church work attract the incurably rude?

The woman's smile faded. "You really don't know about it, do you?"

"Your pronouns are driving me nuts," Sandra said, "and no, I don't know anything about anything."

The woman tilted her head toward the back room. "Come on. I'll show you."

Walking the thirty feet or so past the young stonecutters, who were ostensibly working at the benches lining the walls, was tougher than walking past a crowd of sailors on shore leave.

At least she'd have known exactly what the sailors had in mind.

Finally the woman stopped near a stack of busts in various stages of completion. Griffins, unicorns, dragons and demons snarled at her from atop wooden cabinets, and a surprising number of them looked familiar in a way she couldn't quite figure out.

But no matter. The brunette had turned her full attention on Sandra.

"You're Michael's old friend, aren't you?"

Sandra nodded. "I'm old Sandra Patterson." *And I'm at an extreme disadvantage here.* "And you're...?"

"Annie Gage." She extended her hand. "I run Altar Ego over in the church basement. We help keep money in their coffers."

"I see."

Of course she didn't see, but Sandra was already suffering from information overload. Wondering how Annie Gage and Michael connected with one another was occupying most of her brain circuits at the moment.

"You look just the way I thought you would."

"Except for the nose?" Sandra wasn't above a quick shot.

Annie laughed. "Except for the nose."

Sandra's eyes narrowed. "Michael described me to you?" That didn't sound like the Michael McKay she knew at all, unless he and this Gage woman were much closer than she cared to contemplate.

"He didn't have to," Annie said. She stepped back and gestured toward the carved torso of what seemed to be an angel-in-progress. "He did this."

It was a female angel, with a tumble of straight hair, but without her glasses on, Sandra couldn't make out the details. Her curiosity piqued, she moved closer, aware of Annie's scrutiny but unable to resist. The hair, the long, slightly slanted eyes, the full mouth—suddenly it all came together in a rush of understanding so overwhelming that she leaned back against a nearby workbench.

"That's me." Her voice was low, hushed. "I can't believe it..."

"Believe it," Annie said. "We've been taking bets on who the Mystery Lady was. As soon as I heard about the Hurricane Henry reunion, I knew."

Sandra took another look at the carved stone. The sensation of seeing her own features staring blankly back at her was disconcerting; it was almost as if she were watching herself sleep.

"He did all this work in less than a week?" It hardly seemed possible.

"You don't know much about stonecutting, do you? He's been at this since last March."

Sandra started in surprise. "That's six months ago."

Annie nodded. "Yup. Stonecutting's a long, painstaking process. Amazing that McKay has the patience for it, isn't it?"

It was Sandra's turn to nod, but it wasn't Michael's patience that she found amazing. It was the fact that she had obviously been as deeply embedded in his heart as he had always been in hers.

This incredible work of art in front of her was the most visible testament of love—or obsession—she had ever seen.

Annie Gage was watching her closely, her huge golden eyes frankly curious and assessing. Sandra forced herself to turn away from her own eerie likeness and meet the other woman's gaze.

"Is something wrong?" she asked.

A half smile tilted Annie's mouth. "You didn't know he was a stonecutter, did you?"

"I knew he worked here at the church," Sandra hedged.

"But you didn't know he was capable of something like this, did you?"

She bristled at Annie's unabashed frankness. "Michael is capable of anything he sets his mind to," she said, he words clipped.

"Did you think he was a construction jock-type?"

"I knew he worked with his hands." Sandra was finding it hard to control her annoyance.

"You think I'm pushy, don't you?" Annie plunged her small, paint-stained hands into the pockets of her jumpsuit.

"Yes," Sandra said. "Extremely."

Annie laughed. "I am pushy. It's a family trait. I just can't help being curious about where you fit in."

That queasy feeling returned to the pit of Sandra's stomach. Annie Gage was an extremely sexy and attractive woman. It wasn't hard to imagine that she and Michael might have progressed far beyond sharing a bagel and coffee in the church cafeteria.

The concept of knowing one another in the biblical sense took on yet another dimension. One that Sandra didn't like at all.

She decided against asking the obvious—and very direct—question, because it was all too apparent that Annie Gage would give a direct answer.

"Is Michael around?" she asked instead. "I know I'm early, but . . ." She let her voice trail off.

Annie checked her watch, a big round-faced Timex with huge Roman numerals. "Davey's plane came in at three. Unless they hit traffic coming back from Newark, they should have been here a while ago."

Sandra stole a quick look at her own Rolex and swore to take a step into downward mobility. Glittery gold watches were hardly the thing to wear in a neighborhood like this.

Assuming she'd ever be back in a neighborhood like this.

"Maybe the plane was delayed."

"No, it wasn't," Annie replied quickly. "I called Delta to make sure."

Sandra stared at the woman. She called Delta Airlines to make sure?

What on earth was going on? Unless Annie Gage was waiting for someone on that plane herself, why would she care if the plane carrying Michael's child was early, late, or on time? Oh, God. The only reason she could come up with was that Annie Gage and Michael had—

"Annie!"

Sandra's disturbing thoughts were stopped in midstream as a small bundle of boy, dressed in a candy-apple-red baseball jacket, catapulted himself across the workshop and into Annie's arms.

She knew it was idiotic, but Sandra's legs began to shake, and she was glad she had the worktable behind her for support.

"Well, look at you!" Annie, who wasn't much taller than the boy herself, ruffled his dark blond hair. "You have a tan, Davey!"

The child's head was turned away from Sandra. All she could see was the curve of his right ear. This wasn't the way she'd had things planned.

"Grandpa Art took me fishing on a boat," she heard the boy say. His voice was high and clear.

"Did you catch anything?" Annie asked.

"Uh-uh." He shook his head, his blond curls bobbing with the movement. "It takes practice. Daddy says we can go fishing in the spring by home."

"Daddy also says you have to learn how to swim first and wear a life jacket, pal."

Sandra's entire body reacted to the deep, thrilling sound of Michael's voice as he walked toward them. She felt as if she were suspended over a flame, yearning toward its warmth but aware of the danger inherent in fire.

On one side of the stone angel, his son stood, hugging Annie Gage. On the other side, Sandra waited, hands clutching the edge of the worktable, heart pounding uncontrollably.

What Michael did in the next ten seconds would determine much of her future.

She held her breath.

He looked at her, his dark eyes unreadable. "You're here early."

She swallowed. "Yes. I decided to make a break for it."

Everyone in the place was staring at them, including the little boy whose face she had yet to see.

She couldn't take her eyes from Michael.

"Risking the wrath of your boss?"

She snapped her fingers. "Piece of cake. I told them I had something important to do."

A slow, lazy smile broke across his face, and her heart turned over. Joy, pure and wonderful, was in his eyes, and she felt that same joy flood her entire body.

Risking the wrath of Citi-National was a small price to pay for a moment of such intense pleasure.

And then he came toward her.

That simple act of singling her out, publicly stating her importance in his life, sent what was left of Sandra's defenses tumbling to the floor.

Michael drew her into his arms and gave her a warm hug. She wanted to bury her face against his shoulder and close out the rest of the world.

"See the resemblance?" he murmured, angling his head toward the lovely stone angel.

"You have an incredible memory," she said.

"No," he said, "not incredible enough. You're more beautiful now than I ever imagined."

"When you said you worked with your hands, I had no idea you meant this."

"It still surprises the hell out of me, too," he said. "When I found out I could create something so beautiful—" He stopped and shook his head. "Hell. I finally knew what I was all about."

Everything she was, everything she'd hoped and dreamed and strived for, was tangled up in this moment and with this man she loved.

Of course, now the man she loved had a small son to care for, and that small son would be at the center of any future she and Michael might have.

God knew, she wasn't a stranger to the responsibilities required by love—the depth of her commitment to Elinor was proof of that—but this was something else again.

Bonds of love didn't exist between her and Michael's child. The easy rapport Annie Gage enjoyed with David was something Sandra wasn't sure she could manage.

She could feel the boy's eyes upon her, and knew it was time to face the music.

Michael released her from his embrace, and she took a deep breath.

"Davey." Michael stepped toward his son. "This is the friend I told you about."

If Sandra had been worried that she would see Michael's ex-wife's face each time she looked at this child, that fear vanished the moment she looked at David McKay.

The dark, midnight eyes of the boy she'd known looked back at her across the years, and only the mop of curly blond hair assured her that she hadn't stepped back in time.

Those eyes belonged to David McKay and no one else, and right now David McKay was wondering what on earth she was doing there.

Good question.

"Hi," she said, bending down and extending her hand for him to shake. "I'm Sandra."

He moved closer to Annie, his right forefinger resting against his lower lip. Sweat began to pop out along Sandra's hairline as she realized her hand was fluttering in the breeze like a forgotten flag.

She pulled it in and swiftly wiped her palm against the side of her expensive skirt.

Gathering her forces, she gave it another try.

"Your father and I went to school together. I knew him when he was just about your age."

Annie Gage's eyes widened, and Sandra felt a wicked burst of pleasure.

David looked up at his father as if the thought of Michael's ever having been five years old was incomprehensible.

Michael swooped the child into his strong arms and laughed. "Sandy was just like you are, pal," he said. "She loves animals, too."

It had been so many years since Sandra had lived a life that was stable enough to include pets that Michael's words surprised her. How many long-ago parts of herself had she lost along the way to discovering who she was—and what she wanted?

She moved closer to them.

"Do you have a dog, David?" Not a brilliant question, but the best she was able to come up with. Thank God Michael had brought up the topic of pets; if he hadn't, she would still be stumbling around looking for something to talk about.

The boy was watching her with those huge, dark eyes of his, and she had the strangest feeling that he understood her uncertainty, could see right through to the fears gnawing at her heart.

You think you have it tough, David? she thought. *At least you know you'll end up with him.*

That was more than she knew at the moment.

Michael caught her eye as he spoke to his son. "Why don't you tell Sandy about Pepper?"

Sandra waited, conscious of the Motown music behind her, of the concentrated interest of Annie Gage, of Michael's apparent discomfort and of her own failure to manage a two-minute conversation with a five-year-old boy.

"Is Pepper your dog?" she asked, her voice sounding strained and false to her ears.

David looked at her, then shook his head.

"Your cat?"

He made a face, then buried his nose against his father's chest.

Two giant steps backward for you, Patterson.

What she wanted to do was blink her eyes and disappear, but since magic was beyond her reach at the moment—and since Annie was watching her with something uncomfortably close to pity on her face—she decided to give it one more shot.

"Then I guess Pepper must be your pet rhinoceros."

He looked at her again, this time with more interest.

"Your hippo?" she continued. "Your dragon? Your dinosaur?"

He squirmed until Michael put him back down on his own two feet.

He looked up at her with his father's eyes. "Everyone knows Pepper's a parrot."

She knelt down so they'd be eye-to-eye. "Pepper's a funny name for a bird. Why did you name him that?"

David looked at her as if she were terribly backward. "Because he eats hot peppers, silly."

Michael cleared his throat. "Remember what I said about that, pal. We don't call people names. This is Sandra."

She started to say that she'd been called a hell of a lot worse things than silly, but caught herself. The last thing she wanted to do was to undermine Michael's authority over his son.

Annie, however, had no such inhibitions. She jumped right in.

"Pepper's a Double Yellow-Headed Amazon. I bought him for David's fifth birthday."

"Double head?" All Sandra could imagine were two beaks, each the size of a cattle prod.

David giggled. Well, at least her monumental ignorance was amusing him. That was a start.

"When he's grown up, he'll have yellow all the way down to his shoulders," David said, sizing her up with the same open curiosity that had been his father's trademark as a boy.

Sandra smiled and nodded, but she didn't understand a thing she'd heard.

"Don't worry," Michael said. "It'll make sense once you see Pepper."

"I hope so. Right now all I can picture is a two-headed bird wearing a yellow cape."

David laughed, then cast a quick look at his father. Sandra knew he was dying to call her silly again—or possibly something stronger—but he was obviously a good kid, and he controlled himself.

Suddenly the beeper in her pocketbook began to shrill. David's mouth dropped open in surprise, and he tilted his head to one side as he listened.

Sandra winked at Michael and Annie and pretended nothing was happening. Michael chatted about the music playing in the background. The beeper in her pocketbook continued to shriek, sounding like a strangled hyena.

Finally David could stand it no longer.

"Your purse is making a noise," he said pointing at it from a safe distance away. "Something's in there."

Sandra looked at him and smiled. "Don't worry, David. It always does that." *True enough.*

"Maybe it's hurt."

She shook her head. "It's not hurt," she said. "It just wants me."

"What is it?" he asked, venturing closer, his eyes as big as half-dollars.

"What do you think it is?"

His index finger tugged at his lower lip. "Is it a bird?"

"It's not a bird."

"Is it a turtle?"

She shook her head.

"A puppy?"

"Not a puppy."

He bent down and put his ear near her pocketbook, giggling as it beeped in his ear.

"I know," he said, his voice shrill with excitement. "It's a kitten."

"Sorry, David. It's not a kitten either." She unclasped her bag and reached inside. "Do you want to know what it is?"

He was practically dancing with excitement. "Yes!" He glanced over at his father and grinned. "Yes, *please!*"

"Put out your hand, David."

He did. His fingers were small, the palm of his hand broad like his father's. A faint streak of orange paint circled the base of his thumb. For some idiotic reason a lump formed in her throat, and she had to look away for a moment.

"Close your eyes."

His eyes closed, and she placed the beeper in the palm of his hand.

"You can open them now."

He did and stared at the electronic marvel squealing in his hand.

"What is it?"

"My beeper."

"Beeper?"

She explained the principle behind the beeper in simple language, but quickly realized that the sound fascinated him more than the reason behind the sound.

"I wish I had a beeper," David said, reluctantly handing the device back to Sandra. "Then my mommy could call me from where she is."

A silence that could only be described as hideous fell over the room.

Michael bent down and put his hands on his son's bony shoulders. "Mommy can't call you," he said. Sandra had never known his voice could sound so soft, so openly vulnerable. "Do you remember what I told you about going to heaven?"

David nodded, his forefinger once more glued to his bottom lip. "I forgot, but I remember now."

Michael stood up. Annie reached over and ruffled David's hair, and Sandra felt a sudden, unexpected stab of envy over the woman's easy rapport with the boy.

"We have some of the baby animals for tomorrow's parade in the workshop," she said. "How about coming over to Altar Ego and taking a look?" Her golden eyes darted from Michael to Sandra, then back again. "We have a litter of puppies that—"

That was all David had to hear. "Can I? Can I?" He leaped around his father, Sandra and her beeper forgotten.

The relationship between Annie and the child was obviously a warm one and, Sandra assumed, one of long standing. It wasn't difficult to figure out that her own appearance on the scene was going to have quite a few repercussions.

Not all of them good.

Michael hesitated, meeting her eyes over his son's head.

More than anything, Sandra wanted to get as far away from that room as was humanly possible. All she had to do was say she had to get back home, move her car out of a tow-away zone, meet Jacqueline Onassis for a quick dinner—pick one—and Michael would instantly back her up.

But she looked at David's face, and something inside her shifted. Maybe she wasn't as far removed from that five-year-old as she liked to think. When she was his age, a litter of puppies was like having a month of Christmas mornings one right after the other.

Anyone who didn't understand that fact was the worst type of Scrooge imaginable.

She winked at Michael.

"You sure?" he mouthed.

She nodded. "I'm sure."

"Ten minutes with the puppies," Michael said. His voice was stern, but his eyes twinkled merrily. "Then we head out for supper."

David's "Thanks, Daddy" was lost as he raced for the door and Altar Ego.

Annie stayed behind a moment. "I'll have him back in time," she said, looking from Sandra to Michael and plainly weighing the import of what was happening between them.

"That won't be easy, Gage," Michael said. "The way he feels about puppies..."

Annie straightened her shoulders and grinned. "Don't worry. I can be tough when I have to be."

With that she went after David, and relief almost knocked Sandra to the floor.

"He'll love you for that," Michael said, drawing her into his arms despite the audience they had in the studio.

"He doesn't even realize what happened," Sandra said, breathing in his familiar scent. "All he's thinking about right now are those puppies."

"It went pretty well, I thought."

"Did it?" Sandra made a face. "I was scared to death. You should have given me a list of appropriate topics of conversation. I never felt so bewildered in my life."

He kissed her forehead. "You did fine. Just remember what you liked when you were five years old, and you're home free."

She shook her head. "I don't think I was ever five."

"Yes, you were," he said. "I was there. I can vouch for it. You were a snotty little girl with shiny blond hair and patent-leather shoes."

"I was not!" Her memories were of a rough-and-tumble tomboy.

"You hated dirt and mud and falling down."

"Sounds sensible." His words were bringing back memories of hopscotch games on the sidewalk, of jumping rope in front of the apartment building, of the sounds of Yankees games floating across the hot summer air as everyone waited for the Good Humor man to show up.

"You were prim and proper, and I think I fell in love with you the day you showed up in first grade in your navy-blue uniform with the bright red ribbons in your hair."

She looked up at him, puzzled. "You can't possibly remember that. I mean, I'd almost forgotten about those red ribbons." Elinor had had a fresh red grosgrain ribbon ready to tie in Sandra's hair every morning. It was one of the small but important things that had somehow given Sandra a sense of family, of security.

His words called up memories so tender that she almost wished they'd remained buried in the back of her heart.

"I haven't forgotten a thing, Sandy. Not one thing."

She glanced at the stone angel, her likeness, and knew he was speaking the truth.

"Your son looks just like you," she said, her voice catching slightly. "I'd know him anywhere."

"He has Diana's hair, but everything else is pure McKay." The look on Michael's face was one of such pride that it was almost painful to see.

"You're lucky," she said quietly. "I never realized how lucky before this minute."

Nothing she had ever done with her life, nothing she would ever accomplish at Citi-National, could come close to the miracle Michael and his wife had created the day David was born.

He kissed her hair. "Now I am," he said softly. "Now I'm beginning to believe in second chances."

He talked of a future she wasn't sure was possible for them. David was a major responsibility and, by rights, Michael's first responsibility.

Raising a child took time and money and love.

So did the care of Elinor Patterson.

Was it fair to entangle Michael's future and his son's in something as devastating—both emotionally and financially—as that?

Was it fair to keep it a secret?

She felt trapped, damned by her promise to Elinor to keep her illness secret.

And damned by her own reluctance to risk losing this miracle she'd just found.

Behind them, the apprentices struggled with the melody of an old Miracles tune, the basses and the baritones battling for supremacy. Finally a clear, trembling falsetto rose above the rest and blended everything together in a harmony so sweet it brought quick, sharp tears to her eyes.

Michael hugged her tight and she said nothing, letting the fierce love she felt for him flow with the music and the moment.

There was no turning back, no playing it safe. This was the man she loved, the man she'd walk through fire for, the man she'd defend with her life.

David came tumbling back into the room with three puppies at his heels, and Sandra's heart turned inside out.

How ironic that it had taken more than fifteen years to return to the place where she'd started.

To the man she'd always loved.

And to the child that could have been theirs.

Chapter Ten

Sandra was sprawled across his living-room sofa, her eyes closed, her long legs propped up on the arm.

"Tired?" Michael asked, sweeping up the last of the pizza crusts Davey had scattered on the rug.

"Exhausted." The word sounded suspiciously like a yawn.

Michael grinned. "The David McKay Show wore you out, huh?"

One eye opened. It was amazing how much outrage one sleepy blue eye could convey. "I have a lot of energy," she said. "I'm just conserving it."

"Conserving it for what?" Michael dropped down next to her, his hand playing lightly with a stray lock of her hair. "Do you have something special in mind?"

"Yes," she said. "Getting myself home in one piece."

"I'll drive you back home." He watched as she stifled a yawn, then sat up on the sofa. "I'll just bundle Davey up in a few blankets and stick him in the back seat."

"It's not far," she said, smoothing her hair down with the palm of her hand. "I'll be okay."

"I don't like you out there on the roads so late."

She laughed, amused. "How did I ever manage without you, Michael?"

Damned if he didn't feel a sting to his male pride, but he refused to let her know it. The truth was, he wanted her more dependent, more needful of the tenderness and concern that hid behind his macho exterior.

The way he needed her scared him. His need was wrapped around his heart; it tore at his sinews and burrowed inside his bones until it became a physical ache.

At times she seemed so distant, so self-contained and solitary that, despite the words of love and the past they shared, he wondered how he figured in her life.

He'd asked her to stay the night, but she'd refused and he hadn't pressed her. This wasn't the time to add any more fuel to Art Bentley's fire—and the presence of Sandra Patterson was enough to start a forest fire.

There'd been another message waiting for him from Art when he got home, and two from his lawyer. None of the messages were good. Art was on the Italian-racing-bike kick again, and Michael had simply fast-forwarded his way past the usual tirade while Sandra and Davey went out to pick up the pizza.

His lawyer's message was something else again. Art had hired a private investigator, and was determined to catch Michael in something unsavory.

Something like having a woman in his house.

He forced the thought from his mind. Across the room Pepper squawked and Sandra laughed.

"Rodan the Flying Monster's at it again," she said, tilting her head in the parrot's direction. "I nearly passed out when David let him out of his cage."

"Rodan weighs two pounds, Sandy. I think you can handle him."

"Two pounds, huh?" She made a face, and Michael laughed. "All of it must be beak."

"You'll get used to him.

"I wouldn't bet on it."

He pulled her to her feet and held her close to his body.

"What about Davey?" he asked. "Can you get used to him?"

She suddenly grew serious. "Maybe the question is, can he get used to me."

"He's like his father," Michael said, nuzzling the side of her neck, savoring the warm pounding of her pulse beneath his lips. "He has great taste in women."

She pulled away from him slightly and looked up into his eyes. "Well, he certainly likes Annie Gage, I'll grant you that."

"Jealous, are you?"

She didn't flinch. "Yes."

"I kind of like that."

"I don't."

"When I saw you with that Ed McGregor—"

"Gregory."

"Whatever. When I saw you standing with that guy in the White Castle I wanted to punch that smug grin off his face."

"I'm glad you didn't. I might have lost my job." A smile twitched at the right-hand corner of her luscious mouth. "Though I must admit the thought of it does have its appeal."

He smiled back. "See what I mean?"

Her smile faded. "There is a slight difference here, though. Ed's no threat. I'm not that sure about Annie Gage."

She watched him intently, but he said nothing. He knew that anything he said now would only foster her insecurities, even though they were without foundation.

"So tell me you two don't have anything going," she said.

"We don't have anything going."

Her blue eyes narrowed. "Now or ever?"

"Ever," he said. He hadn't wanted to risk the friendship or his son.

"I'm surprised," she said. "She's very attracted to you."

"It's mutual."

She gave him a quick jab in the stomach. "I want honesty," she said, "but that's carrying it a bit far."

"And I want you to know you have no competition." He put his hand beneath her chin and tilted her face up to his. "You never have, Sandy. You never will."

"I love you," she said. "That was the one thing that never changed."

He took a deep breath and moved closer to the edge of his emotions.

"So what are we waiting for?" he asked, trying to make himself sound more lighthearted than he was. "Why don't we take the plunge?"

She laughed, sounding as nervous and uncertain as he was feeling. "You want to swim?"

"I want to marry you."

She fluttered her fingers inside the opening of her silk blouse. "Why, Mistah Butler, I do declare—this is awful sudden."

"No jokes, Sandra." He captured both her hands in his and wished it were as easy to capture her soul. "We've been heading toward this since we were six years old. Why wait any longer?"

"Your son, for one reason," she said, looking more uncomfortable than he would have liked. "And the fact that I'd like a courtship."

"A what?"

"A courtship," she repeated. "Flowers, candy, candlelight dinners—all the things we never had."

He thought back through the years. "You mean, I never gave you flowers?"

She shook her head. "Never."

"What about at the senior prom? I know I gave you flowers then." He had a hazy memory of a yellow orchid on a wrist corsage. He'd never quite figured out why a woman would want to wear a flower like a watch.

"That doesn't count," she said. "That was part of the prom package."

"I never gave you roses?"

Her laugh was soft, slightly melancholy. "We were kids," she said. "You couldn't have afforded them."

"And this is important to you?"

She nodded again. "Yes. We missed a lot of things, you and I. I'd like to make up for lost time."

He pulled her even closer, letting his body make a few suggestions of its own. "Making up for lost time sounds like a good idea."

She put her hand flat against his chest. "Not with David in the next room."

"When you marry me you'll have to get used to that."

"When I marry you I will, but have pity, Michael. I've only known him a few hours. It takes a little getting used to."

He drew his hand over the beautifully sculpted planes of her face, then down the length of her throat. "Fair warning," he said, unable to control the brief stab of anger that sharpened his voice. "I'm not a patient man."

Her eyes widened and he thought he saw fear in them, but before he could put a name to the emotion, she smiled. "I'm not asking you to be."

"I want to marry you," he stated flatly. "I don't want to turn around fifteen years from now and wonder why I let you go a second time."

"I don't want that either," she whispered. "I just need time—"

"Damn it! Who the hell knows how much time we have, Sandy? Do you have any guarantees? I sure don't."

"I think we have a few good years left, Michael." Her voice came at him with an undercurrent of irony that puzzled him, but he was too angry to pursue it.

"We've wasted too much time already," he said, resisting the urge to toss her over his shoulder and drag her back to the Cathedral of St. Matthew the Divine and marry her. "I love you. I want to spend my life with you." He spread his arms wide in a gesture of exasperation. "I don't know how to make it any clearer than that."

"You don't have to make it any clearer," she said. "I understand."

"Then let's do it," he said. "Let's call your mother, wherever she is, and get things started."

"Well," she said, with an embarrassed grin, "would you believe I don't know exactly where she is?"

He had to laugh. It was terrific to think of Elinor Patterson, who had sacrificed so much to give her daughter a start in life, finally kicking up her heels. "They don't have phones in Pago Pago?"

"I don't know," Sandra said, her grin sliding into a real smile. "I'll have to see if I can dig up her itinerary."

"I'm kind of surprised you don't know where she is. Elinor must really be cutting loose."

"She is," Sandra said, looking down to adjust the top button of her blouse. "She is."

"Are you going to tell her we're engaged?"

"Not yet," she said. "First I'll tell her we're courting."

"You're serious about this courting business, aren't you?"

She raised herself up on tiptoe and kissed him on the mouth. The scent of her perfume rose up and around Michael, dizzying him.

"I want everything," she said, telling him with her eyes that she would give everything in return. "I want everything we've missed: the courtship, the engagement, the plans. We owe it to ourselves—we owe it to David. He needs time to get to know me, time to accept me. You can't just add water and have Instant Mom pop up in the kitchen." She kissed him again. "Let him feel he's part of the process, too. It's only fair."

"I thought you didn't know a damn thing about kids."

"I don't. That's just logic."

And he was powerless before her logic, just as he'd always been. Michael had always followed his heart while Sandra followed her head, and although it had infuriated him at times, it was one of the many things about her that had always fascinated him.

"Two months," he said. "Two months of flowers and champagne and candlelight and trips to Adventureland with David, then we make it legal, lady."

The sparkle in her eye was back. "Six months?"

"Two."

"Four and a half?"

"Sixty days. Take it or leave it."

She wrapped her arms around his waist and pressed her lips against the underside of his chin.

"I'll take it," she murmured.

"I thought so."

"You drive a hard bargain, McKay." Her hands slipped inside his shirt and he thought his heart would burst through his rib cage at her touch.

But it really didn't matter.

Sixty minutes, sixty days, or sixty years from now, she would still be his.

Her heart had always belonged to him as his had belonged to her, and nothing—not music or flowers or candlelight—could ever change that.

SANDRA DIDN'T BREATHE NORMALLY until she pulled into her driveway an hour later and turned off the ignition. She closed her eyes and rested her head against the back of her seat, letting the dense throbbing silence of the October night wash away some of the tension tugging at her nerves.

The mournful wail of a foghorn floated in from the Sound, and she shivered and pulled her jacket closer to her body. It was the kind of night that called to mind crackling fires and long kisses—not sitting alone in a car wondering why the happiest experience of her life, this miraculous reunion with Michael McKay, was suddenly going wrong.

All evening she'd felt off balance, as if she were moving one beat behind everyone else. The second Michael had mentioned marriage—which was the obvious, the inevitable next step for them—she'd had to hold herself back from making a run for the door.

And it wasn't even David who was the problem.

Not really.

Oh, she'd had her weak-kneed, sweaty-palmed moment when he'd first exploded into the room, a forty-pound package of energy and enthusiasm who'd learned more about sorrow and loss in five years than a more generous fate would have allowed.

But when he looked up at her and she saw those onyx eyes, so like his father's, she knew she was in trouble. Watching David was like being put into a time capsule and whisked back thirty years to Cornish Avenue, back to the long summers when people slept on the fire escape or sat up on the roof to get away from the stink of hot tar and the metallic blare of *Murray the K and his Swinging Soiree*.

Michael wanted a wife, and he needed a mother for his son. Like Sandra, he wanted the chance to recapture the past, the opportunity to build their future.

It was no less than he deserved.

And no more than she wanted, as well.

He'd built a good life for himself, Michael had, a life that far exceeded what she'd imagined he would have years ago, when the need in her for security overshadowed even love. That big house in the good neighborhood was more than she'd expected. Oh, he was mortgaged to the hilt just as she was, but his sturdily almost-upper-middle-class life-style had come as an enormous surprise.

But medieval craftsmen weren't in great demand. Once the work on the cathedral was over, where in hell did a master stonecutter go?

And what happened to a master stonecutter with a son whose needs doubled and tripled with every passing day?

He had responsibilities of the heart, just as she did, responsibilities that were bred into the blood and into the bone.

Michael would no more turn away from his son than she could turn away from her mother. In that they were alike.

He was a man of honor, but sometimes even a man of honor could buckle beneath the pressure.

Andrew Maxwell had, and unfortunately there was no guarantee that the same thing wouldn't happen with Michael.

She was sure of one thing: she had come too far to let Michael go now. He had always been part of her and always would be, and now his son was laying claim to a part of her heart.

A future she hadn't dared dream about was suddenly opening up before her, and there seemed to be but one way to ensure it.

A branch crackled somewhere to the left of the blacktop driveway. She knew she should gather up her purse and briefcase and make the fifty-yard dash to her front door, but she was at the edge of something important.

For the last few days she'd been avoiding the obvious, but now, in the darkness of her car, there was no escaping it.

This mythical trip of Elinor's finally had to come to an end.

Sandra had argued and demanded and pleaded with her mother not to keep her illness to herself, but to no avail. Elinor Patterson was a proud woman, and a vain one. Her beauty had been a source of strength for her when strength had been in short supply; her physical grace had been a source of joy.

When ALS had begun to strip her of control over her own body, she had made the conscious decision to remove herself from her old friends, her old routines, and "disappear."

The thought of seeming vulnerable, of appearing ugly, was as difficult for Elinor to accept as the inevitable result of the disease itself.

Sandra had hoped that the reappearance of Michael McKay in her life would open a new door for Elinor. She'd had every intention of pushing the issue each time she visited.

Elinor's self-imposed isolation had seemed both foolish and unfair.

Sandra laughed in the silent darkness.

"Who are you trying to kid?" she said out loud. A part of her—a part she hated—wanted to take the easy way. But no, not this time.

When she drove up to see Elinor tomorrow after work she would tell her about Michael and his phenomenal work at the cathedral; she would tell her about David and his gold-

en curls and his eyes black as the night; she would tell her
about Annie Gage and Leon and that incredible stone angel,
and she would try just once more to force her mother out of
hiding.

"YOU SHOULD HAVE CALLED FIRST, lovey," Lucie said, the
following evening. "If I'd known you were driving up, I
would have saved you the trip."

Sandra disengaged herself from another of Lucie's hid-
den-tape-measure hugs and tried to hide her dismay.

"Mother had a bad day?" she asked, keeping her voice
light. "Another Fair Oaks party, I suppose."

Lucie smiled, but Sandra couldn't help noticing the sad-
ness in her eyes.

"Elinor has no control over her extremities today, and
she's had some difficulty with her speech. She's sleeping
now."

Sandra sank down onto the couch in the hallway. It was
an overstuffed colonial in a gay chintz pattern that belonged in front of a roaring fireplace. She'd give anything
to be in front of that roaring fireplace, to be as far away
from this reality as possible.

"Here," Lucie said, handing her a cup of ice water from
the cooler near Elinor's door. "Drink this. You look terrible."

Sandra took a gulp of water. "Am I that obvious?"

"I know you too well, lovey. You can't fool me."

Sandra patted the woman's hand. "Wonderful," she said,
a trace of amusement in her voice. "Now I have two mothers to nag me."

Lucie picked up her knitting and started to untangle a
length of beige yarn. "You can never have too many mothers," she said. "That's an old English saying I learned at my
own mother's knee."

"I thought your family was French," Sandra said, fascinated by the way Lucie's hands quickly picked up the rhythm of the knitting.

The older woman's dark eyes flashed as she glanced at Sandra over her stitches. "I'm flexible," she said. "I can bend to fit the occasion."

Sandra patted her hand. "Advice from every nation?"

Lucie laughed. "The international Ann Landers."

A young, red-haired nurse bustled by in a cloud of Shalimar and Ivory soap, and Sandra was once again reminded she was in a hospital, not a drawing room.

"Mother seemed so well the other day," she said. "I was actually beginning to wonder if—"

Lucie put her knitting back down on the sofa and met Sandra's eyes.

"No," she said quietly. "As much as we love Elinor, she isn't going to get better. You know that, Sandra. Don't let yourself get caught up in that trap."

"Damn it, Lucie. Sometimes she seems so healthy that I expect her to kick aside the wheelchair and head out to the jogging track." Her laugh caught on the jagged edge of a sob. "It's so damned unfair."

"That it is, lovey."

"This isn't—I mean, this isn't a serious setback, is it?"

"A minor one, but she'll gain back the ground she's lost," Lucie said.

"It's so difficult not knowing," Sandra said. "Days, months, years—every time the phone rings late at night my heart stops."

"She still has time ahead of her. Time enough to see you married and settled down with a family of your own."

Sandra tried to ignore the fact that, thanks to her self-imposed banishment, Elinor could never be a part of the family she created.

"Subtle pressure, Lucie?" she asked, trying to avoid a head-on collision with a problem she couldn't solve.

"Not too subtle, I hope."

"Have no fear. You'll never be accused of that."

Sandra closed her eyes for a moment, blinking back tears. "It's the ups and downs that get me. Sometimes I feel like I'm on a roller coaster and someone is about to jam on the brakes."

"Elinor is a strong lady, Sandra. She can bear what needs to be borne. It's you she worries about."

Sandra's head jerked up. "Me?"

"You. She wants more for you than you want for yourself."

"Meaning what?"

Lucie picked up her knitting again. "It's not my place."

Sandra's laugh was genuine this time. "Since when has that stopped you?"

Lucie swatted her with a ball of yarn. "Don't be impertinent."

"Answer my question, Lucie."

"She has high hopes for you and your young man."

"What young man?" Sandra asked cautiously.

Lucie's eyes twinkled. "How many young men are there?" she countered. "I mean Michael."

"How do you know about Michael?"

"I have my ways."

"So my mother's been talking about me, hmm?" She thought of Larry's words to her the other day on the same subject. "I never knew she was such a gossip."

"Neither one of us cares for *Dynasty*," Lucie said, "and, try as we might, we can't watch *Magnum* forever."

"So you gossip," Sandra said.

"We talk," Lucie amended.

"About me?"

"Among others."

"Tell me this: have I any secrets left?"

"Not many."

"I was afraid of that."

Once again Lucie put her knitting down. At this rate, Sandra's sweater would be finished sometime early in the next century.

"If you want to make your mother happy, you'll marry your Michael."

Sandra said nothing, but could feel a telltale flush creeping up her throat and flooding her cheeks.

"Has he asked you?" Lucie persisted.

There was no use trying to hide it; her idiotic grin was a sure sign. "He's asked me."

"And you've accepted?"

She thought about her demands for a courtship, for flowers and candlelight.

For time to balance reality with her dreams.

"I'm working on it."

"Don't be a fool, lovey. You're not getting any younger."

"Lucie!"

"Well, you're not. Before you know it you'll be a middle-aged spinster with your hair tucked into a bun."

"That's a rosy picture of my future that you're painting, Lucie."

"I'm only speaking the truth, lovey. If you're smart, you'll grab up that young man before someone else gets her manicured fingers on him."

An image of Annie Gage popped into her mind, but she pushed it down.

She reached over and hugged Lucie, knitting and all. "I promise you can dance at my wedding. Does that make you feel any better?"

Lucie grinned. "Only if I'm not too old to dance by the time you decide to say yes."

It had been a long, emotionally wearing day—both at work and here at the hospital—and suddenly a wave of fatigue rolled in on Sandra that was strong enough to lower her defenses.

"I haven't told him about Mother yet."

Lucie's face was impassive. "She wouldn't want you to."

"I know," Sandra said slowly, "but it doesn't feel right. Michael knew her and loved her. Maybe this time it would be different—"

"Elinor's a proud woman," Lucie said. "She wants to build a life away from her past."

"And I understand that," Sandra said, "but this goes beyond visits from old co-workers and PTA pals."

"Have you spoken to her about it?" Lucie asked. "Perhaps if you put it to her bluntly, she'd understand."

"I was going to talk to her today," Sandra said. "I thought maybe if I explained the way I felt, she might—"

The buzzer in Elinor's room interrupted her. Lucie put her knitting down and went to see what Elinor needed.

Sandra could hear Lucie's soothing voice and the low sound of her mother as she tried painstakingly to form her words.

At least she was able to speak. On her worst days, Elinor couldn't even say hello.

Such a small, meaningless victory, but Sandra had learned early on to wring whatever joy she could out of each one as they came along.

She looked up as Lucie bustled back into the hallway.

"How is she?"

"*Comme ci, comme ça.* Better than before, I'll admit."

"Can I see her?"

"She's tired, lovey. I don't think she's up for a major mother-daughter gabfest."

"Five minutes," Sandra said, standing up and smoothing the back of her skirt. "I won't tire her out. I promise."

Lucie said nothing for a moment; then her expression softened. "Just remember one important thing: Elinor is as sharp now as she was before the disease struck. She can make her own decisions. She doesn't need a caretaker when it comes to matters of the heart and mind."

The words stung Sandra, and she lifted her chin. "I resent the implication, Lucie. I've never undermined Mother's autonomy, and you know it."

"And I never said you did. I just want you to be prepared for her decision." She put her arm around Sandra and squeezed. "It may not be the one you want."

How could it be?

She didn't even know what she wanted herself.

TEN MINUTES LATER, it was over.

Elinor had come down squarely on the side of maintaining her self-imposed isolation. The panic in her lovely eyes when Sandra had proposed telling Michael the truth had dissipated only when she promised her mother she wouldn't bring up the idea again.

"You must think me a fool," Elinor had said as Sandra bent down to say goodbye. Her lovely face reddened with the painful effort of forming her words. "The worst kind of vain fool."

"No," Sandra had said, touching her hand. "I understand. I honestly understand."

More than you know.

She said goodbye to Lucie, then hurried down the hallway, past the nurses' station, past the telephone booths and the coffee machines and the doctors lounging near the lobby.

It was Elinor's life. It was Elinor's decision.

And—God forgive her—Sandra was finally about to accept it.

She pushed her way back out into the cold night air that dried the tears on her cheeks before she even realized she was crying.

LUCIE HAD BEEN WATCHING HER over the top of her knitting for the past hour.

"Don't look at me like that," Elinor said over the theme music to *Moonlighting*. "Stop pursing your lips."

Lucie's silver needles caught the light as they flashed through the yarn. "You didn't even give her a chance to explain her side, did you?"

Elinor's brows drew together in a frown. "I know what's best." She paused for breath, to gather the strength necessary for speech. "I want her to be happy."

The knitting needles clicked together defiantly. "Best is being truthful, Elinor, not hiding you away."

"I heard you tonight, Lucie. You said it was my decision to make."

"It is. I'm just going on record as thinking it's a horrible decision."

"Duly noted."

Lucie looked at her knitting and made a face, then threw the mess of yarn to the floor.

"How can she make a life built on a lie?"

"Other people manage," Elinor said. "It's better this way." The yearning had been all over Sandra's face that evening. The same soft, lovestruck look Elinor remembered from years ago had returned, as if time had somehow reversed itself and Elinor had been given a second chance. "She loves him and he loves her. They belong together. *That* is all that matters."

"Someday she may hate you for pulling away from her like this."

She closed her eyes and feigned fatigue. For a long while she felt Lucie's gaze upon her, then finally the rhythm of the knitting picked up again and Lucie lost herself in her needlework and the relentless banter on the television screen.

Two months. That's all it would take. Sandra had said Michael had given her two months in which to be courted, and then he fully intended to marry her.

What Elinor had to do was pull away from her daughter for a while.

Clumsily scheduled therapy sessions when Sandra was planning to visit. A number of days when she was simply too ill, too tired, too debilitated to make conversation. Lucie would help her. She was certain she would.

Just sixty days, and Sandra and Michael would finally have the chance to build a life together, as they would have more than fifteen years ago if she hadn't been so arrogant as to think she could play God with her daughter's future.

What she was planning now wasn't playing God.

She was simply making amends, drawing upon the boundless love she felt for her daughter—and the affection she'd always had for Michael—and channeling it into a way to make their dreams come true at last.

Someday Sandra would understand.

And if she didn't—well, Elinor would be long gone, and it wouldn't matter a bit.

Knowing her daughter was finally happy would be enough.

She sighed and turned her face into the pillow.

It would have to be.

Chapter Eleven

The hawk rose up from the block of limestone in all its primitive glory. His eyes snapped with fire; his wings were flared, his body poised for flight.

All morning Michael had been working on the bird's right leg, trying to free it from the stone, and all morning he'd been finding it difficult to concentrate.

Sandra Patterson and the bizarre progress of their relationship were making it difficult to keep his mind on anything else.

Something had gone wrong between them, but he'd be damned if he could figure out what.

After all, Michael was a man of his word.

He'd promised her a courtship and, by God, that was exactly what he'd been giving her.

For three weeks now he'd been plying Sandra with champagne and candy and elaborate floral arrangements—complete with helium balloons—sent to her office.

Twice they'd gone out to Montauk for dinner and dancing at Gurney's, a terrific watering hole of the rich and famous that prided itself on the Atlantic Ocean that crashed and roared right outside the dining room window.

Romantic?

Definitely.

Effective?

He wasn't so sure.

He had been determined to play this game according to her rules, but so far it seemed as if maybe he hadn't quite understood them. Instead of this courtship drawing her closer, it seemed as if she were pulling away.

Only when they were together with David in a more familial setting did she seem to relax.

Strange that the one thing he'd expected to be a problem had turned out to be the greatest source of joy.

Never in a million years had he expected the sophisticated, career-oriented Sandra Patterson he'd met that night at the White Castle to become enamored of a five-year-old boy for whom "soap" was the ultimate four letter word.

There was a tenderness in Sandra he hadn't expected, a deeply nurturing side to her personality that she'd managed to hide from him until now. David had been wary at first, bringing up Annie's name at least once every half-hour, but Sandra had hung in there, managing to turn a sticky situation into something wonderful.

He changed his position a fraction of an inch and kept working on the hawk's right talon, ignoring Leon's curious look as he struggled to regain his concentration.

It wasn't easy when your whole life seemed to be wrapped up in one woman.

Just five more weeks, he thought as he chipped away a millimeter of limestone. Just five more weeks until she was his forever—

"The angle is all wrong."

He looked up. Annie Gage, wearing a bright red sweater and faded jeans, was leaning against his workbench.

"What are you talking about?" He put the chisel on the table and brushed some dust from his eyelashes. "The angle is perfect."

She pointed to the bottom curve of the bird's leg. "Here," she said, drawing her index finger across the spot he'd been working. "Make it flow this way. See?"

He saw, all right. She was right on the mark.

"Since when did you get so good at stonecutting?" he asked, grimacing. "I thought paints and papers were more your thing."

"Someone around here has to keep you in line, McKay. Love's doing terrible things to your perspective."

He laughed. "And how am I supposed to take that statement, Gage?"

Her look was one of wide-eyed innocence. "Any way you want to," she said. "All I'm doing is making a simple observation..."

Leon and the others had been eavesdropping openly since Annie had come into the room. Enough of his life was already public domain, so Michael led her outside into the yard.

"Your attorney called," she said as soon as they were out of earshot. "He wants you to call him back ASAP."

His neighbor Jim Flannery had stepped in to handle the increasing custody threats from the Bentleys.

"How did he sound?"

Annie thought for a second. "Serious."

"Did he talk to Art and Margaret?"

"He didn't say."

"Can I use—"

She laughed, and linked her arm with his. "Of course you can use my phone. Come on."

Ten minutes later he hung up the phone and stared blankly at the silk screen on the wall across from him.

"Go to Florida," Jim had said. "Talk to them face-to-face. Give it one last shot before we start flexing our muscles."

The last thing he wanted to do was talk with the Bentleys face-to-face.

The last thing he wanted to do was go to Florida.

Hell. The last thing he wanted was to be away from Sandra right now, when it looked as if the future he'd always dreamed of was finally within reach.

"Bad news?" Annie stood in the doorway.

He nodded. "Flannery wants me to go to Florida to have it out with Art and Margaret."

"When?"

"Day after tomorrow."

"I thought the day after tomorrow was Davey's school pageant."

"You're right." He dragged his hand through his hair. "What the hell am I going to do?"

"Perspective," Annie said gently. "You're going to go to Florida. I don't see as if you have much choice in this, McKay."

"It might take a couple days."

"Then so be it. It's a small price to pay to keep your kid, isn't it?"

He looked over at Annie and smiled. "And who said women aren't logical?"

"Not me," she answered. "Will Davey go with you?"

He shook his head. "Bad move. I want to keep him out of this, physically and emotionally, for as long as I can."

Annie's mouth opened, then she caught herself.

"What?" he asked.

"Forget it."

"You were going to say something, Gage. Out with it."

She met his eyes. "I was going to say I'll take care of Davey while you're away, but given the circumstances..." She let her words trail off. "It just doesn't seem like the provident thing to do."

"Provident? Since when do you use words like 'provident'?"

Her saucy grin reappeared. "That's what happens when you work in a cathedral basement. Just forget I said anything."

"They get along beautifully," he said, referring to his lover and his son. "I didn't expect it, but—"

"Please," Annie said. "I get the drift. Even Davey has jumped ship."

"Annie, I—"

"I'm teasing," she said. "Don't take me seriously."

"I've always taken you seriously, Gage. You know that."

"How about the two of you?" she asked. "Are you as serious about each other as I think you are?"

"Yes." He felt the tug of something close to regret at the flash of sorrow on Annie's face.

"Then go to her," Annie said. "If the two of them are going to be a family, now's as good a time as any for them to get started."

He bent down and gave Annie a swift hug, and as he did he saw the glitter of tears in her golden eyes.

"Thanks for the good advice, Gage," he said, his voice soft. "I can always count on you when the chips are down."

Annie blinked rapidly, refusing to acknowledge the tears trailing down her cheeks. "Damn it," she whispered fiercely. "I wish I hated her."

He looked at the woman who'd been his friend for so long, and he couldn't think of a thing to say that made any difference.

McKAY THE YOUNGER was spending the night with his pal Sean Flannery, while the elder McKay spent the night with his pal Sandra.

When Michael had told her they'd be able to spend a whole night together, she'd surprised herself by suggesting he come to her house for a home-cooked dinner.

To be honest, she was getting a little weary of the moonlight-and-roses aspect of being courted, and the opportunity to be alone together without hovering waiters and smarmy maître d's was too wonderful to pass up.

Being courted had turned out to be more wearing than she would have imagined, and it was beginning to take its toll on her work. A steady diet of candlelit dinners and dancing and trips to the theater could be exhausting. Ed had made more than one pointed comment about her obvious fatigue, and she'd had to hold herself back from snapping, "None of your business!" when he'd asked why.

He'd been doing his share of hinting around about a new opportunity coming his way, but Sandra had been too preoccupied to pay much attention. Her work for Citi-National had finally slid into second place in her life where it belonged.

Oh, she was still hardworking Sandra Patterson, but the fever was gone. She no longer felt the burning need to prove herself over and over and over again.

There were other things in life that deserved her attention.

Elinor's condition had taken a sudden, mysterious turn for the worse, and Sandra had driven up to Fair Oaks a number of times only to be turned away. Lucie had been urging her to call first before making the 150-mile round trip, and Sandra had finally given in.

Not being able to share her happiness with her mother was one of the few dark spots on an otherwise happy, if hectic, horizon.

"This feels wonderful," she murmured, as she stretched out on her sofa after a late dinner. "A night without an orchestra."

"All danced out, are you?" Michael was busy stacking wood for a fire.

"I may never tango again," she said, kicking off her shoes and putting her feet up on the arm of the couch.

"We could cut this courtship short and get down to business, Sandy."

"Five more weeks," she said, closing her eyes. "I'm entitled to thirty-five more days of moonlight and roses."

He chuckled, and she heard him throw another log on the pile. The truth was, she didn't want more moonlight or more roses or another fancy dinner. The fact that they were ready to take the next step was painfully obvious in everything they said and did.

Their connection was deep and strong. It spanned years and continents and other alliances. Marriage was only a way of confirming what already existed, what would always exist.

However, the fact that marriage should be based upon truth lodged in her throat like a stone each time the words "Let's marry now" tried to escape her lips. Michael had been painfully honest about his son, about his marriage and his in-laws and the years that had gone before.

She had told him about her need for a career. She had told him about her broken engagement, about the powerful ambition that made her always want to be the best in her field. She had told Michael that these weeks with him and his son were the happiest she had ever known.

But she hadn't told him about her mother.

She hadn't told him about the heavy burden of emotional and financial responsibility that colored every move she made, every decision that came her way. The promise made to Elinor was a promise made in blood.

Elinor had sacrificed so that Sandra could be where she was. Honoring Elinor's wishes was the least her daughter could do.

Despite the sixty-day courtship and the silly jokes about wine and candles and music and her wanting an old-fashioned engagement, Sandra knew she couldn't take her wedding vows until she told him the truth.

And yet how could she change her mother's mind when her mother was too ill even to see her?

Until she could, she was powerless to follow her heart.

"Are you okay?"

Her eyes flickered open. Michael was kneeling next to her, his eyes darker than the night. She wanted to hand herself over to him, body and soul, and be absorbed into his power and healed by his strength.

"Just tired," she said, making room for him on the sofa. "I usually settle for a frozen pizza and a glass of wine."

"The lasagna was great," he said, fitting his body against hers in a way that made her forget about her fatigue.

"You sound surprised."

"I am. I didn't know you could cook."

"I'm a woman of many accomplishments."

He bent his dark head and kissed the throbbing pulse at the base of her throat. "So I've discovered."

"There isn't enough room on the couch for that," she whispered as he slid his hands up under her silky robe.

"Sure there is." His fingers splayed out over her bare hips and grasped her firmly.

"You'll fall off."

"The hell I will. Watch."

He lifted her up as easily as if she were a doll, then positioned her atop the length of his body. He was all coiled muscle, tense and ready to strike.

"You're quite a man," she said, kissing the contours of his jaw. "It must come from carrying all that limestone around the workshop."

His hands slid over the backs of her thighs and found what they were seeking. Her entire body trembled with longing as his fingers moved within her, coaxing, demanding, urging her on.

"Do you still hate men who work with their hands?" His voice was rough with desire; his breath burned against the curve of her ear.

"I was a fool," she managed as her mind soared higher. "A total fool..."

His laughter was the last thing she remembered for a long while.

TWO HOURS LATER they were curled together in the middle of Sandra's bed. She'd been right: the couch hadn't been large enough to contain the love they needed to express.

Her heart certainly wasn't large enough. The emotions he brought out in her were so violently tender, so overwhelming that each time she saw him, each time he touched her, each time they came together, she wondered how it was she didn't die from pleasure.

"This is wonderful," she mumbled against his chest. "And to think I once thought pajama parties were the ultimate."

His laughter rumbled beneath her ear. "Marry me and we can do this every night."

"Unfair bargaining practice," she said, looking up at him. "Bribery is against the law."

He touched her intimately, then brought his hand to her lips. "Nothing between us is wrong," he said. "Nothing."

She moaned low in her throat, an almost animal sound of pleasure that shocked her with its intensity.

"You make me feel things I never imagined," she said. "Things I never knew were possible to feel."

"Then take a chance, Sandy." He moved away from her, and she felt desolate without his touch. His power over her was incalculable. "Track your mother down and let's set a date. Let's start living."

The mention of Elinor worked on her like a splash of ice water. Lust moved aside and reason took its place.

"Remember your son," she said. "I think he could use more than three weeks to get accustomed to me."

There was a long silence. She raised herself up on one elbow. "Michael?"

"This is a hell of a time, but I have a proposition for you."

She laughed. "I think we've run the gamut, Michael, but if you have any suggestions..."

"It's about David."

"David?" She was at a loss to figure out what he could possibly be talking about.

"I spoke to Art Bentley today at my lawyer's request."

She listened carefully as he explained the Bentleys' escalating demands and Jim Flannery's advice to take one last shot at a civilized solution.

"...so I'm leaving for Florida the day after tomorrow to take a stab at it."

"You don't sound very positive."

His laugh was grim. "Oh, I'm positive, all right. I'm positive we'll end up at each other's throats."

"So don't go."

"I have to." He paused. "For my son's sake."

Ah, yes. Responsibility.

She swallowed hard. "And where do I fit into this scenario?"

"How would you feel about keeping David while I'm gone?"

She sat up straight. "What?"

"How would you feel about keeping David for the two days I'm away? Jim said he and his wife would be happy to take him, but it occurred to me that if we're going to become a real family one day, maybe you two should—"

She put her finger to his lips to silence him. "Shh. It's not that I'm against the idea, Michael. It's just that I didn't expect it."

"Don't feel pressured, Sandy. I know this is short notice."

The idea of getting to know his son had a definite appeal. "I still have to work. I mean, I can't take a day off or anything."

"You wouldn't have to. He'll go to school same as always. In fact, he has a pageant on Wednesday evening. I was going to go, but—"

"Could I go in your place?" What was she saying? She knew about as much about school pageants as she knew about nuclear physics. Had she gone mad? "Would that embarrass David?"

The sheer joy in Michael's voice brought tears to her eyes. "Hell, no! It would probably make his day." The other kids in David's kindergarten class had begun to ask questions about his missing parent, and David was finding it hard to answer them. Each question probed deeper into feelings of loss and abandonment that were more than a child his age could handle.

That was something Sandra understood well.

"Okay," she said, at last. "You've got yourself a baby-sitter."

Ah, Mother, she thought. *What am I going to do?*

The chains binding her to Michael McKay were growing stronger, and she wondered how she would ever break free.

"I DON'T BELIEVE THIS!" Ed Gregory stepped around a tricycle in her foyer and nearly tripped over a small sneaker in the living room.

"Believe it," Sandra said, slipping a cracker into Pepper's seed cup and praying he'd keep his beak shut.

"Don't we pay you enough?" he asked. "Did you have to open a sleep-away camp for Munchkins?"

"Keep your voice down," she said, pushing a Hulk Hogan coloring book off her elegant sofa. "I don't want Davey to wake up."

"Davey?" Ed lowered himself down on a Queen Anne chair, then reached behind him to retrieve a chestnut-brown Crayola from the seat cushion. "What's going on—anything I should know about?"

"I'm taking care of a friend's child. His name is David. He's five years old, and it took me two hours to get him to go to sleep. If you wake him up, Gregory, so help me, I'll kill you."

The school pageant had been a lot of fun and afterward they'd gone off to Chi-Chi's for Mexican food, which David seemed to love. He'd slept in her car on the way home, but the second they'd gotten inside, he'd been wide awake.

David had had to have a room-by-room inspection of Sandra's house, complete with a closet check, before he went to sleep. He seemed to have a vivid imagination that ran the gamut from the usual bogeymen under the bed to a water monster that managed to creep throughout the plumbing until it popped out of the hot-water faucet in the bathroom sink. How the water monster had managed to get from Michael's house to hers was something she hadn't pursued.

Just getting him off to sleep was enough of an accomplishment.

Fortunately, however, Ed Gregory hadn't come by to check up on her private life. He had other things on his mind.

"I want to talk to you," he said as she brought him a cup of coffee.

"There's such a thing as a telephone."

"I tried," he said. "No answer. And since you refuse to get yourself a machine—"

She pointed to the end table near the door. "I got one," she said. "I just set it up an hour ago."

"Finally," Ed said. "Welcome to the age of enlightenment."

She ignored the gibe and sat down opposite him. "Whatever this is, it couldn't wait until morning?"

"No way. We needed some privacy. McGrath and Richter seem to have a grapevine that won't quit."

She took a sip of coffee in a crazy attempt to calm herself down.

"We could've had lunch tomorrow afternoon."

He laughed. "You're never around these days, Patterson. I've tried to book a dinner with you three times in the past week, and you're always busy." He drained the cup of coffee, then put it down on the table in front of him. "I figured I'd catch you in your own den while your guard is down."

Her hand began to shake and she gripped her coffee cup more tightly. He had come over either to proposition her or fire her, and at the moment, she wasn't certain which idea bothered her more.

He leaned forward, his eyes intense. "Have you un-packed yet?"

A nervous laugh rippled through her. "No. I keep prom-ising myself to do it on the weekend, but things just haven't worked out that way so far."

"Don't."

"Don't?"

"Don't. You may be on your way out."

The room seemed to swirl in front of her, as if she'd had too much wine.

"If there's a problem, Ed, I wish you'd told me about it sooner. Perhaps we could have—"

"The only problem I have is getting a word in edgeways. Quit hyperventilating for a moment and listen. I've lined up a dynamite job for myself in Geneva and I want you to go along as a full vice-president."

Geneva.

Geneva, Switzerland.

The job she'd always wanted, in the perfect location.

Why, then, did she feel as if she were being sent to the electric chair?

"Did you hear me, Patterson? The big enchilada! Swit-zerland. Banker's paradise."

He looked as excited as a kid out of school, and she had to laugh. "I hear you, Ed. I think it's great."

"You *think* it's great? Let me tell you, Patterson, it's the greatest thing that's ever happened to me. A 20K-per-year raise. Perks up the ying-yang. I get to pick my own staff. From now on, the sky's the limit, and I intend to take you with me."

"Is your transfer final yet?"

He waved a hand impatiently in the air. "Almost. Bur-gess still has to sign the papers, but it's as good as done."

"You haven't put through any papers for me yet, have you?"

His sandy brows drew together in a frown. "Not yet, but that's only because I have to get on the Swiss payroll before I can do anything." His expression lightened. "Is that what's bothering you? I'm not going to pull a fast one on you, Patterson. I promised to take you to the top, and I'm going to keep that promise." He grinned. "And you can bank on that."

Her first instinct had been to blurt out everything about Michael and her mother and the growing sense of destiny surrounding her return to Long Island, but some other instinct, honed by time, had blessedly triumphed and kept her silent.

Ed Gregory was prone to these fits of "I'm-on-the-stairway-to-the-stars" hysteria, and his grandiose schemes were subject to quite a few false starts. She had no doubt he'd end up with that cushy position in Geneva someday; but she doubted it would be now.

There was absolutely no point in jeopardizing her current position by refusing his offer at this stage of the game.

Instead she fed him a few questions, and he filled her in on a Byzantine series of negotiations that left her speechless.

"You're a devious man," she said over their second cup of coffee. "I'm glad we're on the same side."

"So am I." He looked tremendously pleased with himself. "You can kiss this little backwater goodbye, Patterson. We're going to play with the big guys."

Something must have shown on her face, because he leaned forward and looked deep into her eyes.

"We are, aren't we, Sandra?"

"This is your scenario," she said warily. "You tell me."

"I've spent a lot of years preparing you for this. Don't let me down now."

She got up to make another pot of coffee. "You act as if you've got your plane tickets for Geneva in your back pocket."

"And you act like you're not going to go."

"All I'm saying is to take things one step at a time, Ed. Get the promotion first, then we'll talk."

"It's that guy, isn't it?"

"I beg your pardon?"

He waved toward the bedrooms upstairs. "That jock from your past. That's what this is all about, isn't it?"

"That's none of your business, Ed."

"The hell it's not. I've brought you along since you were fresh out of grad school, Patterson. You don't go deserting me now just because you've got the hots for some guy who pushes all your buttons."

"I won't dignify that with an answer." What she wanted to dignify it with was a good right hook, but she knew that would be professional suicide.

"If I go, you go, Patterson. I've invested too much time and money in you to let you bury yourself here on Long Island."

She laughed and poured herself a fresh cup of coffee. The caffeine wasn't doing good things to her nerves, but she needed something to keep her hands busy.

"Five months ago you were telling me Long Island was the Citi-National equivalent of Shangri-la."

He dismissed her words with a wave of his hand. "That was five months ago. I would've told you anything to get you on my team."

"Wonderful," she said, sitting back down opposite him. "Now I find out I was conned into taking the job."

He laughed. "You weren't conned, Patterson. You know you wanted the promotion as much as I wanted you to have it."

He spoke the truth. Five months ago her entire life had revolved around promotions and upward mobility. How quickly her focus had changed. Suddenly there seemed to be so much more to life than Citi-National was capable of offering her.

"Well, now I have the promotion." She took a deep breath and willed herself to stay cool. "At the moment I'm very happy here."

"You'll be happier in Geneva. Trust me."

"We'll talk about that when it happens."

"It's going to happen, Patterson. Don't think that it won't."

"Fine," she said. "We'll deal with it then."

His face hardened, and he put his cup down on the coffee table with a bang. It was a wonder the fragile china didn't shatter into a million pieces.

"I don't think you understand, Patterson. If I go, I take your future with me."

She stiffened. "And what exactly does that mean?"

"You want it straight?"

She nodded.

"I'm the key to your success. Without me behind you, you won't amount to anything here."

A fine anger rose inside her, and she stood up. "Would you repeat that, Ed? I want to make certain I understand you."

He stood up and faced her, his hands jammed into the pockets of his grey flannel pants.

"If I leave here, you can kiss your chances for advancement goodbye."

"I resent that."

"Doesn't matter, Patterson. It's the truth any way you slice it. Understand?"

"What I understand is that I have value of my own, Ed. I don't need you to act as a human safety net."

He listed the various positions that he'd intended to promote her to, one by one, on her way to the top. They didn't sound as appealing as they once had, but she felt a stab of anger and fear that what she'd assumed to be a result of hard work and talent was turning into the product of patronage.

"Can you do that without me, Patterson? Can you climb the ladder here without someone to give you a push?"

She was about to answer him when she heard a sound from upstairs.

Ed raised an eyebrow. "What's that?"

"Shh." She tilted her head to listen.

David's voice, thin and shrill, floated down the stairs. "Daddy! Daddy!"

Her body galvanized into action and she turned for the stairs.

Ed grabbed her arm. "Patterson! We're not finished yet."

"David needs me."

"He can wait a minute."

She jerked her arm away. "The hell he can."

"Give me an answer."

"Not now," she said. Her heart was pounding so wildly that she was surprised she didn't collapse on the floor. Was this what professional suicide felt like? "I have to go to him."

Ed stared at her as if she'd lost her marbles. "I may not be here when you come back downstairs."

"That's your choice," she said. "Right now I have a little boy to tend to."

"Sandra, I—"

She turned and raced up the stairs before he could say another word.

Before she could change her mind.

Chapter Twelve

David was sitting up in bed when she reached the guest room. Michael had brought over a cot from his place, and they'd fitted it out with David's Spiderman sheets and pillowcase so that he'd feel at home.

From the look of terror on the little boy's face, however, they hadn't done quite enough.

His dark eyes were huge as he watched her come into the room. He looked past her to the doorway, and when he didn't see his father bringing up the rear, he burst into loud, heartbreaking tears.

"I want my daddy! Where's Daddy?"

She sat down on the edge of the bed. Harvard Business School hadn't touched on anything like this and she felt woefully inadequate.

"Don't you remember, David? Your daddy had to go to Florida to see your grandpa."

David rubbed at his eyes and looked at her suspiciously. He wasn't sobbing. She took that to be a good sign.

"You and Pepper came to spend the night with me at my house. I took you to the school pageant."

"Oh." His sniffles eased up. "Pepper bit you when you tried to take him out of his cage."

She made a face and rubbed her index finger. Damned parrot. "Pepper's a monster," she said. "And all I was trying to do was give him a slice of pizza."

"He doesn't know you yet," David said sagely. "When I tell him you're nice, he'll be good."

She leaned back against the wall and cuddled the little boy in her arms.

"Pepper's a flying monster," she said, making him giggle. "I think he wants to put me in the cage."

The child's giggle turned into a laugh. "You're too big to put in the cage."

"Too big!" She feigned outrage. "I could so fit in the birdcage."

"Could not!"

"Could."

David launched into a detailed description of the limbs that would be left dangling outside the monster's cage, and she was about to defend her honor as an adult when she heard the sound of her front door slamming shut.

"What was that?" David asked, suddenly wide-eyed and very much a little boy.

"My boss was just leaving," she said.

"He slammed the door. Daddy yells at me when I do that."

"Well, I yelled at Ed," she said. "I guess he's getting even."

David yawned and burrowed more deeply beneath the covers. She arranged the blanket and rested her hand on his shoulder. My God! He was so small, so fragile, so vulnerable.

He yawned again, and she saw the spaces where his second teeth would soon pop up.

"You ready to go back to sleep, honey?"

"Mmm." He opened one eye. "Will you stay with me?"

She nodded. "I'll stay with you, David."

"Promise?"

She crossed her heart. "Promise."

He smiled, and in moments his breathing was soft and even and the room was filled with the sweet smell of a sleeping child.

"Sorry, Ed," she whispered.

Geneva didn't even come close.

As USUAL, flights into JFK were delayed, and Michael shifted in the narrow seat and looked out at an unappetizing view of New York as seen from fifteen thousand feet. The pilot was performing one of those lazy, time-wasting circles that kept the jet at a constant angle and usually turned Michael's stomach inside-out.

Today, however, he was too preoccupied to notice.

Art Bentley's threat had lingered with him all the way up from Florida, his last words repeating themselves over and over again like some insane litany.

"You can live in the dirt, boy, but I won't let my grandson live there with you. If you don't have the decency to shield my daughter's child from your sex life, then Margaret and I will."

He drained the rest of the Scotch in front of him and barely managed to keep from asking the flight attendant for another.

That bastard ex-father-in-law of his had had him tailed by a private eye who'd compiled a dossier on his habits—with special attention paid to his sexual proclivities. His one and only slip from grace, and now this...

"Damn it!" He ignored the look of concern from the man next to him and stared out the window. He'd lived like a monk for the last year, devoting his time and energy and love to the son who needed him.

When he'd turned to Sandra it had been out of love, not lust. And now that bastard Bentley was going to twist the facts into something ugly and sordid.

Something a judge just might take seriously.

The plane banked sharply and began the final descent into Kennedy Airport. In a little while he'd be back at work. In a few hours Sandra and David would be at the Cathedral for the Blessing of the Animals in honor of the Feast of St. Francis.

Waiting any longer was ridiculous.

The only thing waiting could do was add fuel to Art Bentley's fire. It couldn't make what he and Sandra had together any stronger than it already was.

This sixty-day courtship had already progressed far beyond the boundaries of moonlight and romance. In their hearts, he and Sandra had been married since the first day they met.

He wanted to tie all the ties there were to bind. He wanted their vows signed, sealed and delivered. He wanted there to be no doubt in anyone's mind that what he felt for her—what he'd always felt for her—was the real thing.

His son deserved nothing less.

And, damn it, so did he.

This time he wouldn't take no for an answer.

IT WASN'T AN ARGUMENT, exactly.

But whatever it was, it followed Sandra and Michael and David all the way from the Cathedral of St. Matthew the Divine to the McKay house on Harvest Drive.

The low-grade bickering stopped while he got his son ready for bed, but by the time she found where he hid his coffee maker and had a pot brewed for them, it was in full swing again.

"What are we waiting for, Sandy?" he said, straddling a kitchen chair. "What the hell is the point?"

She fumbled around for a reason to delay something they both wanted more than anything. "We've only been back together a few weeks, Michael. Let's enjoy what we've got before we take the next step."

"You're admitting there'll be a next step?"

"Damn it!" She threw her teaspoon into the sink, and it landed with a satisfying metallic clang. "You've been hanging around too many lawyers, Michael. I feel like I'm on the witness stand." She leaned against the refrigerator. "What on earth happened in Florida? You're wound up tighter than a mainspring."

"Nothing happened in Florida," he said, looking away. "Bentley started throwing his weight around again, and I suddenly got damned tired of being his whipping boy. It's an old story, and I'm sick of it."

"Well, don't take it out on me," she snapped, suddenly fighting back tears. "I'm not your enemy, Michael." She crossed her arms in front of her chest and tried to regulate her breathing. "A new location, a new job and a new family are a bit much to handle all at once. I need a little time."

His expression softened visibly. "I know I'm pushing you, Sandy, but you got away from me once. You can't blame me for running scared."

"Don't run," she whispered, moving toward him. "I'm yours. I always have been."

"Then marry me now," he said, pulling her into his arms. "Let's tell the world to go to hell."

She said nothing, and he took her silence as encouragement.

"You don't have to let Citi-National push you around. I earn a damned good living, Sandy. I can take care of us."

During dinner she'd told him about her argument with Ed Gregory and the uneasy truce they'd been working under. Now she regretted it.

She stiffened in his arms. "I can take care of myself," she said, thinking of her mother's medical bills and what they would do to his dreams. "I'm a worker. I can't change that."

"I'm not asking you to stop working," he said. "I'm just saying you don't have to be bound to Citi-National if you don't want to be. You can tell Gregory to go to hell and find another job."

Oh, God, she thought. *You just don't understand.*

But then, how could he? Her promise to her mother was forcing her to keep the man she loved in the dark.

Quitting Citi-National was an impossible dream. She needed the security of her job in order to do the things that mattered. The idea of pounding the pavement in search of new employment made her physically ill. Unfortunately, sophisticated medical technology didn't come cheap. Her savings would be eaten up in a matter of weeks, and Elinor would lose whatever freedom she now enjoyed.

"My job's important to me," she said finally. "I shouldn't have to explain that to you, any more than you should have to explain your responsibilities to me."

"Are you talking about David?"

"Yes. No—damn it! I don't know what I mean." She pulled away from him and tried to recover her equilibrium. "All I know is you're pushing me, Michael, and I don't understand why."

"I love you," he said. "I can't see why we should wait any longer."

"Do it for me," she said, meeting his eyes. "If you love me, give me a little more time."

He didn't say a thing. He simply nodded and turned away and Sandra wondered if he'd ever know how much her words had cost her.

THE FEELING OF DESPERATION Sandra felt when Michael turned away from her didn't leave, and two days later, Sandra found herself doing the unthinkable.

She called in sick, then drove up to Fair Oaks in an attempt to speak with her mother.

She and Michael had been polite and friendly and civilized, but the wonderful joyous spark between them had dimmed. He wanted a commitment and he wanted it now and that commitment was the one thing she couldn't give him.

Not until she made Elinor see things her way.

"Sandra!" Lucie looked up from her knitting as Sandra bent to kiss her cheek. "I thought you said you'd call this afternoon."

"I had a few free hours," she lied, trying not to think about the bad time Ed was bound to give her. "I decided to say hello to Mom. It's been weeks since I've seen her."

She was about to head for her mother's door when Lucie cried out, "Wait!"

Sandra turned around as Lucie leaped to her feet. Her knitting slid to the floor unnoticed.

"Is something wrong?" Sandra asked.

"Elinor's not in there."

"That's okay. I'll catch up with her in the PT room."

Lucie plucked the half-finished sweater from the floor and brushed it off with the heel of her hand. "She's not in there, either, lovey. She's—umm, she's with Dr. Gardstein."

Sandra felt a distinct chilling of her blood. "Has there been another setback?" Lately it seemed as if Elinor's life was one setback after another.

Lucie reddened, and Sandra feared the worst.

"Tell me, Lucie. I'm her daughter. I have the right to know."

Lucie looked absolutely miserable. "It's just tests. He's just running a battery of tests. She'll be busy with him all day."

"She was well enough for tests? That's a good sign."

Lucie fiddled with her knitting needles, trying to make the stitches lie flat. "Everything she's doing is necessary," she said. "She was sure you'd understand."

"Understand?" Sandra was puzzled. "Is she worried about the money?"

Lucie, looking relieved now that Sandra realized the problem, nodded. "She's worried about your working so hard."

"None of that's important," Sandra said. "You tell her that. There's more than enough money to make sure she gets the help she needs."

Lucie gave her a bone-crushing hug. "You're a good daughter, lovey. She's a lucky woman."

Sandra laughed and straightened the hem of her jacket. "You're certainly in a strange mood today, Lucie. Are you sure things aren't any worse?"

It had been the longest uninterrupted relapse Elinor had experienced since the onset of the disease, and the anxiety was beginning to wear on Sandra. And on Lucie, too, if her nervous attitude were any indication.

"Things are no worse."

"Honestly?"

"Honestly."

"You'll call me when Mother is up to visitors?"

Lucie crossed her heart with a #13 knitting needle. "Scout's honor."

Sandra toyed with the idea of hanging around the hospital for a while on the off-chance Elinor would return from the tests early and be well enough at least to listen to her side of things, but decided that the time would be better spent trying to defuse Ed's firecracker temper.

Better to get on the road before the lunch crowd and get a few things done around the office. That steady paycheck seemed more important than ever before.

She was about to push her way through the double doors leading to the main lobby when a familiar voice behind her called out her name.

Larry, in a red silk robe with a white handkerchief jutting jauntily from the breast pocket, whizzed up to her in his motorized wheelchair. His white hair was slicked back, and the unmistakable scent of English Leather hovered over him.

"Well, well," she said, bending down to kiss his cheek. "Look at you! Do I have competition I should know about?"

"You don't," he said with a grin, "but from what I hear, I sure do."

"And what have you been hearing?"

His grin widened. "Oh, a few things here and there about some big strapping Irish boy."

Sandra laughed. "I'm going to have to slap a restraining order on Lucie," she said. "That woman talks entirely too much."

He looked puzzled. "Lucie isn't the only one who talks," he said. "Your mom had a few things to say, as well."

The emotional roller coaster she'd been on since her mother's illness was diagnosed revved up again, and all it took was an innocent reference to Elinor. It had been weeks since Elinor had felt well enough to say much about anything.

"I miss your phone calls. The Fair Oaks gossip line doesn't seem very active these days."

"Nothing much to say lately. Things are just going along as always."

Why had she put him on the spot like that? Did she expect him to call her every single day just to chronicle her mother's steady decline? No one would be that cruel.

"Don't be such a stranger, missy."

"Well, you know the situation . . ."

His eyes twinkled. "I certainly do!"

Leave it to Larry to turn a potentially maudlin conversation into something cheerful.

"I'll be up again next week," she said. And the week after that and the week after that—however long it took to make Elinor see the light. "Call me, please, if anything happens before then."

"Nothing's going to happen, missy. Things are just fine."

"You don't have to shield me, Larry."

He looked puzzled. "I'm not shielding you from anything. Everything *is* fine."

Idiot, she thought as she said goodbye. *Don't push him.* Larry wasn't there as a paid observer, after all. He was a patient, just like her mother and a hundred other patients, many of whom would never leave Fair Oaks again. His point of view was bound to be obscured by his own hopes and dreams.

Trust Lucie, she thought. Lucie loved her and Elinor. Where Dr. Gardstein would sometimes slough her off with a "What can you expect with ALS?" Lucie would take the time to explain the ramifications of each step along the way.

When the time was right to talk with Elinor, Lucie would let her know.

Until then, all Sandra could do was wait—and hope Michael could do the same.

MICHAEL COULDN'T GET IT RIGHT.

He bent down and approached the hawk's wing from another angle.

Dead. Lifeless. The worst piece he'd attempted in all his years as a stonecutter.

He positioned his hammer and chisel and tried to capture the layer upon layer of feathers covering the raptor's mighty wings. He tapped once against the chisel, then tapped again, harder this time. A huge chunk of limestone flew out and shot across the workroom, catching Leon in the back of the neck.

"Hey, man!" Leon called out. "If you want something, ask for it."

"An accident," Michael hollered over the noise of the Temptations and the Four Tops. "I'm sorry, Leon."

"It's gettin' so you need a helmet around this place," Leon muttered as he went back to work on the finial for the north tower.

All eyes in the workroom were focused on Michael. It was bad enough knowing that Art Bentley's flunkies were detailing his every move; lately it seemed as if even his apprentices were watching him, the way people used to gather around St. Helen's when the eruption was imminent.

He zeroed in on the hawk again, determined to get it right this time. Limestone chalk flew as hammer met chisel.

Don't think about Sandra. Don't think about David. Don't think about all of the things you can't control.

Keep the focus where it was. Block out everything but the work. This work was the one thing that would go on long after he and everyone he loved had passed into dust. The mark he was making would be seen hundreds of years from now. It would last. It would matter.

Leon and Angel were fighting over the snarling face of a dragon.

"It needs fire. No dragon I ever seen had no fire."

It needs nothin', man. It's fine the way it is."

"I ain't puttin' my boast on that."

"Who the hell asked you to, man? Why don't you—"

Ignore them. He was their teacher, not their baby-sitter. Let them work out their own problems.

Concentrate on what was important.

The cathedral. It would—

The table moved. His chisel gouged the face of the hawk, and six weeks' work was ruined.

"Son of a bitch!" He whirled on Angel and Leon, whose argument had erupted into a minor shoving match. "What the hell is the matter with you? Can't you keep your problems in line?"

The young men stared at him in shock. Michael was known for his temper, but this was beyond anything they'd seen before.

"We didn't mean it, Mike," Leon offered, making sure he was out of target range. "It got out of hand."

"Yeah," said Angel, his dark eyes wide. "We didn't mean nothin' by it."

You're scaring the hell out of them, you fool. One shoving match in two years and you're bringing the wrath of God down on their heads.

The hawk had already been severely damaged by the chunk he'd snapped off it minutes before. He was looking for a way to vent the towering frustration he felt about Sandra and the Bentleys, and he'd picked the easiest target.

"Just be careful," he said, backing down somewhat. "This isn't a gym, you know."

They continued to stare at him.

"Am I paying you to watch me or am I paying you to produce? A hundred years' work isn't enough for you guys? You wanna make it two hundred?"

They scrambled back to their workbenches. He felt violent, powerless, trapped in a way he hadn't been since he was a teenager looking for a way out.

If he went to Sandra like this, she'd run back to Sioux Falls before he had a chance to explain.

"Don't look," he called out to the apprentices in the workroom. "Don't turn around." He picked up the stone hawk and held it up. "Don't anyone say one damned word."

The crash echoed in the silent room. Pieces of stone scattered across the tiled floor and bounced off the walls. Dust from the limestone covered his shoes and pants. He glared at the astonished faces that had, of course, turned to see what happened.

"And don't clean anything up." They weren't getting paid to learn how to sweep.

He stormed out of the workshed.

"YOU NEED A LONG REST, friend," Annie Gage said as she poured him a shot of ecclesiastical brandy in her studio a few minutes later. "A *very* long rest. I mean, six weeks work down the drain..."

He gulped down the brandy and waited for the fire. "I wrecked it before I wrecked it," he said. "Besides, it was either that or kill someone."

Annie shivered and made a point of sitting down as far away from him as possible. "Fair warning," she said. "Love turns people into monsters. No wonder Leon uses you as his gargoyle model."

He snorted in disgust. "I'm at the end of my rope, Gage."

"So I've noticed."

He leaned back in the rickety wooden chair and closed his eyes. "Bentley's closing in on me. The way things are going, if I keep seeing Sandra, I lose my son. Bentley's determined to make me look like a sexual deviate who entertains women in front of a five-year-old."

Annie's soft laugh made him open his eyes. "How have I missed out on the fun?"

"Don't," he warned. "Not now, Annie."

She shrugged, and her black sweater slipped down over her shoulder. She yanked it back into place. "I may not be the right one to ask for advice," she said, her voice low. "After all, I have a vested interest in the outcome."

"Help me, Annie." He righted the chair and reached for the bottle of brandy. "As a friend. I don't know what the hell to do."

"I'd like to tell you to give up the woman for the child."

He felt her words like a blow to the heart. "But?"

"But that would be my jealousy talking." She took a sip from her glass and watched him, her golden eyes level and sad. "Did you ever think there might be something else going on here besides her wanting a courtship?"

"Something else?" he asked. "Like what?"

"Another man, perhaps?"

His whole body reacted to the thought. "There's no one else, Annie. No one." The idea of another man anywhere near Sandra made the anger he'd felt in the workroom a few minutes ago seem like a gentle spring rain.

"Maybe not," Annie said, sounding less certain than he would have liked, "but there sure as hell is something that's holding her back."

He let his thoughts wander over the weeks since their reunion. The one driving force, the one constant through everything, had been the importance of her work. Her ambition, her need to excel, was as keen today as it had been years ago.

He stood up and paced the small studio, oblivious of Annie's open curiosity. He understood the need for work; he understood the need to use one's talents to the fullest. He also understood the value of family, of love.

What he didn't understand was why Sandra felt she had to play one against the other.

He wasn't the kid he'd been almost twenty years earlier. He didn't believe he could be everything to her, didn't think he could fulfill all her needs. He wanted a woman who was comfortable within herself, and if that meant a woman with a career, so be it.

As long as that woman was Sandra Patterson.

"Sandra's coming here tonight for the dedication," he said, turning back to Annie. A huge stained-glass window was being dedicated that evening, complete with the crazy media hype that only New York City could produce. "I'll lay it on the line."

"Wait a few days," Annie said, touching his hand. "You're too angry. Cool off and think before you say anything."

He glanced out the studio window and saw the dark green Buick that had been tailing him for weeks. Jim Flannery had warned him that Bentley was ready to strike.

If Sandra didn't know by now what he was about, then they didn't stand a chance.

And he was running out of time.

Chapter Thirteen

There was one thing to be said for the dedication party for the new stained-glass window: it wasn't hard to keep the names straight.

In the past half-hour, Sandra had been introduced to hundreds of people, and it seemed most of the men had been named Matthew.

Annie Gage had told her that the cathedral staff had decided inviting every Matthew in town to the ceremony would be a terrific publicity hook, and from the number of cameras and media people buzzing around, they'd been right.

If not for the fact that Michael was conspicuously absent, she might actually have been enjoying herself. As it was, she was finding it difficult to make small talk.

A handsome blond-haired Matthew smiled at her as he grabbed a glass of champagne from the table next to her.

"You're the only Matthew I recognize," she said to him. "You play for the Red Sox." He was also the husband of the stained-glass artist responsible for the magnificent window.

"*Played* for the Red Sox," he corrected. "I hung up the cleats this season. Now I get to hang around the house and loaf."

His beautiful—and extremely pregnant—wife, Lainie Randall Ward, came up to them. "Don't you believe it," she said to Sandra after thanking her for her compliments on the cathedral window. "We have two kids at home and another on the way. He'll be so busy he'll be counting the days until he hits the road as the new Red Sox announcer."

Matthew and Lainie began bantering back and forth, and Sandra found herself suddenly envious of the obvious deep love between the two.

Tell me your secret, she thought, moving away from them slightly. *Tell me all of these problems will disappear and Michael and I will be where you are.*

Right now it was hard to imagine that they would ever not be at odds with each other. She took a sip of champagne and scanned the room for his face. God knew, their history had been one of such strife—such passion—that it was almost impossible to envision a future for them.

Especially if she had to withhold the knowledge of her mother's illness, the one thing that was at the core of her dilemma.

She turned and was about to slip into the anteroom for a breath of fresh air when she felt a hand on her shoulder. She looked up.

"Sorry I'm late," he said.

His eyes were shadowed, and the faint hint of a beard darkened his skin. He looked tired and worn, and her heart turned over with fear. Something was very wrong.

"That's okay," she said, handing him a glass of champagne from the table. She forced a smile. "I never knew there were so many Matthews in New York."

"Have you met many of them?"

"At least three dozen," she said. "It's been an amazing evening."

A silence fell between them. The band was playing a slow, dreamy tune, and she began to sway with the music, but he didn't pick up the cue and ask her to dance. She didn't feel confident enough to ask him. She stopped swaying and fiddled with her champagne glass.

He put his own untouched glass down on the table and looked at her. "We need to talk."

She nodded. Her throat was tightening up so that she could scarcely breathe, much less speak. "Where?"

"My office."

She followed him through the crowd and out a passageway that led across the deserted lot to the workshed and his office. The ground was hard and rocky and she had a difficult time navigating in her strappy sandals, but she didn't ask him for help. There was something terribly forbidding about this Michael McKay, something dark and brooding that warned her to keep her distance.

"Drink?" he asked after he closed the door behind them.

She shook her head. "I've had one champagne already tonight. That's it for me. I still have to drive home." Another long, throbbing silence. "You wanted to talk?"

He dragged his hand through the mop of black curls she loved so well, then loosened his tie. He looked strange to her in a suit; civilized clothing seemed barely able to contain the raw and powerful spirit within.

Suddenly she knew that before the night was over, her future would be decided.

One way or the other.

DAMN IT! Say something.

He'd dragged her off for this final confrontation, and now he couldn't get the words out past the fear snaking through his body and strangling his vocal chords.

Just spit it out.

"Something's wrong," he said finally, without any preamble. "We've been saying all the right things, but something's wrong between us, Sandra."

She said nothing; she simply waited, watching him with those beautiful eyes of hers.

"I need to know what it is."

"I don't know what to say to you, Michael. Nothing's wrong." She looked so blond, so cool, so untouchable. He felt as if she were drifting away behind a scrim of ice.

His curse crackled in the air between them. "You've put a barrier up between us, Sandy. It's been there since the day we started this damned sixty-day courtship, and I can't seem to break through."

"Your imagination is running away with you, Michael. There's no barrier between us. What a silly thing to—"

He grabbed her by the forearm. His fingertips roughened by years of hard work, snagged the delicate silk of her dress. Her eyes widened, but she didn't flinch. She wouldn't, not his Sandra. She was too proud, too strong for that.

She was everything he'd ever wanted, everything he'd ever dreamed of in a woman, and she was slipping away from him faster than he could stop her.

"Who is it, Sandra? What is it? Until you level with me, we don't have a chance in hell of making things work."

For the first time she looked away, and he knew he was losing her.

"Don't push me, Michael," she whispered. "Don't push me this way."

The years were falling away from him faster than he could think, and he was eighteen again and losing her to a world he couldn't compete with.

"Forget the courtship, Sandra," he said, pulling her into his arms. "Forget the candlelight and the candy and the flowers. Marry me tonight."

She was like a cardboard cutout, stiff and unyielding. "You're talking like a fool."

"Then I'm a fool. I don't give a damn what you call me, Sandy, just show me how you feel."

"Don't do this," she said, pushing him away with both hands. "Just give me a little more time. I promise you soon I'll—"

"Soon!" He let her go as if she were on fire. "What kind of game are you playing?" He was wild with fear and anger. If he was going to lose her anyway, he was going to say what was in his heart. "Was this part of your plan all along—to shoot me down at the last minute?"

She stared at him as if he were crazy. Maybe he was. "What on earth is your problem, Michael? Why this rush to the altar?"

"I've waited my whole life for you, Sandra. How much longer do you want me to wait?"

Her control snapped just as his had. "Until I'm ready, damn it. Until I can give you what it is you need." Her voice broke on the last word and she wiped tears away with a jerky swipe of her arm. "I can't do it now, Michael. No matter how much you want it, I can't."

"Who is it, Sandy?" He moved toward her. She took a step backward. "Is it Gregory?"

"You must be mad."

He hadn't really thought it was. The real truth was the same truth that had broken them apart years ago. "Your job?"

She hesitated.

"Come on, Sandy. Tell me. I have a right to know my rival, don't I?"

She still said nothing.

It all came down on him then: his fears over losing his son, his terror at losing Sandra, the intense, terrifying love he felt for both of them; his heart broke wide apart.

"What is it, Sandy?" he roared. "Tell me. *Tell me!*"

"I can't!" Her voice was a raw, aching scream. "Trust me just once, Michael. I love you, but I just can't tell you what you want to know."

"Not even if our future hangs on it?"

She shook her head. She was crying openly, but he couldn't span the distance between them to comfort her. "Not even then. Oh, God, Michael, I'm—"

He put his hand up to stop her. "Don't," he said. "I heard it before, Sandy, eighteen years ago. I'm not going to listen to it again."

He was in his car and headed toward the highway before the pain hit.

WHAT AMAZED SANDRA was that she could feel so much pain and still live.

When Michael walked out that door and his truck's engine roared to life, an iron fist clutched her heart and twisted until she wondered how she could keep on breathing.

How could she ever have believed it would be any other way, that what they shared could come to any other end? It should have been obvious to even the most lovestruck of fools that they weren't meant to share anything more than an interlude that she would hold inside her for years to come.

She'd been an idiot to think otherwise. Those midnight dreams of a home and a son and a life shared with Michael McKay were just that, dreams that couldn't stand up to reality.

He wanted everything, Michael did, and he wanted it now. He was the same demanding, impractical rebel who'd ried to sweep her off her feet years ago. Back then she had been too caught up in her own dreams of the future to yield.

Now she understood his dreams and shared them and wanted nothing more than to make those dreams come true, but the complicated, heartbreaking reality of her vow to her mother was making those dreams impossible.

God forgive her, but she would sell her soul for a chance to make him understand.

She cried until her entire body ached—until there were no tears left—and then she got up and washed her face at the utility sink on the other side of the workroom. Her eyes felt as if they'd been bathed in salt and sand; her skin felt raw and hot as the cold water touched it.

"Are you all right?"

She jumped at the sound of a woman's voice. Annie Gage, looking lovely in a beaded black dress, stood in the doorway with her arms wrapped around her against the cold.

"I've been waiting for you to come out, but I finally decided to stop being discreet and make sure you're okay."

"I'm okay," Sandra managed, folding the coarse white towel over the edge of the sink.

Annie stepped inside and closed the door behind her. "Are you sure?"

Sandra nodded. "I'm sure." She forced a shaky smile. "Despite the evidence to the contrary."

"I heard him leave."

"I'm sure everyone heard him leave," Sandra said. "He burned rubber from here to the Midtown Tunnel."

Annie's laugh seemed loud in the quiet room. "I always thought they outgrew that kind of behavior when they hit their thirties. McKay seems to be disproving that notion."

Sandra reached for her purse on the worktable. "Well, it was nice of you to check up on me, but I think I'd better be going."

Annie didn't move. "It was a bad one, wasn't it?"

"Look, Annie, I appreciate your concern, but I'm just not up to discussing my private life with you."

"You don't know the whole story, do you?"

Sandra took a deep breath. "I don't know much of anything at the moment except that I want to go home."

"He's been under a lot of stress," Annie continued, talking over her. "I know he seems pushy, but there are reasons—"

Sandra raised her hand. "I don't want to hear the reasons, Annie. If he wanted me to know something, he'd tell me."

"Not this," Annie said. "This is the one thing I know he wouldn't tell you. He didn't want to pressure you into anything."

Sandra looked closely at the dark-haired woman. "You're in love with Michael," she said, her voice flat. "Why would you want to help me keep him?"

"Because I'm crazy," Annie said. "Because I can't stand seeing him torn up inside with love for you." Her shrug was eloquent. "Because if I can't have him, I think you're the one who should."

"I don't know whether to thank you or punch you in the mouth."

Annie relaxed visibly. "Then that makes us even, because I contemplated a little hemlock in your champagne."

"This is a ridiculous situation," Sandra said, sitting on the edge of the worktable in a pile of chalk dust.

"Agreed," Annie said, perching on a stool a few feet away. "I have no business breaking my word to McKay."

"I wouldn't ask you to." Sandra hoped her disappointment wasn't too obvious.

"You won't have to," Annie said. "I'm going to tell you anyway."

"Are you sure?"

"I'm sure. I just can't stand seeing him so damned unhappy."

"YOU'RE A GOOD FRIEND, Annie Gage," Sandra said fifteen minutes later as she hugged the other woman. "And you won't regret it."

"I already *do* regret it," she said, "but that really doesn't matter, does it?"

Annie followed her out to her car, then gave her a fierce and angry hug. "Take good care of those two," she said, "or you'll have me to answer to."

Michael and David could have done a hell of a lot worse than Annie Gage. She was a friend in the truest sense of the word.

What Annie had told Sandra about Michael and the way he had risked all for her love had blasted away one of the two barriers remaining between them.

Tomorrow morning she would go to Fair Oaks and blast away the other.

LARRY WAS BUTTONING HIMSELF into a new pair of silk pajamas when she knocked on his door.

"When I kiss 'em, they stay kissed," he said as she came into the large suite that he shared with another patient. "Back so soon? Elinor wasn't expecting you."

"That's exactly why I'm here." She unceremoniously sat down on the chair near the television. "I have a few questions."

Larry lowered himself onto his bed and leaned his crutches against it. "Shoot."

"Why haven't you been calling me lately about Mom's condition?"

Larry's lower lip curled under for a moment as he frowned at her. "No need to call you. Her condition hasn't changed."

"It's been that bad?"

"Hell, no!" His frown disappeared. "She's been doin' better than any of us."

Sandra gripped the edge of the chair. "Would you say that again?"

"Be glad to. Elinor's doin' great. She's been taking PT every day, and—"

"She hasn't had a relapse?"

"Not that I know of."

"She hasn't been in her room, sleeping all the time?"

"Just her naps."

"You're telling the truth, Larry?"

He looked indignant. "I don't have no reason to lie, missy."

She jumped up and grabbed her purse.

"Where are you going?" he called out. "We only just started talking..."

"Later!" she said, heading for the door. "I'll tell you everything later."

Lucie, as usual, was sitting on the sofa knitting. Her jaw dropped when she saw Sandra standing in front of the door to Elinor's room.

"Sandra!" Her knitting needles clicked together, and she dropped a stitch. "What are you doing here? Is something wrong?"

"You tell me," Sandra countered.

"What do you mean?"

"I want to talk to Mother."

"You can't . . . she's . . . I mean—"

"You're a terrible liar, Lucie. I don't know why I didn't realize it before." She put her hand on the doorknob.

"Don't go in there," Lucie hissed. "She only wants to help you, lovey. Don't let on—"

Sandra opened the door and stepped inside. Elinor, lovely in a dressing gown of rose-colored silk, sat in a chair near the window. No respirator. No cardiac monitor. No crisis.

"You're looking well, Mother."

Elinor's eyes closed for a moment, then she slowly turned toward her daughter. "I didn't expect you today."

Sandra laughed hollowly. "Evidently not. This is hardly the room of a woman who's taken a turn for the worse." She sat down on the edge of the bed near her mother. "Why, Mom? Why did you do it? What on earth were you trying to gain?"

Elinor's eyes were fierce with love and pride. "I was trying to make things right for you," she said, her voice low but clear. "I wanted to step away long enough for you and Michael to work things out."

"By withdrawing from my life?"

"I wasn't withdrawing, honey. I was moving aside for a while."

Sandra waved her hand in disgust. "Do you really think I can forget you exist?" she asked. "Can you really believe I would want to?"

"It's my choice," Elinor said, looking away. "I expect you to respect my wishes."

"Bullshit!" Sandra's words shocked both of them into momentary silence. "No more of that, Mother. I just won't buy it."

"My condition," Elinor managed. "Don't force me to humiliate myself by letting people see me this way."

"What way?" Sandra asked, standing up and grabbing the mirror from the dresser. She held it up to her mother's face. "You're a beautiful woman, Mom. You always were; you always will be. Nothing's going to change that." She took Elinor's hands in both of hers and knelt down in front of her. "My invincible mother. You're just afraid to let anyone know you're as vulnerable as the rest of us."

"No, honey," Elinor said, closing her eyes. "Don't. I'm not going to listen."

"Oh, but you are, Mom. You're going to listen for the first time in your life. What you're doing is wrong."

"It isn't wrong. It's the best way. It's what I want."

"No!" Sandra's voice rang out. "This isn't good for either one of us."

"Sandra, I—"

"This *stinks*, Mom. It really stinks, and now that I'm on to you, I'm not going to let it continue a second longer."

"But Michael, your engagement, the—"

"To hell with Michael," she said. This wasn't the time to talk about their problems. "We're talking about you."

"My life is out of my control now, Sandra. There's so much I can't do—"

"Not good enough," Sandra interrupted. "I just won't buy it. Don't deny yourself what you *can* have because of the things you can't."

Hope suddenly broke out in her mother's eyes. "Such as?"

"Such as a family," Sandra said. "Such as being part of a family every minute that you're able."

A huge smile began to blossom. "You and Michael and David?"

"No guarantees," Sandra said, "but I'm going to give it my best shot."

"You're going to tell him about me?"

Sandra offered up a silent prayer. "Yes," she said, embracing her mother. "I'm going to tell him everything."

"You might lose him."

"I'm willing to take that chance."

If he was half the man she thought he was, they'd be home free.

And if he wasn't—well, then she'd already lost him a long, long time ago.

MICHAEL HAD GIVEN his apprentices the day off, and he didn't pull into the lot behind the construction shed until well after noon. He parked the car haphazardly, then got out, squinting against the weak late-autumn sun.

He was physically tired and emotionally drained, and had seriously considered giving himself a day off, but the thought of being trapped at home with his pain was more than he could handle.

He'd rather grab a new piece of limestone and begin to free another hawk. That, at least, made some sense.

He pulled the key to the workshed out of his pocket and was about to insert it into the lock when he saw someone had already beaten him to it. He pushed open the door and stepped inside. The smell of hot coffee was everywhere.

"Annie?"

"No," the voice behind him said. "It's me."

He whirled around and faced the woman he loved. Love battled with anger; at the moment, anger was still winning.

"What are you doing here?"

"I want you to take a drive with me."

He went to pour himself a cup of coffee. "I have work to do."

"Skip work," she said. "I did."

Whatever she wanted, it was important. "Have you been here long?"

"Long enough. Come with me, Michael. I have a few things to say to you."

"I think we said everything last night."

"I don't." She reached out and took his hand. "I don't think we even came close. Come with me this once and I won't ask another thing of you."

He grabbed his cup of coffee. "Can I bring it with me?"

She nodded, but didn't smile. "Be my guest."

They drove through Upper Manhattan and the Bronx in silence. He didn't know if it was the caffeine or his nerves that made his blood pound crazily in his head. She headed up into Westchester and he looked over at her, but her jaw was set and her expression so grim that he didn't ask.

This was it. The explanation he'd been waiting for was right around the corner, and suddenly he wanted to fling open the car door and jump out onto the Major Deegan to avoid it.

She was already married/engaged/a mother/a father/a bank robber—a thousand crazy ideas were tangled in his head. She didn't love him/she loved him too much/she loved someone else/she—

He forced himself to look out the window at the scenery whizzing by, but the changing autumn leaves couldn't compete with his imagination.

She exited the highway near Tarrytown, drove a few miles of curving country roads, then turned into a private driveway marked Fair Oaks. She belonged to a country club?

They passed a huge swimming pool that was closed for the season. He whistled softly. "Pretty impressive."

She glanced at him. "Think so?"

He said nothing, but broke out in a cold sweat.

She whipped her car into a spot in the visitors' parking lot.

"You're a member here?" he asked as she turned to face him.

"No one's a member here, Michael."

"This isn't a country club?"

Her gaze was locked on him. "No," she said softly. "It's a hospital."

"I don't understand."

"How could you? I've done my best to hide this from you."

God, not her. Please, God— He reached for her hand. "Sandy, are you—"

She shook her head. "I'm fine. It's Elinor."

He stared at her. Elinor Patterson was hale and hearty and in Pago Pago. "Elinor? I thought she was abroad."

"That's what she wanted you to think." He watched, helpless, as she took a long, shuddering breath. "My mother is dying, Michael. She's been dying for the last three years, and it might be tomorrow or ten years from now before I lose her." She squared her shoulders. "But I *am* going to lose her."

"No," he said. "Not Elinor." Not the vibrant, loving woman he'd known. "What? How?"

"Amyotrophic lateral sclerosis," she said, her tongue moving smoothly over the strange-sounding words. "Lou Gehrig's disease."

"I don't understand."

"No one does. It shouldn't have happened to her, but it did."

He sagged against the car door, feeling suddenly very old. "What about you?" he managed. "Will you—?"

"There's a five-percent chance I'll inherit it," she said. "I can't lie to you about that."

He would cling to the other ninety-five percent.

"She's my responsibility," Sandra was saying, looking straight ahead out the windshield. "My problem. I want you to know that right from the outset. I don't expect anything from you except understanding."

He was beyond words. He was still trying to accept the reality of Elinor's illness.

"She wanted to disappear from my life so we could make a life of our own. She swore me to secrecy."

"And you're breaking your promise?"

"Yes," she said. "I told her last night that I was going to."

The terrible puzzle of the past few weeks finally fell into place. Sandra talked dispassionately about the disease, the medications and treatments available, the blunt facts and figures surrounding the high price of quality care.

"I want you to see her, talk with her," she said as they walked into the hospital together. "I want you to understand what this is all about before we go any farther."

His hands began to shake, and he jammed them into his pants pockets. He kept thinking of his accusations, the damning things he'd said to her—unfair lousy things aimed at her heart—and he hated himself for it.

They stopped in front of a room on the first floor and Sandra, his Sandra, turned and looked up at him.

"Whatever you decide," she said softly, "I'll understand. Nothing will change the way I love you."

She pushed open the door, and he found himself looking down at Elinor Patterson. She sat, regal and straight, in a chair by the window.

"Pago Pago?" he said, crossing the room to embrace her. "Where's your suntan?" It was hard to speak over the sudden, unexpected lump in his throat.

She touched his face, his hair, tears brimming at the corners of her eyes. She was older, yes, but the beauty that had always been there still remained.

"Michael," she said, her speech halting and slurred as Sandra had warned him it would be. "Don't you know? This is much better than Pago Pago."

"You should have written," he said. "I've missed you."

She looked over at her daughter, who stood in the doorway flanked by an elderly man in a red bathrobe and a woman with a knitting needle stuck in her bouffant.

"I've made a few mistakes along the way," Elinor said. "I hope there's still time to make up for them."

He stood up and walked toward Sandra. His Sandra. His woman. A woman whose courage and loyalty and capacity for love embraced everything wonderful life had to offer.

"You tell us, Sandy," he said. "Tell us if there's still time."

Tell me if my dreams are going to come true after all.

HIS WORDS CAME TO HER as if through layers of thick fog.

"Would you say that again?" she asked. She'd been waiting thirty-five years for this moment, and she wanted to be sure.

"I want to know if we can have just one last chance."

Her breath caught. Everything in the room vanished except for Michael. "Are you sure?" she whispered.

"Positive." He looked so strong as he stood there, so powerful, so *good* that she found herself starting to cry. He touched her cheek, brushing the tears away as quickly as they came. "How could you doubt me?"

The years they'd spend apart began to fade as the future opened before her.

"I love you," she said, relishing the feel of those words upon her lips. "I've always loved you." Her love for him had been as certain as her heartbeat, as predictable as the tides. Neither time nor distance had been able to change that constant.

He pulled her close. "Say it again," he said.

"I love you, Michael McKay," she said, her voice loud and strong. "I'll love you until the day I die."

Michael's deep chuckle vibrated against her ear. "I'm going to hold you to that," he said lowly. "We have witnesses."

Reality rushed back in at her for a moment.

"It's a lot to ask of a man," she said, wanting to be certain paradise was really so close at hand. "She isn't your mother, after all."

His embrace tightened. "And David isn't your son. Does that change what you feel for him?"

She thought of the rush of emotion that small boy had brought to life within her. "No," she said, starting to laugh. "It doesn't change a thing. I love him." Such simple words; such powerful meaning.

"Raising a kid takes a lot of hard work."

She snapped her fingers. "I'm used to hard work."

"There's a lot of responsibility."

"I'm used to responsibility."

"This is your last chance to get away."

"Go ahead," she said. "Try to scare me off."

"Then listen to me now, Sandra Patterson, because I'm not going to say it again: I love you. I've always loved you. I'll love you in this life and beyond. Elinor is part of my past; she was my friend long before today. Being part of her family is one of the best things to ever happen to me—and to my son." He kissed her, long and deep, and the last of her doubts vanished. "Understand?"

She looked up at him. "No more courtship?"

"No more courtship."

"Should we set a date?"

"How about tonight?"

"How about the spring?"

"Thanksgiving?"

"Christmas."

"December 2." His tone brooked no argument. "That's it."

"December 2," she said with a mock groan. The truth was her entire body had suddenly come alive with excitement. "I'll barely have time to put together a trousseau."

His grin was wicked. "You won't need one."

She started to laugh. "I'll never find a wedding gown in time—"

"You will," he said.

"That sure of yourself?"

"That sure of *us*."

"You win," she said, willingly giving herself over to the inevitability of love. "December 2."

"Are you sure?" Michael asked softly. "This is a lifetime deal you're getting into."

"Ah, you sweet talker," she said, wrapping her arms around him. "Don't you know those are just the words I love to hear?"

Michael's kiss only sealed a bargain that had been made a long, long time ago by two kids who hadn't known much, but had known the real thing when they found it.

Behind them Elinor, Lucie and Larry burst into cheers.

"Mom," Sandra said finally, still wrapped in Michael's embrace, "let me tell you all about your new grandson."

December 2 couldn't come fast enough for her.

Epilogue

"Quit pacing, McKay!" Jim Flannery's voice echoed in the small anteroom. "You're wearing a hole in Father Anthony's carpet."

Michael cadged a Marlboro from his best man, took a drag, then stubbed it out in the marble ashtray on the mantel. "Gimme a break, Flannery. It's my wedding day. Pacing's my God-given right."

"You've got your chronology skewed, friend. Pacing's reserved for the delivery room, not the altar." A wide grin split his ruddy face. "Unless..."

Michael laughed for the first time since the wedding-day jitters had attacked him that morning.

"Don't say it, friend. We haven't even had our honeymoon yet."

Jim straightened his bow tie and adjusted his boutonniere. "That son of yours has been telling my Amy that he's going to have a little brother by the end of the year."

"I'm going to have to have a talk with that kid," Michael muttered. "He's getting too damned smart. Maybe when Sandy and I—"

"Gentlemen." Father Anthony appeared in the doorway, resplendent in his ecclesiastical robes. "The bride has arrived and we are about to begin."

Michael tugged at the jacket of his tux and took a deep breath.

"Nervous?" Jim asked.

Michael nodded.

"Any second thoughts?"

He thought about it for a moment. "Only one," he said finally. "Why did it ever take us so long?"

THE INSIDE OF the Cathedral of St. Matthew the Divine looked like something out of a fairy tale.

Early December sunshine poured in through the huge stained-glass windows, spilling pools of ruby and emerald and topaz light across the marble steps to the altar.

Music, joyful and triumphant, rose up to the vaulted ceiling and swooped down again. Huge arrangements of white daisies and yellow roses lined the sides of the altar, and masses of red tulips stood proudly near the pulpit.

Leon, nattily dressed in tails and high-tops, was serving as official wedding photographer and he was perched to the right of the vestibule, ready to capture the action—if it was ever going to begin.

Finally the familiar strains of the "Wedding March" filled the vestibule.

Annie Gage, beautiful in a dress of watered silk the color of fine brandy, winked at Sandra, then began the long glide down the aisle—to the accompaniment of the clicking of Leon's camera.

Right on cue, Sandra's hands started to shake.

"What's this, Patterson? An attack of nerves?" Ed Gregory, who had finally adjusted himself to her changed priorities, looked over at her with a grin. "It's not too late," he said, gesturing toward the door. "There's a limo warming up at the curb. We could be in the Bahamas before they knew what hit them."

"No good, Ed," she said as Leon got ready to snap his first photo of the bride. "I'm going to the Bahamas, all right—on my honeymoon."

Ed winced, and she slipped her arm through his for the procession to the altar.

"Honeymoons," he mumbled. "Bah, humbug!"

She flashed him one of her newly acquired serene smiles, the ones that drove him crazy. Ed couldn't fool her—at least, not anymore. It had been a long and rocky road to get Ed Gregory to accept the fact that she wanted more from life than balanced ledger sheets, but he'd finally accepted the inevitable.

The fact that he was giving her away today in marriage was testament to their long-standing friendship.

Not to mention the fact that she'd noticed a few sparks flying between him and Annie Gage. Wouldn't that be an interesting combination? Now that his Geneva transfer was postponed, maybe when she and Michael came back they could—

Mrs. Elston, the lady from the flower shop, gave a final tug on the ribbons on Sandra's bouquet, then nodded.

"Off you go," she said, casting a cautionary look Ed's way. "And remember, this isn't a sixty-yard dash. Slow and steady. Slow and steady."

Sandra straightened her shoulders and lifted her chin. A huge smile spread across her face as she and Ed stepped from the vestibule into the church proper, to the accompaniment of a chorus of "oohs" and "aahs" from the guests assembled there.

The cathedral was built on a grand scale, and the walk down the aisle seemed to last forever.

Sandra loved every second of it.

She loved the blur of faces as old friends and new waved at her from pews at either side of the center aisle. She loved the unfamiliar weight of the crown of flowers atop her head, the soft swish of the veil each time she turned her head.

All the sweet and silly daydreams girls have about their weddings blossomed around Sandra Patterson in her thirty-fifth year.

Except none of them were daydreams.

It was real.

It was happening.

Standing there at the foot of the altar, tall and splendid in his black tux and looking fittingly nervous, was Michael McKay.

Her Michael.

The man she'd always loved, and would love into eternity.

Another twenty feet, and Ed would put her hand into Michael's, the symbolic passing of allegiance from one family to another, although it wasn't really that.

She saw it more as a joining together, a blending of all that belonged to him with all that belonged to her, forming a family that was stronger for it.

And she had one person to thank.

There, in the front pew on the bride's side, sat her mother and Lucie. Lucie was dressed in a powder-blue wool suit and matching hat, and she was blubbering into a lace handkerchief that wouldn't last through the ceremony.

Elinor's wheelchair had been pushed into a corner of the church and she sat straight and proud on her own. She wore a silk dress the color of the inside of an oyster shell, and her eyes shone with a joy matched only by the joy in Sandra's own heart.

Although Miss Manners might not have approved, Sandra knew there was time for this one unscheduled stop.

She bent down and embraced her mother, sweet, warm tears wetting her cheeks and falling on the lace of her gown.

"I love you," she whispered in Elinor's ear. "Thank you for everything."

Elinor said something, but it was difficult for Sandra to understand it over the music and the sound of her heart beating in her ears.

Suddenly she felt a hand on her shoulder and looked up into the dark eyes of Michael McKay. He bent down and embraced Elinor, and said something low that made her mother smile.

Then he straightened up and took her hand.

"Come, Sandy," he said. "It's time."

"I NOW PRONOUNCE YOU man and wife." Father Anthony's smile was wider than the sky outside. "What are you waiting for, Michael? You may now kiss the bride."

As Michael's lips met hers, Sandra's heart soared up to the top of that vaulted cathedral, and all the colors of the rainbow exploded inside her soul.

"I love you," she said out loud. "I'll always love you."

"Sandra McKay." His voice was low, almost reverent. "My wife."

The church had erupted into cheers and laughter and the thrilling sounds of the recessional. Michael went to draw her into his arms for one last kiss to seal this sacred bargain when she saw David, beaming in the way only a five-year-old can beam, standing next to Jim Flannery.

His little body was straight and proud in his tiny black suit, his blond hair slicked back off his forehead except for one unruly lock that kept slipping over his right eyebrow.

He was the image of his father thirty years earlier.

And now he was her son.

She turned and spread her arms open wide. David looked at her, then that smile of his grew even broader as he tore across the altar and disappeared inside her hug.

Michael, his eyes suspiciously bright, swept their son onto his shoulder.

"Come on," he said, taking her hand. "It's time for this family to start celebrating."

"Yes," she said, giving herself up to the joy of love. "It's time this family got started."

The McKays turned and walked out of the church.

Together.

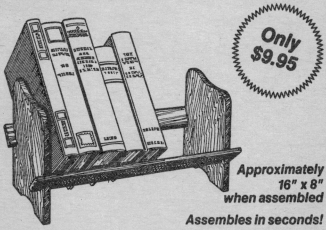

Keeping the Faith

by
Judith Arnold

It renewed old friendships, kindled new relationships, but the fifteen-year reunion of *The Dream*'s college staff affected all six of the Columbia-Barnard graduates: Laura, Seth, Kimberly, Andrew, Julianne and Troy.

Follow the continuing story of these courageous, vital men and women who find themselves at a crossroads—as their idealism of the sixties clashes with the reality of life in the eighties.

You may laugh, you may cry, but you will find a piece of yourself in *Keeping the Faith*.

Don't miss American Romance #201 *Promises* in June, #205 *Commitments* in July and #209 *Dreams* in August.

KFaith-gen